# The Ruby Ring

## Casting The Die

Stephen Gilbert

Stephen Gilbert

# DEDICATION

I first met Garrett Allen in the summer of 2014. He was fourteen years old, battling leukemia, and had already been hospitalized for over a month. I had the opportunity to visit him occasionally in the hospital over the next months and got to know a young man whose strength of character and sense of humor in the face of his many medical challenges were a source of inspiration to everyone who met him. When I discovered that he enjoyed reading and might be interested in this book, but only if it was in paper form, I decided that was time to get to work and finish a project that had been sitting idle for far too long.

Garrett Allen, this book is dedicated to you.

# CONTENTS

## Part 2:  Birth Of A King

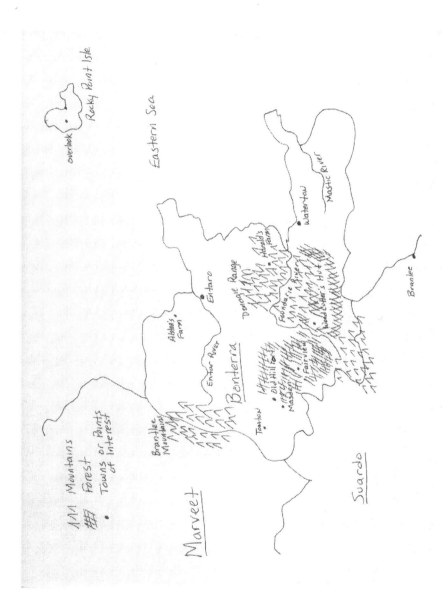

Stephen Gilbert

# PROLOGUE

The woman digging in the garden was neither young nor old. Her hair, tied back in a simple green bandana, had that salt and pepper quality that might come at any age. Her drab brown dress was long and flowing, and any observer would be able to tell from looking at her hands that she was accustomed to hard work.

She paused in her digging to wipe a stream of sweat from her brow, leaving a brown smear that traveled across her forehead. The night was hot, just as she remembered it being eighteen years earlier. She shuddered suddenly, squeezing her eyes tightly together. One lonely tear broke free, staining a path through the dirt on her cheek and giving voice to her sadness. There was much to do though, and grieving would have to wait until later. She paused to compose herself with a drink of water from a chipped clay jug, and then resumed her digging.

When she judged that the hole was deep enough, she let go her spade and dropped to her knees. Working swiftly now, she used her hands to cast out small piles of soil. Presently, she hit a hard surface and grimaced. She'd remembered. The object that she had been seeking was to one side of the hole, so she used the spade to enlarge the space, and then bent down and using her fingers, carefully scooped away the remaining dirt. She looked carefully about her before reaching into the hole with both hands, and prizing out a small box, approximately the size of an apple. The rotting cloth in which it had been wrapped tore as she pulled the box from the hole, so she slowed and carefully wound it again to hide the wooden container.

Laying the package to one side, she took up the spade again and quickly filled in the hole, taking the time to sweep dry dirt and leaves over the opening so that it might appear to the casual observer to have been undisturbed. With a satisfied nod, she picked up her treasure and made her way back to the house, stepping carefully around the beans, squash, and tomatoes.

# PART ONE
# ROBERT OF MASDEN

## CHAPTER 1
## MASDEN

Robert breathed deeply and grounded the heavy wooden practice sword. His father, sweat rolling off his muscular chest, drove his own sword into the dirt and panted, "Enough?"

Robert's shallow laugh betrayed his eagerness to train, "Never. But it looked like you could use some water." He went to the basin in the corner of the stable and dipped a tin cup, bringing up some of the clear, cold water.

His father looked at him, his lips forming a comical grin, "I could use some water! Why you young pup! Sixteen and brash as can be!" He chuckled and said, "Well, I suppose a drink would taste good." Pointing his finger at his son, he chuckled, "You were about to get whipped and you know it!" Still, he took the offered cup and drained it in a single gulp. He scooped another cupful and splashed it across his upper torso. "You're getting better. I do believe that one day soon, you'll pass me up." He patted his son's shoulder and added, "but not today, and not tomorrow!" Then he laughed, "enough play. We've both got work to do. Have you finished the repairs to the miller's saddle?"

Robert shook his head. "Not yet. A few hours work, and I'll be done." He pointed to the horse in one of the stable's larger stalls. "He does have a fine horse, doesn't he?"

His father laughed. "He does indeed, much too fine for stable masters like us." He hung the cup on the hook by the basin and turned serious. "You get your chores done. I want some help with the books later this afternoon. It's time you learn how the business is run."

§§§§

Later that evening, father and son walked slowly through the village, their day's work done. Already, candles were starting to flicker in the windows, a testament to long hours spent at the stable. Several times, Robert started to open his mouth, but then held his tongue, and walked on. Finally, as they rounded a corner and saw the welcoming glow coming from the windows of their own small cottage at the end of the lane, he decided to speak.

"Father, I don't understand."

His father turned to him and wiped away a shock of tawny hair just starting to give way to gray. "What don't you understand son?"

Robert paused, as if trying to find the proper words. His father was a big man, a man of authority. Though he sought no position of leadership in the village, others naturally listened when he spoke, and several sought his counsel. Robert had always been awed by the man's strength and bearing and had noticed that even his friends treated his father with a deference that they seldom showed to others. He paused and then plunged ahead. "Why do you work me so hard? Johnny and the others went fishing today, but I've been working. Last week while I practiced ciphers after work, they were down at the river swimming. It doesn't seem fair."

His father nodded slowly and grunted. "It doesn't, does it? So you think you'd prefer to be down at the river?"

Gaining his courage, Robert blurted, "Yes." He was about to add more when his father waved him to an old log lying under a grove of pine trees near the house.

"Have a seat. Maybe it's time that we talk."

Robert went to the log and then watched as his father eased himself carefully down with a sigh. He'd noticed him limping slightly on the walk home and wondered if the old jagged scar that wrapped across the front of his left leg was bothering him. He'd asked about it once when he was a young boy and been told only that it was from an old injury, and not to worry. "Is your leg bothering you today?"

His father waved his hand as if to silence him. "I probably just tweaked it a bit during the sword practice. It'll go away." Then he smiled. "Do I work you too hard?" Robert nodded and thinking that this was his opening, started to speak but his father interrupted him. "You're no longer a boy, Robert. You're becoming a man." He looked at his son. "And that means that you have to be willing to take on the responsibilities of a man. And a man..."

Robert interrupted him. "I understand all that father, but the others. They do their chores and then they have freedom to do other things. I study at school and do my chores, and then I must practice reading and writing and figures. And lately I have to read and write in the old tongue. It seems a waste of time!"

"Are you done?" asked the older man with a wry grin.

Robert started to speak and then shrugged his shoulders. "I think I've said my piece."

His father looked at him and smiled. To look into his son's face was like peering into a looking glass that erased the age from his own. "How many of your friends can read?"

Robert started. "Well Johnny can read pretty well, and some of the others can read some, at least from the simpler books."

"And you?"

"I think I read well, Father. At least, I don't know of any books that I can't read."

"Neither do I. Why do you suppose that's the case?"

Robert smiled ruefully. "I suppose it's the work." Then he added quickly, "but what's the need? If I'm to be a stable master like you, what will I need to read?" Sensing a strong argument, he added, "And I certainly won't need to read and write in the old tongue!" He looked up at his father's face triumphantly but what he heard next shattered his victory.

"And why would you be a stable master?"

Robert didn't know what to say. He sputtered, "I...but... doesn't every boy take over his father's trade?"

"Is that what you want?" his father asked seriously, "to spend your life covered in manure and tending to the needs of travelers? To care for fine horses while riding nothing better than a nag yourself?"

As he stared at his father, Robert was struck speechless. "I...what else could I do?"

The older man smiled and stretched out his leg. "Ah, now we get to the heart of the matter. Always remember this. Set your goals high, and let your effort define your character."

Robert frowned. It was a phrase he'd heard often from his father. He was about to speak when his father looked up at the glow from the cottage window. "Go up to the house and tell your mother that we're home and that we'll be in for dinner shortly." Robert rose and he added, "and bring us each a flask of ale. This talking is thirsty work."

When Robert returned, he could see that his father was standing, flexing and stretching out his injured leg. He watched for a moment until his father noticed him and waved him over. When he handed him the flask, the man took a long draft and then sighed and wiped his mouth with the back of his sleeve.

"Ah, that was good. I thank you." He motioned Robert back to his seat on the log and settled himself. "So you want to know why you must learn to read and write in both the common verse and in the tongue of the ancients." He looked across at his son.

Robert nodded.

"You said yourself that most of your friends struggle to read at all, and yet you read fluently. Am I right?" Without waiting, he continued. "You have great ability Robert." He tapped the side of his head with one finger. "A fine mind and a curiosity that places you above the others. Your mother and I have known that since you were a babe. Your sister shares these traits, for all that she is a girl, and that is why I teach you together."

Robert nodded. It was most uncommon for anyone to bother to teach girls in the village, and yet his sister if anything, could read and write better than he, though she had little interest in numbers.

"It is said," his father continued, "that to those who receive great gifts from the gods shall come great responsibilities." He took a large mouthful of beer and swirled it around before swallowing with a sigh. "The gods have a plan for you Robert, and I would be remiss in my responsibilities were I to fail to prepare you."

Robert's head swirled with this new information. The thought of not following his father into the stable was more than a little bit frightening, but somehow he knew that the man was right. He would not be happy as a stable master. His friends, while fine companions, often teased his learning and seemed uncomfortable with him when he referred to something that he had read. He looked at his father, "But what am I to become?"

The man smiled. "Ah, so I have your interest." He rose and flung the remnants of his beer onto the grass. "Don't forget that we live in uncertain times, and you must be prepared for whatever may come your way. That is why you must work hard to master both the new and the old tongues. It is also why a stable master's son trains with the wooden sword." He patted Robert on the shoulder. "I fear though, that that is a much longer conversation than we have time for tonight." He paused and then smiled indulgently at his son. "Tomorrow's Saturday. I'll work the stable alone, and you can take the day to relax with your friends. Come. I smell dinner."

# CHAPTER 2
## JOHNNY TUPPENCE

Robert looked enviously at the tall young man walking next to him. "What bait were you using? I didn't get so much as a nibble, and you've got what, eight fine trout?"

Laughing, Johnny Tuppence said, "Ah, the secrets of the trade my boy. We dug the worms together this morning. Did you forget? It was my superior skill."

"Bah," continued Robert. He looked at his partner's tackle. They had similar equipment, rough hewn fishing poles whittled from willow branches along with fine woolen thread and hooks fashioned from metal fragments scrounged at the blacksmith's yard. "Johnny…You are planning to share, right?"

His friend draped an arm around his shoulder. "Of course," he replied seriously. "I managed to hook a little sunfish earlier. It's all bones and fins, but you're welcome to it!" Seeing Robert's scowl, he burst into laughter. "I'll tell you what. I need four fish for dinner tonight. The rest are yours. I'll throw in the sunfish as a bonus."

The two friends continued up the lightly forested trail, chattering about their fishing trip, and soon made their way over a small rise. From the top, they could see the village of Masden laid out before them. It was a small community of some thirty homes, surrounded by a patchwork quilt of vegetable gardens and fields of grains. The center of the village was dominated by church and inn, standing across from one another, one representing the spiritual and the other the temporal heart of the community.

As they started down the slope, Johnny squinted and said, "Do you see the cloud of dirt in the distance there?"

Robert laughed. "Your eyes are better than mine. I see something. What do you suppose it is? Horsemen?"

Shading his eyes with his hand and taking a long look, Johnny answered, "I'd guess so. They're probably a couple of hours away." Then he looked at Robert, "Say, let's stop by the tavern. My uncle's just cracked a new keg of beer."

His friend glanced at him and shook his head. "I've no money for beer. Besides, I need to get these fish home to my mother."

"It's on me," Johnny insisted. "Just one and then I'll send you on your way."

"On you?" replied Robert. "I've never known you to pay for beer. On your uncle you mean?"

Johnny laughed. "Not at all. I figure I'll give him my share of the trout, so he'll be more than happy to draw us a couple of mugs."

Laughing, Robert pounded him on the shoulder. "Always the schemer. That must be why I stick around you."

§§§§

Two hours later, Robert sat down with the family for dinner. His father led them in a quick prayer, and then everyone dug into the fresh trout. After taking a bite and savoring the buttery flavor, he turned to his son, "It would appear that your luck was good. Where'd you go fishing today?"

Robert looked at him. "You know the old willow on the far bank of the creek? Just beyond it's an inlet where the moss overhangs the water. The fish like to rest there."

His father chuckled, "I know it well. And Johnny? How'd he do?"

Robert grimaced, "Actually, these are his." He shook his head. "He says he talks to them, warns them about my hook and tells them to come to him." Then he laughed and took another bite of his fish. "Can you imagine? Talking to fish?"

His father smiled and said softly, "His father used to say the same thing to me."

Robert looked surprised, "Really? I just thought it was something Johnny was putting on. Good fish though." He took a bite and looked up at his father, "Oh, by the way, where were the riders from?"

His father looked at him. "Riders?"

"Yes. Johnny and I saw them coming down the east-west road. We figured they'd put their horses up in the stable before they went on to the inn."

"I saw no riders. How far out were they?"

"We could just see the dust on the horizon from the hilltop. A couple of hours I'd suppose. Maybe they're still on the road."

His father stirred the fish around on his plate, as he snuck a nervous glance at his wife. "Maybe." Then he smiled. "After dinner I'll go check with the innkeeper. I'm sure they'll want a place for their mounts." Forcing a smile back onto his face, he looked around the table, his eyes lighting on his daughter. While Robert took after his father, his twin shared her mother's dark hair and brown eyes. Though her features were soft and delicate, there was an underlying strength that seemed to radiate out from her. "And you, Marie, how was your day?"

"Busy," she said with a smile. "Sally was here. We worked on a new cable stitch on the sweaters we're knitting and after that, we read from the book of poetry."

Robert groaned. "It's Saturday. Take a break from schoolwork!"

His father turned to him, "Don't forget our talk. You'd be wise to work on your own lessons a little more."

He was about to say more when Marie interrupted him, "Robert does well in school father. He's the top scholar in the class in all subjects, without really seeming to try and he's far more fluent than I am in the old tongue that you've been teaching us." She grinned at her brother. "Besides, had he been working with me on computations, we'd be eating potatoes instead of this trout."

"That's right Father. I…"

His father interrupted him. "Well mister hard worker. I trust you're well rested after spending the afternoon under that willow tree. How about if you finish your dinner? I'll need your help at the stables when those riders come in."

Robert nodded curtly, "Yes sir."

§§§§

The riders didn't show up that night. Robert spent two hours mucking out the stalls and laying new straw for the horses they boarded before returning to his work on the miller's saddle. His father had passed the time pulling out the old worn tack, and setting it aside for repair the following week. He was replacing the leather in one of the harnesses when Robert came up to him. "It's getting dark, Father. I imagine they've passed us by."

His father nodded and continued working the tough leather straps. "Possibly. Doesn't seem likely though. They'd have had to go through town. Maybe we'll see them tomorrow. They could have camped on the road." He finished tying a knot and stretched the harness out on a worktable. "Well, this will wait until tomorrow. Let's head for home."

Once out in the street, he looked across to the inn. They could hear the raised voices of the Saturday night revelers. "I hear you and Johnny tasted William's new porter. How was it?"

Robert smiled. "Good. Better than the last batch, I think. A little bitter, but it went down well on a hot day. Shall we go in?"

"I think not son." He continued walking down the dusty road. "You're mother and sister will worry if we're late." He looked up the road to their home. The warm glow of a candle flickered in the front window. Throwing his arm around his son's shoulder, he said, "Those were fine trout you brought today. I wish we could eat like that every Saturday night." He grew quiet as they walked along, finally saying. "I was thinking of riding up to the old hill fort tomorrow after church. Why don't you bring Johnny along?"

Robert was puzzled. The hill fort had been abandoned generations ago. So far as he knew, it was empty and run down, an isolated place. He looked at his father. "Sure. What do you want to do?"

His father punched him playfully in the shoulder. "You'll see."

# CHAPTER 3
## ATTACKED!

Robert woke to the sound of pounding on the front door. Bleary eyed, he looked out the window in the loft and saw that it was still dark outside. He heard rustling downstairs and then his father's voice calling, "Who's there?"

In response, the door slammed open with a splintering crash. Robert jumped from his bed and sprinted to look out over the rail to the main room downstairs. A heavily armed man stepped into the living room. He could see two others directly behind him. His mind flashed on the dust cloud on the road earlier that afternoon. Could these be the riders? Why were they here? Before he could react, he heard his father roar, "Get out of my house!"

The man turned toward the voice in the bedroom that his parents shared and motioned to the others. He pulled a short sword out of a scabbard at his waist and raised it as he stepped cautiously forward. Just then, Robert saw the flash of a blade come from beneath him, and the sword went clattering to the floor. With a howl of pain, the man pulled back the bloody stump that remained of his arm.

Wide eyed, Robert saw his father emerge from the bedroom, wearing his bedclothes and carrying a heavy two-handed broadsword. The other two men were in the room now, each armed with a short fighting blade. They circled Robert's father warily, looking for advantage. As each man lunged forward, his father parried their thrusts, leaving them frustrated. Slowly the taller of the two men worked his way around to the side of the room. Like mad dogs, they continued to thrust and parry until they had forced him back into the corner.

Robert raced down the stairs and grabbed the poker from the fireplace. He lifted it over his head and was about to advance when his father shouted, "Get out of here. Take your mother and sister and run to the place we were going to tomorrow. I'll meet you there."

"Father," he yelled and stepped forward with the poker.

"Go," he shouted, but Robert wasn't listening. With a thud, he brought the poker down on the shorter man's right shoulder, stunning his arm and forcing him to drop his weapon. The man turned, and pulling a dagger from his belt with his left hand, jumped at Robert.

Robert leaped back and struck out with the poker, barely missing the man's weapon.

The other man looked aside in confusion, and then pressed his fight home against Robert's father. He lunged, and then skittered to one side as Robert's father parried with his long sword. Back and forth they raged, the invader attacking and Robert's father skillfully parrying his jabs.

Warily, Robert and the shorter man circled one another, each looking for an opening. As Robert stepped back into the doorway to his parent's bedroom, he caught sight of his mother, arms wrapped around Marie, holding her head to her breast. "Run Mother," he yelled. "Out the window!" Just then the man slashed with his dagger and Robert thrust his hips back as the blade cut the front of his nightshirt. As the man was recovering, he slashed at him with the poker and was rewarded with a crunch of bone as the heavy end bit into his cheek. He folded onto the floor and Robert yelled again, "Run now!" He looked back in time to see his mother pushing Marie out the window, and then returned his gaze to the fight. The man he'd struck was rising to his knees, his face a mass of blood. Robert swung down hard, slamming the poker through the top of the man's skull and dropping him to the floor.

He looked back into the corner to see that the taller of the robbers had taken advantage of his greater maneuverability with his short blade to push his way inside the reach of the long sword, and was grappling with his father. Robert reached down and grabbed the dead man's sword and leapt into the fight just in time to see his father's bad leg buckle. As he reached out to save his balance, the man plunged a dagger into his chest.

"No!" he yelled and jumped forward with the sword. His opponent turned lightly on his feet, letting Robert's father slump to the floor, grappling weakly with the blade that protruded from his body.

As Robert charged him, the tall man slashed his blade to the side and then grazed him on the head with the hilt of the weapon. Dazed, Robert dropped to his knees and rolled into the wall. The man smiled wickedly and walked to where Robert huddled. As he raised the weapon to finish him off, Robert plunged his sword up and into the man's stomach. The man's eyes went wide and he looked down at the bloody stain that had appeared on his robe. Then he slumped backward and fell slowly to the floor.

Robert rose carefully and looked around at the carnage. Two of the invaders were lying on the floor, their eyes rolled upward in the posture of the dead. The third lay whimpering in a pool of blood in one corner, trying weakly to staunch the bleeding of his stump.

He turned to his father, still pulling weakly at the knife that protruded from his chest. Kneeling tenderly by his side, he brushed his hand across his forehead. "You'll be OK. I'll get the doctor."

His father shook his head wearily. "It's too late. You must listen to me now. Take your mother and your sister and go to the hill fort. I've left a cache of food and supplies in a cavern under the old temple. You'll be safe there for a few days."

"But…"

His father's response was savage. "No time. You've got to get out of here. They'll be back. Go quickly; take your mother and flee!"

"But they're dead father, we've killed them."

His father shook his head and whispered, "There will be more. Look at their uniforms, their weapons. These are the Duke's men. When these men don't report in, he'll send more." He dropped his chin to his chest and took a few haggard breaths. Raising his head slightly he said, "Remind your mother to take the coins I've hidden in the attic and the old box she buried in the garden." He lifted his head slowly and looked weakly into Robert's eyes. "You've been all I could have hoped for in a son. Go now and make me proud. Be gone before sunrise." With a last rattling breath, he dropped his head and slid to the floor.

Robert sat still, stroking his father's forehead as the tears streamed down his cheeks. He was roused out of his lethargy by a scream from outside.

Leaping up, he grabbed a sword and ran to the door in time to see a horseman flying down the road, his mother screaming in pursuit. She stopped and slumped to her knees, wringing her hands in despair. Robert raced to her side and lifted her to her feet. "There was another man outside," she wailed. "He's got Marie!"

# CHAPTER 4
## THE DUKE'S PALACE

The small group of soldiers huddled nervously in one opulent corner of the great hall of the palace. They were shabbily dressed, and looked as if they had been riding hard. One chanced a glance around. Tapestries hung from stone walls, blocking drafts and adding a touch of elegance. The ceilings, nearly twenty feet above, were covered with murals depicting hunting scenes as well as glorified caricatures of Duke Henry and his family. The floors were covered with fine carpets, but the room was strangely devoid of furniture. One chair, the large gilded throne, with its purple velvet cushions, was centered on a raised dais at the far end of the room.

They heard shouting before anyone entered from the door behind the throne.

"Are you telling me that three of my finest men at arms are dead and all they've got to show for it is one scrawny girl?"

"Sire..."

"Bah. Where are they?"

Duke Henry stomped into the room and looked about for the soldiers. They shrank back as his eyes landed on them.

"You," he demanded in a cold fury, "Approach."

Their leader, taller and possessed of a grey grizzle in his beard, stepped toward the duke. The other two followed meekly behind him. At a signal from their general, now standing just behind the duke, the three soldiers dropped to one knee before the throne and saluted by slapping their right fists against their left shoulders. Duke Henry glared down on them and they lowered their heads.

His tone was icy. "Explain!"

The leader of the small band raised his head. "Sire, we experienced unexpected resistance. We, we had expected to take them by surprise."

Duke Henry silenced him. "So I hear. I'm told that you were confronted by a man and a boy in their night clothes." He paused, as if to let the charge sink in, and then continued with a bellow, "in their night clothes!" Suddenly he jumped down and slashed the man viciously across the cheek with a short leather crop. The soldier stumbled but then returned to his rigid position on one knee, blood welling from the ragged wound.

Lowering his voice to a near whisper, the duke asked, "Tell me, what was your assignment?"

The bleeding soldier looked up again and said, "We were to capture the man and the boy and bring them to you."

Duke Henry raised his hands and gestured toward the empty chamber, "So they should be here, right? Why is it that I don't see them?"

The soldier gritted his teeth and said, "The man was armed with a broadsword. The boy had a weapon as well. We hadn't expected resistance. I take full responsibility. We weren't prepared for that possibility."

Duke Henry raised the crop again and then lowered it before going to his chair and settling onto the cushions. He turned to the general, "You told me that you were sending six of your best men. These were the best?"

The general hurried to his side and motioned the soldiers back to the wall. As the men began to rise, the duke stopped them with a hand, "Not yet." He looked back to the general, "Well?"

"Sire, they've never disappointed me before. Believe me, I will deal harshly with this failure."

"See that you do." He spat toward the soldiers. "Get them out of here."

The general slapped his hands and pointed to the door. "Wait for me in the barracks office."

As the men left the room, Duke Henry asked, "So you say the man is dead?" When the general nodded, he asked, "Where is the boy?"

The general took a deep breath and answered, "I have a troop searching the area for him. We'll find him soon. There's no place to hide. We're going door to door and searching every building. Someone will give him away."

Duke Henry turned to him and sneered, "Be sure of it. I want you to close the inn and then take three children. For each day that you can't find the boy, hang one of them."

The general started to protest, but seeing the vicious look on the duke's face, simply turned, and saying, "As you wish," left the room.

§§§§

Marie opened her eyes slowly and looked around her. She was in some kind of dark room. She could feel through torn clothing that the stone floor was cold and damp and when she took her first wakeful breath, she gagged at a miasma of fetid odors. She started to sit and winced at bruises that screamed with pain.

"Where am I?" she thought. She heard a shuffling sound off to her right and looked in that direction. She could make out a shape, possibly another body, through the dark. As her eyes became accustomed to the dim light, she could tell that it was indeed someone else, but they were clearly asleep.

She looked around the room. She was huddled in one corner and as she reached out, her hand touched a rough stone wall. The window high above her head allowed just enough light for her to tell that the room was small, maybe ten by fifteen feet. There appeared to be three others in the room besides her, but so far as she could tell, she was the only one who was awake. She shivered, "or alive," she muttered. She tried to stand, but hit her head on the ceiling and abruptly sat down again. Looking around, she realized that she was in some kind of cell, possibly a dungeon. "But why?" she mused, "What's happened?" She flashed a glance back at the others, wondering if they could be Robert and her parents.

Carefully, she crawled to the form nearest her, one with the rounded hips of a woman. Reaching the body, she gently pulled on her shoulder, "Mother?" As the woman's face flopped toward her, Marie lurched back in shock. Maggots crawled in and out of the woman's mouth and nose and her eyes were the dull gray of death. She'd clearly been dead for a couple of days.

Huddling back in her corner, she wrapped her arms around her knees and began to rock back and forth. "Where am I?"

# CHAPTER 5
## THE OLD HILL FORT

Robert looked around the crypt beneath the old hill fort. They'd entered through a trap door that had been cleverly concealed behind what remained of the alter in the tumble down chapel. The room was dark, but not so dark that he couldn't make out the stone coffins that seemed to be scattered randomly around the room. He shivered involuntarily. Probably the final resting places of the old priests who'd used the chapel, he guessed.

His mother called out to him, "Hurry. Have you closed the door?"

He nodded, and then realizing she couldn't see him, whispered, "It's latched."

"Good," she said, "follow me." She slid back the wooden cover on one of the caskets and climbed in.

Robert's eyes widened in horror. "We're not going to hide in there, are we?"

She looked back at him. "No. It has a false bottom." He looked over the top of the casket and could see that she'd slid aside the bottom and was carefully climbing down a ladder. She looked up. "Come along, and remember to close the trap doors on the way down!"

Warily, Robert climbed into the casket. As he went down into the dark hole beneath it, he slid the lid back on, muttering to himself, "I feel like I've just sealed my own grave."

When his feet touched ground again, Robert looked around. The room was absolutely black. He could hear his mother scurrying about off to his right, but when he looked, could see nothing.

"Stand with your back to the ladder, she called out to him. Do you feel the wall to your right?"

He reached out. He had expected dirt, but was surprised when, his hand made contact with a finished stone wall. "Yes."

Her voice sounded farther away now. "Good. Keep your hand on the wall and follow me. We'll be there shortly."

Wondering where 'there' was, Robert stepped cautiously forward. He encountered no obstacles in his way, so increased his pace, constantly mindful of his hand scratching along the stone wall. Once his hand slid across something wet and slimy, causing him to gasp quietly, but he guessed that it was simply water seeping down into the ground from the recent rains. He figured that they'd walked about a hundred feet when he bumped into his mother.

"Feel here," she said, and directed his hand to an indentation at the top of the wall. "There used to be a place for a lamp there. That's your marker. Can you feel it?"

"I've got it," he whispered.

"Good. Don't forget. For you, it will be about forty paces down the wall, but keep your hand high so that you can feel for it in the future. Wait here." She turned and continued another few feet down the tunnel, and he could hear that her rustling sounds started to come from higher on the wall. "I want you to continue down the wall, holding on as you have. Go ten paces. You should feel the tunnel start to veer to the left. Can you tell that?"

By now it was clear that her voice was coming from behind and above him. "Yes," he called back.

"Good. That way leads out of the tunnel at the base of the hill, behind some bushes. Now come back to my voice. Just beneath me, you'll find a shallow step about knee high. Use it to climb the wall to me."

The steps were only about two inches deep, but Robert found a series of hand holds that made it easy to scale the wall even in the blackness. When he reached the top, his mother reached for him and pulled him over the edge. "We're almost there. Stay close behind me." She turned and went forward again, still holding his hand.

This tunnel zigzagged through the mountain for another fifty paces before coming to a stop against an old wooden door, set on leather hinges. Cautiously, his mother pushed it open, and stepped inside, pulling him in behind her. Once inside, she closed the door and said, "Wait here. I'll light a candle."

Robert stood quietly for what seemed a long time, but probably was only a minute or two. "It's funny how darkness affects your sense of time," he muttered. Finally, a match flared and he began to see again. As his mother went about the room, lighting candles, he could see that he was in some sort of cellar. The walls were lined with wooden shelves that held a wide assortment of things. One section seemed to be a pantry, packed with dried fruits, grains, and salted meat. Against another wall, he could see a simple kitchen, complete with dishes, a cook pot, and other gear. Clear cool water flowed through a channel in one corner of the room and he nodded thoughtfully as he looked around. There were even a wardrobe and beds on the far side of the room, and he wondered idly if anyone had ever stayed here before. Looking toward his mother, he could see that she was busy stuffing a blanket into a crevice in the roof of the cave. "What is this place?"

"Just a moment. I need to block the light from getting out." She worked the blanket into the crack before collapsing into a chair and dropping her face into her hands. After a few seconds, she looked up at him, grief etched on her face. "I never believed him," she moaned. "He told me that one day they would come, but I never believed him." She buried her face in her hands again and began to sob.

Robert rushed to her side and took her into his arms, holding her as he felt the first tears start to roll down his own face. They had been so busy just trying to survive the night that neither had time to think of what had happened. Now that they were safe, the events of the evening came crashing down upon him. He was as tired as he could ever remember, and completely confused right now.

Slowly, lovingly, he directed his mother to one of the beds at the far end of the room and covered her with a blanket. Then he sat stroking her head and holding her hand until her breathing changed and he could tell that she was asleep. Finally, he stepped to the other bed and lay down.

His mind raced with the events of the evening. Someone had attacked them. That much was clear. And that someone wore the colors of the Duke, but why? His father was dead; his sister abducted; and he and his mother were hidden in this strange underground chamber. As he lay there, he allowed the grief to wash over him, tugging at his heart, and drawing rasping sobs from his throat. The anger, he knew, and the burning desire for revenge, would come later. For now though, he needed time. He lay awake for a long time before drifting into an uneasy sleep.

§§§§

Johnny Tuppence rose before dawn the next morning. He and Robert had talked about fishing by the mill five miles up the river, and they wanted to arrive there by sunrise. He took his pole, and smiling, walked up the lane to his friend's house. When he arrived, it was still dark and he didn't notice that the front door swung by one broken hinge until he began to knock on it. Startled, he pushed the door cautiously open and peered inside. A dim glow from the coals in the fireplace provided enough light for him to see the chaos in the main room. Broken furniture was strewn about haphazardly, and as he stepped cautiously inside, he was struck by the nauseating smell of death. His foot stuck to the floor when he tried to move, and he looked down into a black pool of blood, seeping out from a man with just one arm. The flies were already beginning to crawl over his wasted stump. Johnny leaped back against the doorframe, vomited, and wiping his mouth with one dirty sleeve, turned to run home.

§§§§

Robert woke to the smells of salt pork frying in a pan. He took a deep breath of the aroma, expecting to hear his mother call into the loft to wake him for breakfast. When he opened his eyes, he was momentarily disoriented, and then the night came roaring back to him in a rush. His father and Marie, gone. He and his mother, hiding in this cave somewhere under the old hill fort. He opened his eyes and glanced toward the sound of the sizzling meat, surprised to be able to see his mother's back. Then he looked up and could see a dim light filtering through the roof of the cave. Rising on one elbow, he looked around the room, taking in again the stores of food and equipment. He was startled to see several highly polished swords as well as a set of chain mail stored carefully in one corner of the room. He looked again at his mother and asked, "Where are we?"

She turned around, startled by his voice. "Quietly," she said. "We don't want to be heard outside." Her eyes were red and her cheeks streaked where the tears had run through the dust from the cave and he choked back a sob. She'd lost her husband and daughter last night, and yet she thought to make him breakfast.

She attempted a smile and said, "This was your father's hide away. He seemed to know that someday someone would come for him. He brought me here shortly after we were married and made me promise to come here if anything ever happened to him." She looked around the room. "It wasn't much when I first saw it. He and Albert built the shelves and equipped it the way it is now."

Robert snapped a look at her, "Albert? Johnny's father?"

She smiled ruefully at him. "Oh yes. He and your father were close back then, like brothers. They grew apart over the years, but still retained some kind of a bond that I never really understood. I expect that we'll be hearing from Albert as soon as things settle down in the town. Meantime, here we are."

Robert stared at her across the gloom, still leaning on one elbow on the bed. Finally he got up and went to the channel of water in the corner. He lifted some and washed the sleep out of his eyes, his mind in turmoil. After taking a drink and running some of the water through his hair, he turned back to her, "What happened last night?"

She shook her head sadly. "I don't know much, just what he's told me over the years. For some reason, your father was hiding from the Duke. He came to this village nearly twenty years ago and took a job as an apprentice to the stable master. Albert came at about the same time. They may have been together, I don't remember." She put the pan of pork on the table along with some biscuits she'd fried in the grease and a pot of coffee. "Come along and have some breakfast. I took a chance and cooked for you. I suppose I needed something to do. After this, we'll only be able to cook at night after any patrols have gone in." She motioned toward the table. "Sit down. I'll tell you what I know. It's time you know. He had plans to tell you himself soon; he just never got around to it. No doubt he'd have been able to fill in the details better than I will."

Robert sat at one of the benches next to the table and reached for a biscuit. He started to eat, and realized that he was famished. After he'd finished several biscuits and most of the pork, he noticed that his mother was picking at her food, stirring it around on her plate, but not really eating.

"Are you all right?" he asked.

She smiled sadly at him. "I will be. It's going to take some time. I guess I always knew that this day would come. I just didn't know it would be so sudden."

She took a small bite of biscuit and a sip of coffee. "I know almost nothing of your father before he came to Masden. He's always been good with horses. I know that. And I know that he was a natural leader. He wouldn't take any kind of position in the town, but whenever the council met, they listened to him. He had a way with people." She let out a long sigh. "I've loved him since the first day I met him. I remember telling my sister the night he came to town that I'd met the man I was going to marry." She smiled. "She didn't believe me, but I did!"

"There was always something secretive, something hidden about him. I knew he'd been a soldier." She looked wistfully into the corner. I saw you checking out his armory there. I suppose those are yours now." She paused for a moment and wiped a tear, and then continued more forcefully, "He insisted from the time you were a little boy that you needed to train with weapons so that you'd be ready as a man. The same was true with your lessons in school, and his insistence that you learn the old tongue. And from the time you could walk, he had you working with the horses in the stables."

She looked at him and Robert smiled sadly, "I remember. I always had to be faster, stronger, and better than any of the others. I didn't understand it, but here I am, and today I suppose I'm glad. If he hadn't trained me so well, …" He grimaced.

"Anyway," she continued, "he and Albert spent a lot of time up here when they first arrived. I suppose that's how they found this chamber. They said it had belonged to old King Ethelbert a couple of hundred years ago, and that he was known to have built an emergency exit from each of his fortresses." She looked around at the small room. "I suppose it's fortunate for us that he did."

They talked away through the morning, and later that day she took Robert back to the passage that had led to the chamber. They hiked several hundred feet out to the exit buried in a thicket, and he memorized the twists and turns so that he could find the hidden chamber without difficulty.

Day followed day, and over the course of the next week, though anxious to leave, they became accustomed to their confinement.

# CHAPTER 6
## VISITORS

On the morning of their ninth day in the chamber, Robert was startled to hear muffled voices coming down through the light column above them. The novelty of the change got his attention, and he started listening intently. At first, the voices were soft and indistinct, and the passage of the sound through the narrow gap distorted the clarity, so though he listened carefully, he couldn't make meaning of them. He thought to call his mother, but she'd hiked down the tunnel a short while ago and hadn't yet returned. He continued to listen and as he did, the voices became clearer, as if the speakers had moved closer to the outlets above.

"...about here," a deep voice boomed through the rocks. "I remember this small cairn. We built it to mark the opening." Scuffling sounds followed, and Robert stared intently at the light source, holding his breath lest he miss any of the sounds. Suddenly, the voice came clearly. "Ah yes. Here we are. You see this crack in the rock here. It goes down into the mountain and provides light down below."

"Kathryn, Robert, Marie, you down there?"

Robert jumped at the sound of his name, and was about to answer when his mother returned. He turned to her and gestured to the ceiling. "Someone's up there," he whispered.

His mother listened and the voice came again. "This is Albert. I've brought Johnny. We'd like to come calling. Sally's here as well. She's brought nine of the village children with her."

Suddenly, his mother stiffened. She clapped her hands and whispered to Robert, "Nine. It's the safe word. It means they're alone. Two is a danger word." She called out, "Albert, it's so good to hear from you. We'll be waiting."

§§§§

By the time Albert and Johnny had climbed down to the chamber, they'd brewed a fresh pot of coffee and set out a meal of biscuits and dried apples. Robert was waiting at the door as they came up the tunnel. Johnny was in the lead, and seemed to have no difficulty finding the narrow pathway up to their hideout. As soon as he reached the top, Robert hugged him and then asked, "How'd you find us so easily? I've been up and down this trail dozens of times and still miss the markers from time to time."

Johnny grinned enigmatically and glanced back at his father. "I've been here before." Then he swept past Robert and into the chamber, "Ah, dried apples. My favorite." He sat at the table and picked up a slice of apple as Robert stared at him, mouth agape.

Albert stepped carefully across the threshold a few seconds later, and took Robert's hands seriously in his. "I'm sorry about your father. He was a good friend. I'll miss him." Seeing his mother, he went to her and wrapped her in a hug and just held her for a long time. Leaning back, he looked into her face, and then taking out his handkerchief, wiped away the fresh tears that stained her cheeks. "I'm so sorry, Kathryn. I'm so sorry." Then he put an arm around her shoulder and they walked together to the table. They sat, and he took her hand as if unwilling to let her go. "We came as soon as we could." He looked about the small room and then suddenly started. "Where's Marie?"

Kathryn squeezed his hand and said wearily, "They took her. That night. One of the men at arms came by on his horse and just grabbed her and dragged her off."

He shook his head. "That devil. We knew we'd never be completely safe here, but as the years went by and nothing happened... Well, I suppose we got complacent." He looked across the table at Robert, and then back at Kathryn, "You're going to have to stay here for a while. It's not safe to leave yet."

§§§§

Albert and Johnny stayed until it got dark, filling them in on events in the town. At one point, Johnny and Robert hiked up to the emergency exit, and sat at the opening, talking in the dim light that filtered through the leaves.

"How long have you known about this place?" Robert finally asked his friend.

Johnny looked out through the brush, as if trying to avoid an answer. After a while, head downcast, he spoke, "Long time. Years. I was sworn to secrecy. I don't think even your father knew I'd been here. I only came with my dad. There were times when he needed help, and he brought me along." He paused and looked sadly at Robert. "I'm sorry about your father. I truly am. And I would have told you about this place if I could have. But I couldn't." Then he grinned and punched Robert softly in the shoulder, "It would have been a great place to play when we were younger!"

"I suppose I understand," Robert said slowly. He looked across the tunnel to where he could see his friend's silhouette in the near darkness. "My father always said that a man is only as good as his word. As hard as it is knowing that you'd been here before, I don't think I'd have been able to trust you in the future if you'd broken your oath to your father. And somehow I have a feeling that my trust in you is going to get pretty important."

§§§§

That night, as Robert lay on his cot, his head swirled with what he'd learned during the day. That his father had found and provisioned this hiding place he'd known now for several days. Why, he still wasn't sure. And Albert and Johnny knew about it! Why was that? He stirred restlessly and looked across the blackness to where he could hear his mother snoring. What else did she know? What was she keeping from him, and more importantly, why?

Finally, he fell into a fitful sleep, full of dreams of battles, and soldiers, and confusion.

# CHAPTER 7
## A CONFUSING HISTORY

Three days later, Albert and Johnny came again. As before, they were careful to announce their presence through the crack above the hidden chamber. When they clambered down into the vault, Robert met them at the door. Before Johnny climbed up, he tossed him a rabbit, still warm to the touch.

He grinned mischievously, "I caught it this morning. If you're not tired of dried meat and beans, let me know and I'll take it home."

Robert just stared at the soft bundle in his hand and then said, "You have no idea how happy I am to see that!" He reached out his hand and pulled his friend up the rest of the way.

Once they'd settled into the chamber, Albert turned serious. "The duke's men seem to have left, but I'm sure they've not gone far. They know you escaped, but don't know where you've gone. I got word that they've been searching a few of the neighboring villages on the pretext of a hunt for escaped fugitives. They've questioned everyone in Masden but nobody other than Johnny and I knew about this place, and your father and I were careful not to seem to be too close for a long time, so nobody has connected us yet. I think you're safe for now."

He looked around the chamber, lit by the dim light that filtered down through the crack in the ceiling as if deciding what to say next. Finally, he took Kathryn's hand and whispered, "Were you able to get the ring?"

Robert looked curiously at his mother and was about to ask what they were talking about when she reached under her cot and took out a small package wrapped in an old stained cloth. Reverently, she unwrapped the material and handed it to Albert. "It's here."

Albert took the bundle carefully and seemed to nod. He brushed off a few crumbs of dirt from the wooden box, and then with a conscious motion, used the sleeve of his jerkin to buff the wood on the box. To Robert's surprise, the wood responded with a mellow richness and began to glow under his touch. They all watched in silence, as he polished first the top, then the bottom, and then the sides. Finally, satisfied, he held up the box for all to see. The effect was stunning. What had previously been a simple dirty wooden box had been transformed to a piece of art. The box itself seemed to have been crafted out of several different hardwoods, each separated by a delicate piece of inlaid silver. A tiny brass button protruded from one side, and he gently pushed that and then opened up the top. Inside, wedged into a bed of satin, was a heavy man's ring, the gold intricately carved with what appeared to be ancient runes and set with a large dull red gemstone. He held it out to Robert. "This was your father's ring. I suppose now that it's yours."

Robert looked at the ring, mesmerized, and then at his mother. He started to reach for it, but Albert pulled it back.

"Before I give it to you, I need to tell you a little more about your father." He looked at Kathryn, "How much have you told him?"

She shook her head sadly, "I know so little, and promised never to talk with anyone."

Albert nodded. "A wise promise." Then he looked across at Robert. "What I am about to tell you is for your ears only. On pain of death, you must not tell anyone of this until you are sure that the right moment has come. Do you agree?"

Dumbly, Robert nodded, and then looked toward his mother and Johnny.

Albert seemed to relax a bit and then began again. "Your mother knows some of what I am about to say, but like you, is sworn to secrecy. Johnny knows some, but he will need to know more because when you leave here, he will be going with you."

Robert looked around him. When his eyes crossed his friend's, Johnny grinned, but then seeing the earnestness on his father's face, became serious again.

Looking back at Albert, Robert said, "All right, you have my attention."

Albert put the box down on the table, but left the lid open so that they could all still see the ring. He pulled at the beard on his chin, as if trying to figure out how to begin, and then leaned back.

"For as long as you have known your father, he has been a stable master. And," he paused and looked at his son, "I have been a farmer since I came to the village." He stopped and smiled. "I apologize. After keeping quiet for so long, it's hard to talk of this now." Gathering his strength, he continued. "Our fathers however, were powerful men. They lived on great estates in Entaro, the capital city, and consorted with the mighty every day. The kingdom was prosperous, and the king was well loved by his people. Duke Henry, as he likes to call himself, was a member of the lesser nobility, related only distantly to the king. He was then, and remains today, a thug, a brute, and a coward. He was however, a prosperous man, though some say that his wealth came from extortion and other criminal enterprises. I don't know, but I wouldn't be surprised." He paused and drank water from the flask in front of him before continuing. "Anyway, he was able to put together a small army of thugs like himself, men of low breeding and lower morality, but also men of great ambition. Through treachery and guile, they waylaid the king as he was traveling to pay his respects at the shrine of his sainted mother, and killed him along with his guards. From there, they raced to his castle, and propping him clumsily on his horse, yelled out to the guard that the king had fallen ill and needed immediate attention from the court doctors. Of course, the guard recognized the king and could see that he was not well, so they opened the gates. Once inside, the murderers, for that's what they were, killed the guard and captured the castle. Henry took over as duke and quickly consolidated his power over the land in a bloody massacre of the nobility. As each of the great estates fell vacant, Henry rewarded one of his henchmen, until all were sated. Our families were among the first to fall under the axe, but your father and I were out hunting at the time and managed to escape."

Slowly, Albert took up the box and held it out to Robert again. "This ring is your inheritance from your father." He passed him the box as he said softly, "guard it with your very life!"

Robert took the box and carefully took out the ring. As he held it up to examine the strange designs, the stone in the ring emitted a soft ruby glow, as if it was catching every bit of light in the room. He began to slide it over his finger and Albert quickly grabbed his hand. "No," he hissed. "You must not wear the ring until the right time has come. This ring will identify you to others. The duke sought out your father across the years and killed him. He's kidnapped Marie. He is certain to be watching for you." He handed him a long thick leather thong. "Put this through the ring and hang it about your neck. Keep it with you at all times, but know that showing it to others could sign your death warrant!"

Carefully, Robert slid the ring over the thong and then tied the ends to form a secure knot. He slipped the thong over his head and tucked the ring into his tunic, so that it hung just beneath his breastbone. Only then did he look back at Albert and ask, "How will I know the right time?"

Albert nodded, pleased. "A proper question, and one that only you will be able to answer." He smiled enigmatically and said, "I've said all that I can for now. Tonight, just after dark, you and Johnny must leave here." He looked at his son who nodded. "Make your way to Waterton and seek out Andrew Jameson. He's a merchant who owns a fleet of ships. Seek passage as seamen with him. He'll be able to tell you more. You'll need to travel overland, and go by night, as the duke's men are watching the roads. Johnny knows the way. Now it's time to pack and rest so that you'll be ready to leave at dusk."

# CHAPTER 8
## MARIE MEETS THE DUKE

Marie had been resting against the back wall of her cell when she heard voices outside. This was common enough that she really didn't pay much attention until one of the men said, "So where is she?" She heard the men coming toward her cell, and assuming then that she was likely the only female prisoner, turned toward the door. Sure enough, the key rattled in the lock; the door swung open; and a large man stepped in.

Even in the dim light, Marie could tell that he was richly dressed in some kind of shimmering cream colored silk. He strode forward just enough to catch the light from the high window. Midway across the cell, he stopped, his cruel eyes staring down at Marie. Finally, he spoke. "Where's your brother?"

Marie just stared at him, uncomprehending. He waited and then repeated, louder and slower than before. "Where is your brother?"

"I, I, I don't know," she stammered.

The man squatted, careful not to soil his fancy clothing in the filth of the cell. "Don't play coy with me, girl. I want your brother."

Marie just shook her head. The last image she had of Robert had been when she'd reached back to help her mother, just after climbing through her parents' bedroom window. He was holding the bloody fireplace poker in his hands, just outside the bedroom door.    She looked up at the man in confusion. "Somebody broke into our house.    He and father were fighting them."

"I know that," the man snarled.    "Where is he now?"

She shrugged her shoulders, "I don't know.    Somebody grabbed me and ... I didn't see either of them again."

"Where would he have gone?"

Marie had difficulty even figuring out what the man wanted.    Gone?    Where would Robert have gone, if not home? She had no idea. "I don't know," she moaned. "I just don't know."

The man stared at her for a long time, finally deciding that he'd get no more from her.    He turned to go, stopping just inside the door and looking back. "I'll find him, you know." Then he stepped through the door.    Just before he closed it, she heard him say, "Cut her rations in half.    Let's see if a little hunger loosens her tongue."

He stomped down the hall and the jailor peeked in. "You hear that?" he asked.    Without waiting for a response, he added, "Won't be no dinner tonight. Duke's orders."

# CHAPTER 9
## OUT INTO THE LIGHT

It seemed to Robert that he'd just fallen asleep when his mother shook his shoulder and whispered, "It's time to go." He opened his eyes and looked about the cavern. Already the light was failing, and areas of the room that had been visible during the day were shrouded in darkness. He blinked once, twice, and then rolled his feet off to the dirt floor. Stretching, he ran his fingers through his blonde hair and looked about for Johnny. His friend was quickly filling a rucksack with cheese, dried fruit, and bread. He wore a light traveling cloak that would keep him warm while blocking the rain.

He smiled when he noticed Robert stirring. "So you're up. Ready for the grand adventure?"

Robert absently fingered the ring inside his tunic and nodded. He noticed that Johnny had brought two rucksacks as well as two traveling cloaks and mused that he and Albert had planned well for this journey. "What can I do to help?"

"We're pretty well set," Johnny answered him. "I've got the bags packed. It's mostly food with a simple change of clothes." He turned back to the bag.

Robert noticed for the first time that Albert and his mother weren't in the room. He went to the door and when he swung it open, could hear their whispered voices outside in the tunnel. They had carried a small candle with them, and he could just recognize their images in the flickering light. "Mother?" he called.

She turned toward him and he noted the worry etched into her face. She stood and walked to him, and then pulled her way up the footholds to the door to the chamber. Albert followed behind her. Once inside, she went to Robert and wrapped her arms around him, pulling him tight for a long hug. "Be safe," she whispered, and then let go. Still holding him by his hands, she looked into his face and repeated firmly, "Be safe." Then she turned away and went to the corner of the room where Robert had previously noticed the small armory. Bending down, she selected two short daggers and then rose. She looked at her son and said, "I'd tell you to take more, but that would make you stand out. Poor country boys don't wear armor or carry swords. These though, won't draw as much attention." She handed one dagger to Robert and another to Johnny.

Robert withdrew the blade from its scabbard and saw that she'd given him a simple but vicious looking weapon. The handle was covered with sharkskin and wrapped in fine wire to give it an abrasive grip. Beyond the pommel was a stiletto blade, about eight inches in length, that narrowed to a razor sharp point. The weapon was simple, but well constructed. He slipped it back into the scabbard and then strapped it to his right calf noticing as he did so, that Johnny had already put his knife away and returned to the rucksack. He cocked his head as he looked at his friend, wondering where this serious side of Johnny had come from. He'd always been so playful when they were together in the past. Then he thought about all that had happened in the past few days and what might occur in the days to come and reflected that he and Johnny were both becoming men in a hurry.

"The sun will be setting soon," Albert said. "You'd best be on your way. Remember, stick to the forests as much as you can, and be careful to cover your trail as you go. If you see the duke's men, find a good place to hide and lay low. They're mostly watching the roads, but you never know." He took Johnny by the shoulders and looked into his face before pulling him close in a crushing hug. "I know you'll make me proud." He held him for a long moment before pushing him away, and then stepped back. "Do you have everything?"

Johnny nodded, unsure of what to say.

"Good. Robert, are you ready?"

Robert nodded as well. Suddenly the hazards of what they were about to do were settling in on him. He'd never traveled more than a few miles from the village before, and then always with his father. Now he was setting out on a trip of over two hundred miles, to a city he'd never seen, to meet a man he'd never known, and all that with a friend whose experiences were as limited as his. He wanted everything to go back to the way it had been before the attack, but knew that it never could. He looked at his mother. "I'll be back," he said, "And when I come back I'll be bringing Marie."

She smiled at him and then inclined her head. "I know."

Albert looked up at the ceiling. The last light of day was gone, and the chamber was lit only by the small candle they'd had in the tunnel. "Time to go," he said simply.

§§§§

That night's journey was uneventful. With Johnny in the lead, they used the moonlight to follow narrow animal trails they'd used as boys when hunting in the forest. Only once did they see any sign of anyone else there, a fire that emitted a flickering light across the valley. They kept their distance, slowly working their way deeper and deeper into the forest until they were sure that they were alone. Finally, after several hours of traveling, Johnny stopped. He motioned Robert up to him and pointed to the east. "Daylight," he whispered. "We'd better find a place to camp."

Robert nodded. Though it was still quite dark under the canopy of the trees, the sky was starting to lighten with the coming day. They hiked for another quarter mile before Johnny broke his way off to the right, along a narrow rabbit trail. They followed it for about one hundred paces until it disappeared into a thicket.

Getting down on their hands and knees, they crawled through the brush down into a small glade, just big enough to accommodate the two of them. To all extents and purposes, they'd be invisible in the unlikely event that anyone else came wandering down the path.

Robert looked around at the dimly lit space. "Good choice," he said softly. Then he took off his knapsack and pulled out a canvas water bag. He took a long drink of the cool water and handed it to Johnny. While Johnny drank, he stretched out his blanket and lay down. "It's been a long day. I could do with some rest."

Johnny finished the water and then rolled out his own blanket. As he lay back, he looked over at Robert, surprised to see that his friend was already asleep.

§§§§

On their seventh night, they came to the Founderie River. Robert slipped through the last of the trees and looked up and down the banks. The moonlight glinted off of occasional clear patches of smooth surface and he could hear the water tumbling through a series of falls. "I don't see anyone, but it's much too dangerous to cross here. I think I can see a bridge downstream."

Johnny peeked out through the brush and agreed. "My father and I talked about that. He said it would be a logical place for the duke's men to be waiting for you. There's a toll taker posted just on the far side of the bridge. He's just a local villager, but who knows if he's alone." He looked again. They were standing at the top of a steep bank that fell away sharply into a boulder strewn stream. Trees grew out of the sides of the riverbank, and he could trace multiple handholds that they could use to lower themselves into the water for an attempt at swimming across. The waterway below them wasn't wide, but the current was swift and the rapids treacherous. Any crossing was bound to be fraught with danger, either from the guard at the bridge or from the river itself. He backed into the brush. Sitting, he took off his backpack and said, "We're pretty secure here. Let's have a bit of lunch and talk it over."

Robert chuckled. "Are you ever not hungry?"

Johnny looked at him as though he was deep in thought and then smiled. "Now that I think about it, no." He cut a slice of apple and some cheese and offered them to Robert. "My father mentioned an old ferry crossing about five miles upstream from the bridge. He wasn't sure if the ferryman was even still there, but according to what he had to say, the river is pretty wide and just drifts along there. It's still too deep to wade, but even if we can't find the ferryman, we might be able to swim across."

Robert chewed thoughtfully on his apple. "No rapids?"

"Not from what he told me."

"We'd be pretty obvious during the daytime. Do you think we could swim it at night?"

Chewing thoughtfully, Johnny considered his answer for a moment. Finally, he answered by standing and shouldering his knapsack. "Only one way to find out. Ready?"

Robert popped a last bite of cheese into his mouth and stood. "Lead on.

§§§§

Backtracking into the forest, they were able to find a series of narrow trails that led along the riverbank. Occasionally, they came out at water level but always, the water was too swift to attempt a crossing. Often, the trails narrowed so that they had to push their way through the underbrush, so it wasn't until just before dawn that they reached a slow moving stretch of river that looked like a logical crossing. Continuing on, they came upon a wider trail, obviously rutted with cartwheels. Looking down toward the river, they could see a small, dilapidated wooden dock jutting precariously out into the water. Nobody was in sight, but the light was still too dim and the river too wide to see if anyone was on the far side.

Inclining his head back into the forest, Robert whispered, "Let's find a place to spend the day. It's going to be light soon, and I'd like to have a look at the crossing when we can see well. I don't want to be caught out in the open during daytime."

"Good idea," Johnny said. "I saw a good hiding place a little way back."

Moving carefully, they made their way back into the forest and up onto a ridge that overlooked the riverbank. The area was thickly forested and they were able to find a sleeping place nestled in the brush. The day brightened quickly, and they found that just a few yards closer to the river, they were able to see clearly through the shrubbery while remaining hidden from view by anyone on the far side.

Johnny wriggled to the front first and carefully scanned through the branches. Coming up softly next to him, Robert asked, "What do you see?"

Johnny crept a little further out, and then focused on the far bank were he could see the partner to the dock at the end of the road they'd just left behind them. "Another dock. This must be the ferry crossing." He smiled and looked across to Robert. See it?"

Nodding, Robert smiled. "This is the place then. If we wait a while we'll probably see the ferryman. That's probably his cottage in the distance." He started to raise his hand to point out a wisp of smoke rising from a structure half concealed in the forest when suddenly he froze, "Wait. There's something there, behind that big tree by the dock." He stared intently through the bushes, and then whispered, "I'm sure I saw some movement. "The ferryman?"

Suddenly, a man stepped out, walked out to the dock, and after stretching his arms to either side, spat into the water. His chain mail caught the early morning sunlight and sent gleaming reflections of light up and down the river.

"Don't move," Johnny hissed as he stared at the man. "Wait for him to turn."

The man in the armor walked out to the end of the dock, and looking up and down the river, grunted and took an apple out of his satchel. Smiling grimly, he bit into the red fruit as he scanned the opposite bank. His eyes passed several times over the spot where Johnny and Robert lay, and seemed to settle there once before moving on.

The two young men clung to the ground, eyes staring straight ahead for what seemed an eternity. Finally, they heard a muffled voice from across the river. Another armored man emerged from behind the trees and walked toward the dock. The man with the apple turned and walked toward his partner.

"Now," whispered Robert. Both boys inched back slowly, careful not to disturb any of the greenery that had hidden them from view. Finally, as he slid below the crest of the rise, Robert let out a soft breath, and looked back to his friend. "Whew. They're definitely looking for someone."

Johnny nodded slowly and then broke into a grin, "And I'll bet you that someone is us!"

"So what do you propose we do?" Robert looked at his friend. "There're probably more than just those two. Do you know of any other crossings?"

Shaking his head, Johnny spoke slowly. "My dad only mentioned this one. I wouldn't want to try the rapids we saw earlier. We're going to have to make this work. There's not as much moon tonight. If we head upstream a little bit, we'll still catch the slow current but should be able to get across without being seen." He walked over to his rucksack. "For now, we wait. Seeing that soldier with that apple reminded me that I was hungry." He grinned. "After that, a little nap, and than a nice swim in the river."

Robert stared at his friend, and then began to laugh softly. "Whatever you say."

# CHAPTER 10
# RIVER CROSSING

Both boys slept through the day and woke just before sunset. Refreshed and eager to get on, Johnny crept to the edge of their clearing and poked his head over the rise that had protected them from view. "All quiet over there," he whispered. He scanned up and down the river, and then stared a while at the trail leading away from the dock. The ferryboat was tied securely to the shore, and a wisp of smoke arose from the cabin on the far side. "I'll bet they're eating dinner right now." He looked up at the sun, hovering just above the western forest. "Time to get ready for a swim. The sun should be well down in another hour."

Quietly, the two ate a light dinner of dried fruits and bread. Chewing thoughtfully, Johnny spoke. "I saw an animal trail going down to the water just downstream from here. That'll take us a little further away from the dock, and as it gets darker, I don't think they'll be able to tell we're in the water. Besides, if we flow with the river, we should drift around that little bend down there, so they won't be able to see us getting out."

Robert nodded his head thoughtfully. "It's so quiet out, our biggest problem will probably be noise. We're going to have to be careful not to splash." He grinned. "We're not likely to sound like fish!"

Chuckling softly, Johnny replied. "Maybe they'll mistake us for really big fish."

Robert looked at his friend seriously. "Yeah. That's what I'm afraid of. According to the duke, we are big fish!"

Johnny tilted his head and took a deep breath. "Right," he said, and took another bite of bread.

As they ate, each lost in his own worries, the sun slowly settled in the west, and the stars came out. The moon was a scant sliver above, and cast little light. Johnny finished his last handful of fruit, brushed his hands, and stood. Shouldering his backpack, he asked, "Ready?"

Robert rose and picked up his pack. "As I'll ever be." He shivered. "I have a feeling it's going to be a cold night." He looked thoughtfully across at his friend. "I don't suppose there's any chance we can risk a fire to dry off after our swim."

Johnny just shook his head and turned. He parted the branches ahead, scanned across the river, and then waved for Robert to follow. Stealthily, they made their way down the trail toward the riverbank. Fortunately, the brush grew lush and tall, and by hunching, they were able to hide in the animal trail. Walking slowly and carefully, the two managed to reach the sandbar below without making a sound. Robert looked over Johnny's shoulder at their crossing. The river was wide and deep, and the water drifted lazily downstream with scarcely a ripple. He sat on the bank and pulled off his boots, and then stuffed his socks inside and tied the laces together. To Johnny's questioning look, he whispered, "Put 'em around your neck. At least your feet will stay dry."

Johnny pulled off his shoes and socks. "I don't see any sign of the soldiers right now. You ready?"

Robert took the lead, crouching around the rocks on the bank. When he reached the edge, he slipped in carefully to avoid making a splash. The water came past his knees, and rapidly got deeper. Whistling against the cold, he struck out for the far side in a smooth, soundless breaststroke, his shoes perched precariously on his back. Looking back once, he saw Johnny's head just above the surface.    Then he turned forward and concentrated on swimming.

The current was gentle, but by the time they reached the other side, they were well around the slight bend in the river. The dock was hidden from view, "just as we are from the dock," Robert whispered softly to himself. As he got closer to the side, he tried to stand, and found that the water was only waist deep. Dripping and shivering from the icy water, he pushed through the last of the river and made his way carefully into the forest on the other side. Once he reached the shelter of the trees, he crawled under a large pine whose outer branches hung almost all the way to the ground, forming a tight chamber in which they could hide.    Johnny followed right behind him, and once he got inside, whispered through his chattering teeth, "I didn't see any sign of anyone, and we should hear them coming with that chain mail, but I'd still like to get a few miles from here before we burrow in for the night."

Robert had stripped off his shirt, and was soundlessly wringing out the excess water. That done, he sat and began drying one foot with a sock.    He nodded quickly, "If we head straight away from the river, we should hit the road just a little way from here.    Nobody's likely to be traveling at night, and if we keep to the fringe of the forest, we should be fine. We'll make better time than trying to slog through the underbrush."

Johnny looked around as he tied his boot, and then he cracked a characteristic grin.    "Ah well, a nice evening swim always brightens the spirits.    Besides, I think we both needed a bath anyway." He wrinkled his nose. "I know you did!" He ran his fingers through his wet hair and then peeked out through the branches. "I think I see a narrow trail up ahead. Let's see where that takes us."

# CHAPTER 11
## THE WOOD CUTTER'S HUT

They walked through most of the cold, wet night and as they'd hoped, nobody was out on the road. Still, they stuck to the edge of the forest, ready to bolt into cover at the first sight or sound of any pursuit. Johnny was nervously wondering where they'd sleep when he noticed an overgrown cart path.

Small aspen saplings grew up in the middle of the path, and the ruts made by the wheels were covered in grass, suggesting that it hadn't been used in some time. Johnny signaled a stop, and then walked a little way up the path. Looking back, he waved Robert to join him. "Do you suppose this belonged to some old forester?"

Robert looked up the trail as far as he could see. The eastern horizon was starting to glow lightly, and he could just make out the winding trail grown over with scrub. "We need to get off the road before the sun comes up anyway. I say we try it. There might be someplace up there to hole up for the day. You found it. You lead. I'll follow."

Johnny bowed with a flourish, "As you command." Adjusting his pack, he struck out down the road, pushing the occasional branch to the side so that he could pass.

Robert figured that they'd walked for a quarter mile when Johnny suddenly crouched and raised his hand. The sun still hadn't risen over the mountains to the east, but the sky had brightened considerably, and they'd had little trouble following the trail through the forest.    Coming up next to his friend, he whispered, "What is it?"

Johnny raised his arm and pointed.  Up ahead, just visible through the branches, was an old woodsman's hut.  As he looked, Robert could see that the place had an abandoned look.  A broken wooden door hung precariously from a pair of leather hinges, and low undergrowth had grown across the clearing in front of the building, mostly hiding the gravel pathway that lead to the porch.

They huddled together and watched for several minutes, before Johnny said softly, "I don't think there's anybody there.  No smoke, no noise.  Anybody living there should be up and about by now.  We'd hear them getting set for the day.  Shall we try it?"

Robert stood and cocked his head.  "You're right.  I don't hear anyone.  We're going to need a place to stay, and I don't think anyone's been here in a long time.  I'm game, but let's be careful, just in case."  He rose and led the way cautiously up the trail to the edge of the clearing around the hut.  Studying the open ground around him, he assured himself that they were alone, and then sprinted for the hut, with Johnny on his heels.  Reaching the door, he flung it open, then jumped back in shock, bumping into his friend.

Johnny pushed past him and brushed aside some cobwebs to look into the hut.  It was a simple dwelling, about the size of a large room.  A fireplace rose at one side, a rusty pot hanging from a metal tripod over cold ashes.  Dirty, tattered clothing hung from nails driven into the walls, and a set of shelves held a few simple possessions.  A plate and cup sat on a rickety table in the middle of the room, gathering dust in the dim light from the newly opened door.  Then he saw what had driven Robert out, and gasped.  Built into the wall at the far end of the room was a narrow bed, the covers lifted by a slender body.  The only thing that stuck out from the head of the bed was a bleached white skull.

He stepped back and looked at Robert.  "Not abandoned," he said.

Robert shook his head.  "I'll bet nobody knows he's dead."

"Or even knew that he lived here. How long do you suppose..." He looked back and shivered again, though not from his cold wet clothes this time.

Robert stepped into the hut and walked to the bed. Gingerly lifting the blanket, he took in the skeleton in front of him. "I don't know, several months at least. Maybe years. He must have died in his sleep." He turned back to Johnny and said. "If you don't mind sharing with the dead, I think we've found a place to dry off."

Johnny grinned ruefully, "I'm so cold right now, I do believe that I could share with a corpse." Then he turned serious. "I'll gather firewood while you clean up in here." He looked across the room. "I see he has a couple of stools, and there's a rack in that corner. We can hang our clothes and dry them off in front of the fire." He looked back ruefully at the skeleton on the bed. "Once we dry off and warm up, I'd like to bury our host and thank him for letting us use his home."

# CHAPTER 12
## OUT OF THE DUNGEON, INTO THE FIRE

Marie heard the rattling of a chain on the metal door and lifted her head. The door was solid, with a small rectangular opening at the bottom through which they'd passed her food and water over the past days, and bars over a small window. As she looked at the door, she wondered, "How long have I been here? One week? Two? Longer?" She had little sense of time passing in the dark room, measuring only her hours of sleep and wake. They'd taken out the others some time ago. All had been dead, and she'd initially wondered that she hadn't smelled their decaying corpses, but then realized that with the stench of the moldy walls and the slop bucket, nothing else would matter much. She found a hole in the floor in one corner and learned to pour the slops in there, but still, the room stank of decay and of bodies left too long unwashed.

The door opened and she winced as the light pierced the darkness she had grown accustomed to. A tall man stepped into the room and she tried to see him, but could only make out his silhouette against the light of the hallway beyond. He wrinkled his nose and spat in disgust. Some of the spittle landed on the hem of her nightdress and she instinctively crawled back in fear. He stared at her and then said, "Well, what have we here? The duke'll be wanting to see you." He turned to someone behind him and continued, "Clean her up as well as you can but don't take too long.  I'm to deliver her to the audience hall within the hour."  He turned and strode out the door.

Marie looked warily out from her corner as another smaller figure stepped into the doorway.  A female voice spoke.  "Come with me girl.  I'm to bathe you and put you into clean clothes." Marie hesitated and the woman spoke harshly, "Unless you wish to have the duke see you like this, you'll do as you're told and quickly."  Still Marie hesitated and she said, "If need be, Randolf will drag you up the stairs and toss you into your bath, but he won't be gentle."  Then she softened her voice, "Come.  You won't be harmed."  She held out her hand and Marie stood carefully, mindful of the low ceiling against the walls.   She stumbled forward, still holding her hand up against the light of the hallway.

The woman took her elbow and pulled her out of the cell, "That's better dearie.  Now follow me."  She turned toward a heavy metal door at the end of the hall.

Marie heard a sound and saw that an armored man wearing a sword had come up behind her, cutting off any possibility of escape in that direction.  She smiled ruefully and thought, "I wouldn't know where to go even if I could get past him.  Best to follow."  Putting one foot in front of the other, and shaking off the stiffness in muscles too long unused, she followed the woman down the hall and up a set of stairs.

# CHAPTER 13
## THE SILVER CHARM

The sun rose early over the forest, and Robert stretched, eyes closed, as he lay in the half sleep of early morning. "I need to finish that harness today," he thought and then sat and started to swing his feet off of the bed. Only when they slid awkwardly across the rough wooden floor did he open his eyes and in confusion, take in the unfamiliar boundaries of the hut. "Huh, right," he thought. Looking to the side, he saw Johnny, also on the floor and wrapped tightly in one of the blankets they'd found the night before, snoring softly.

Robert stood, and carefully folding his blanket, put it back on the cot where they'd found it. They'd worked hard much of the previous day, ignoring their fatigue, drying off and then making the hut comfortable. Finally, as the sun began to set, they gave in to their exhaustion and prepared for bed. Neither had been willing to sleep on the small cot against the back wall where they'd found the skeleton that morning. Even after burying him in the clearing outside the hut, they'd only looked longingly at the bed before deciding to sleep on the floor. With a sigh, Robert raised his arms over his head, and then bent and twisted at the waist, trying to work out the stiffness in muscles still not accustomed to sleeping on the ground. Then he walked to the door, pushed it open, and stepped outside.

The sun hadn't yet risen over the hills in the east, and the cold cut through his clothing, making him glad to be dry again. The sky was lightening more with each passing minute though, and he could see easily around the clearing. They'd taken pains to mask their trail the previous day, certain that they'd found a safe place to stay and plan for a few days. As he looked around, Robert could see no signs that any of their markers had been disturbed, so he sat on the front porch and began to think about all that had occurred over the past weeks. His father dead and his home gone; his mother hiding, and Marie... He winced softly and wondered what had happened to Marie. Nodding his head resolutely, he thought of the duke's men who had wreaked such devastation on his family and vowed softly to himself, "I will have my vengeance. I don't know how, but somebody's going to pay for this."

Then shaking his head as if to clear his thoughts, he rose and walked up the path that led back to the main road. They had found a side trail the previous day, but hadn't had time to explore it. Now, with Johnny snoozing in the hut, seemed just the time. He walked up to the trailhead, and then pushed through a group of leafy green aspen branches and stepped forward. The path was narrow, but clearly had been made by a man. The aspen trees to the left and right grew tightly over thick underbrush, but the path was clear and bore the scars of the woodsman's axe. He stopped, listened carefully, and then made his way silently up the trail. Occasionally he detected a flash of movement in the brush, a bird or a small rodent scurrying away from the intruder. He estimated he had traveled a hundred yards when the trail broadened out and he stepped into a large clearing. Scattered as if by chance, tree stumps stuck up from the ground, each surrounded by a pile of wood chips. He whistled softly. This must be where the man had made his living, and a hard one at that. He reflected on the torn furrows on the trail behind him and imagined the effort involved in pulling a log out from the forest. "I hope you rest well, my friend," he thought, "You've earned it."

Robert was about to hike back to the hut to see if Johnny was stirring yet when a soft glimmer caught his eye. He walked over to the shine and then squatted down. As he reached out, his hand blocked the sunlight and the fire went out of the object, but when he moved his hand aside, the glow returned. He reached down and pried the object loose from the soil. Brushing off dirt and leaves, he held it up to the sunlight and tried to make out what he had found. It was a piece of jewelry, round, about two inches across, and finely wrought of silver with an eagle overlaid upon it in gold. He turned it over and brushed away more dirt revealing a clasp, such as one might find on a brooch a man would use to hold his cloak at the shoulder. He reversed the brooch and using his fingernail, cleaned away more of the dirt. He could detect some pattern of words, but they would need cleaning before he could read them. He stood slowly, still looking at the piece of jewelry in his hand and muttered softly. "Now what in the world might this be doing here?" Still puzzled, he walked slowly back up the trail to the hut.

When he arrived, a wisp of smoke drifting lazily up from the chimney told him that Johnny was up. He smiled. "Hungry again, I suppose." Then he quickened his pace.

Johnny had plainly been up for a while. His blanket too, was folded and stacked atop Robert's on the cot. He was bent over something on the table and looked up as Robert came through the door. He grinned broadly, "I told you those snares we set yesterday would pay off." He pointed down to the table with his knife and Robert could see that he had been hard at work skinning a fat brown rabbit. "This should give us meat for a couple of days." Robert simply nodded and walked to the corner where they'd filled a pail with water the previous night. He dipped a rag in the water then returned to sit on the stool by the table. Johnny continued working on the rabbit, but watched as Robert went to work cleaning the brooch. "What do you have there?" he asked.

Robert looked up at him. "I'm not sure. I found it in the forest. There's a clearing up that little trail we found yesterday.

Lots of trees cut down. This was off to the side, half buried in the dirt. If the sun hadn't just been coming over the hills and hit it just right, I probably wouldn't even have seen it." He held it up for Johnny to see. "Some kind of jewelry I think."

Johnny stopped skinning the rabbit long enough to look the brooch over closely. "Now how would something like that get lost here," he asked.

Robert shook his head. "I was wondering the same thing myself." He poured a little more water over the brooch and scraped away the last of the dirt. "There's some kind of writing on it. Strange. It seems to be in the old tongue." He squinted in the dim light of the hut, and then walked over to the sunlight that was filtering through the door. "Interesting."

Johnny walked over next to him, still holding the bloody knife. "What's it say?"

"It seems to say 'Lord High Treasurer.'"

Johnny scrunched his face up and looked closely at the brooch. "Hmm," he said. "You're right." He looked at his friend, "What would a man like that be doing out here? Suppose somebody stole it?"

Robert gave him a puzzled look, startled that Johnny could read the ancient language, and then shrugged it off. With everything he'd begun to learn about his friend, nothing seemed to surprise him any more. He just nodded. "A good question. A good question indeed."

§§§§

Later that day, the two young men sat on the porch and planned their next moves. The rabbit had been filling and they both felt a sense of contentment they hadn't experienced since before the attack.

"I say we stay here for a while," Johnny ventured. "There's plenty of food and we've got a nice warm place to shelter. Moreover, I don't think anyone knows about this place."

Robert nodded thoughtfully. "I don't disagree," he said slowly, "but I'm worried about Marie. The more time we spend here, the less time we'll spend searching for her. Besides, your father told us to find Andrew Jameson. How far do you suppose we are from Waterton?"

Johnny thought for a while, and then picked up a stick and started to draw in the dirt. He drew crudely, but clearly, and Robert could follow his markings well. He drew an X and said, "Here's Masden." He placed another mark not too far away, "And here's the old hill fort where you hid for a while. When we left there..." He drew an irregular shape in the dirt, then bisected it with a line. "We wandered through the Hidden Forest. At the edge," he drew a double line that curled around the forest and then trailed off on either side, "runs the Founderie River. We crossed that here," he drew in the ferry crossing, "and then ran along the road most of the night." He drew in another forest crossed by a winding road, and then drew a reasonably accurate portrayal of the woodsman's hut. "That should put us about here. We want to get to Waterton, which I'd guess is another two week's travel, pushing through the forest, or less by road." He drew another diagram, showing that the road through the forest would end amid a crosshatch of houses and wharves up against a wide bay.

Robert traced his finger along the road and then popped it down at the edge of the bay. "A few days then. Tomorrow we rest and gather food. The day after, we leave." He looked at Johnny with an air of command. "If we travel by night, we should be able to go by road.

Johnny looked slowly at his own map. "We'll have to be careful. The duke's men are out there, and as we get closer to town, there'll be others." He looked up at Robert, "Are you sure you wouldn't like to go overland? The forest at least offers some shelter. The road could be trouble."

Robert shook his head, having made up his mind. "No," he said. "I have a feeling that time is important now. We take the road."

Standing, Johnny said resignedly, "I'm going to check the snares again then. I'd like to catch another rabbit before we leave."

# CHAPTER 14
## FOOLING THE SOLDIERS

They left at dusk the following day, having rested and re-provisioned.  Robert, in a jaunty mood, whistled softly under his breath as they hiked along.  Johnny, less sanguine, walked quietly, searching frequently behind him, as if he suspected that they were being followed.  The night passed uneventfully, and as the sun started to rise in the east, they burrowed into a thicket a couple of hundred yards up an animal trail to sleep away the day.  Johnny insisted that they keep watches, and volunteered for the first. Robert though, waved him off.  "We haven't seen anyone on the road.  I'm sure we're safe."

"I don't know," Johnny said.  "I'm feeling nervous."

"We're fine," Robert said with finality.  "We're well off the road, and even a fox would have difficulty finding us here.  He rolled over, settling his head onto his knapsack, and almost immediately fell sleep.  Johnny sat up for over an hour, listening to the sounds of the forest, before he too fell into an uneasy sleep.

They were awakened just before sunset by the sound of horsemen ranging back and forth on the road.  Robert started to rise and reach for his dagger, but Johnny stretched out his arm and held his friend, "Quiet," he whispered.  "They don't know we're here.

Robert lay back down and listened.  In the distance, he could hear a man giving orders, and others seemed to be beating at the bushes with their swords. The sounds grew gradually louder as the men moved further off of the main road and closer to their hiding place. One man grumbled to his partner, "Captain's crazy, there ain't nobody here."

"Who we lookin' for anyway," replied the other.

"Don't know. Highwaymen I guess. Nobody else in these woods. Captain thinks he saw footprints."

"What, in this light?" He stomped across the small animal trail. "Don't know what's got everyone so excited over the last couple of weeks."

"Me neither. Duke's worked up about somethin'. They say he hanged a couple of kids in one of the villages out to the west. Masden, I think it was."

"Well I guess we've come far enough," said the first man. "I'm going to have a smoke." He settled onto a log and pulled his tobacco pouch out of his jerkin. "Join me?"

"Sure," the other man answered. "We're so far off the main road, Captain won't know, and I sure ain't tellin'." He laughed and set his sword down with a loud clatter.

Johnny made eye contact with Robert, willing him to stay still as the faint aroma of cheap tobacco floated over them. As they lay, the two men continued to talk, and they could hear others some distance away, thrashing through the underbrush. Finally, they heard one of the men strike his pipe against the log to dislodge the remaining tobacco. With a clatter of metal, he rose, "You ready? I'm for goin' out to the road and tellin' the Captain nobody's here. What do you say?"

The other man rose equally noisily. "Yeah," he answered. "I don't see nothin' here worth beating myself up over." He hawked and spat noisily into the forest, and then turned toward the road.

Johnny and Robert stayed motionless for what seemed like forever, until the sounds in the forest receded. Finally, they heard the sounds of horses moving up the road in the direction of the ferry. Robert let out a long sigh, "That was close," he said, "They couldn't have been ten feet away."

Johnny rose silently. "Just over there," he said, and then as if musing aloud continued, "I saw that log when we came in. It's where I wanted them to stop."

Robert tilted his head and looked at him curiously. "Where you wanted them to stop?"

Smiling, Johnny said, "Like fishing. I didn't want them to take your hook, so I told them to leave it alone."

Robert looked at his friend for a long moment, and then shook his head. "Sometimes you make me wonder. I suppose you're ready for breakfast?"

Johnny reached into his knapsack and pulled out a hunk of roasted rabbit along with the last stale crust of their bread. "Did you hear what they said about Masden?"

Taking the offered meat, Robert stuffed a piece into his mouth and chewed thoughtfully. "I heard," he said coldly. "I heard."

"Do you think he really hanged a couple of kids? Would he do that? Why?"

Robert stared for a long time into the forest. Finally he turned to Johnny. "He's looking for us. For me." And then for the first time in days, he reached up and fingered the ring that rode on the leather thong around his neck. "And this has got something to do with it." Putting the last of the meat into his mouth, he rose impatiently. "You ready? We need to go see Jameson."

# CHAPTER 15
## INTERVIEW WITH THE DUKE

Duke Henry slowly walked around the girl, appraising her. She was in surprisingly good shape, considering she'd spent the past three weeks in his dungeon. He noted that she smelled fresh and clean, and the dress she wore was simple, but she carried it well. From what he'd been told, they'd done a thorough job of cleaning her up.

"So tell me," he asked, "do you know why you are here?"

Marie looked at him. The man had a cruel cast to his eyes, and she knew that she had to answer carefully. "No sire. I do not."

He watched as he continued to circle, like a hawk with its prey. "Tell me about your father." She started, and then regained her composure. He smiled grimly, noticing that he'd struck a nerve. "Well?"

"My father is the stable master in Masden."

"And?"

She looked at him, genuinely curious. "And what? He sometimes advised the village council. I know little else."

"Did you know that he was a traitor?"

She gasped. "My father? Never. He was ever loyal to you sire. He was not involved in any politics outside of our village."

"And your mother?"

She looked at him. "She took care of the home. She raised her children. She taught me to cook and sew. What of my mother?"

Duke Henry leaned in and spat into her face, "Was she not a traitor as well?"

Marie paled and resisted the urge to wipe the spittle from her cheek. Was this the cause of her nightmare? "My mother? When would she have found the time? And even if she had, who would have followed a woman into treason?"

The duke looked at her. It was a good answer. Who indeed would follow a weak woman. "Tell me, who do you favor?"

"Sire?"

"Take after? Who do you look like? Your mother? Your father?"

She shrugged her shoulders. "I suppose I look most like my mother. At least that's what the villagers have always said. She had the same dark hair and brown eyes." She looked at the duke. What did he want? And then she knew.

"So who does your brother take after?" he asked.

Marie started, knowing that for some reason this was his most important question. She steeled herself and lied. "He looks much like me. And like my mother. He used to complain that he hadn't inherited our father's stature or his blonde hair." She looked directly at the duke. "I suppose you could call him bookish."

Duke Henry surveyed the girl warily. Something didn't ring true, but he wasn't sure what. Not to worry. He had some villagers locked up in Masden. A little torture and they'd be more than happy to give up their secrets. He decided to change the topic. "I'm told that you can read."

Marie answered warily. "My father believed that all children should learn to read."

"And who taught you?"

"I attended the local school."

"A boys school?"

She blushed. "Yes. Like I said, my father believed that all children should learn to read."

He leaned into her face, so that she could smell the garlic on his breath. "Why teach a girl to read, or to cipher for that matter?"

Marie fought her urge to reel backwards, knowing that it would only enrage him. Standing still, she said softly, "He wanted me to help him in his business." She hesitated and then added, "He also thought that it might help me to attract a husband with more substantial means."

Duke Henry backed away, and slowly circled her, like a snake trying to mesmerize its prey. Suddenly he leaped forward and slapped her savagely across the face, sending her sprawling onto the floor. "Liar!" he shouted.

Marie's face burned with the blow, yet she knew instinctively that he had not meant to injure, only to frighten her. Her face stung, but as she clutched it in her hand, she knew that he hadn't broken anything. "I...I..." she began.

He reached down and grabbed her by the hair, lifting her to her feet. She winced and he raised his hand as if to strike her again, so she quieted, watching him warily.

"Three of my best men are dead, killed by your father," he hesitated and then growled at her, "and by your bookish brother! Two died of sword wounds and one had his head caved in by blows from a fireplace poker." He paused, "I am certain that they fought two men. I am equally certain that your father used a broadsword. So I'm left to wonder, who so viciously used the fireplace tool." He tilted his head, "bookish?" He moved right up to her face again and hissed, "Now tell me again. What color is your brother's hair? Who does he favor?"

Marie knew that he knew, and her shoulders sagged. "He took after my father. His hair was blonde and his eyes blue. He is still growing, but he will be a powerful man."

The duke snarled. "If he gets there." He turned to one of her guards. "Take her out of here."

He watched her leave, and then returning to his throne, sat contemplatively for a few minutes before one of the men approached him. He was young, and clearly nervous. "Sire?" the man inquired.

Henry looked toward the voice. He waved toward another chair. "Sit." The man sat expectantly on the edge of the chair next to the duke. After a moment, Henry said, "They all lie, you know. Every one of them. Part of the job is figuring out the lies and squeezing out the truth." He looked up into the face of the other man, and had anyone been looking now, they would have been able to tell that his partner's face was simply a younger version of his own.

"Do you believe that she knows where her brother is?"

Henry was silent for a moment before answering slowly. "No, but I believe she knows where he might be, and she's unwilling to tell me that." He clasped the other man's knee and squeezed. "They want your birthright," he said softly. "They want me out, and you as well. Tell me, you'll be Duke one day. What would you do?"

The younger man looked at him, thinking furiously. He was about to answer when Henry continued. "A thorny little problem, isn't it. Well, we've got the girl. I expect her brother to come to us."

# CHAPTER 16
## IT'S STILL A PRISON

That night they took Marie to one of the suites on the upper floors of the palace. She looked around her and took in the lavish furnishings. The centerpiece in the room was a canopied bed, done in green and yellow, and priceless artworks hung on the walls. The windows opened onto the countryside hopelessly far below.

The woman who had bathed her was waiting by the door when she entered. "You'll sleep here tonight," she said. Her businesslike tone startled Marie. "I'm to stay with you." She gestured toward a small bed by the window. "And there will be a guard on the door at all times. Believe me, this room is every bit as secure as the dungeon below. It's still a prison. It's just a more comfortable one." She looked sternly at Marie. " Follow the rules and you get to stay here. Attempt to escape and it's back to the dungeon." Then she softened and said, "Come. Sit over here. Let me see to your face."

She guided Marie to a dressing table where she applied a cold cloth to her cheek. "You'll have a nasty bruise in the morning, but no more."

Marie looked at her, and then around her at her confinement. On the one hand, her heart sank, knowing that she was still a prisoner, but on the other, it sang. Robert was safe, and Duke Henry didn't know where he was. Now if she could just figure out why they were looking for him!

# CHAPTER 17
## WATERTON

They arrived in Waterton late in the afternoon. After asking around, they settled on a disreputable inn near the waterfront district. The beds were rough, and the clientele rougher, but the food was filling if not tasty, and the place seemed to offer anonymity.

After a fitful night's sleep, Robert and Johnny Tuppence rose early. It was a gray day, the thick steel colored clouds threatening but not quite delivering rain. Johnny pulled a piece of stale bread and some cheese that they'd bought from a street vendor from his knapsack and they breakfasted quietly in their room, thinking of the events to come. Finally, Robert broke their silence.

"Well, we'd best be on our way."

Nodding, Johnny pushed a last morsel of the bread into his mouth and rose. "I asked around a bit last night. Jameson won't be hard to find. His office is on Long Wharf. They said that he spends his days there, supervising the trade. It's all the way out Water Street."

As the two made their way out of the inn, the innkeeper's wife stopped them. "Well, if it isn't the young gentlemen from the country. I trust all was well last night?"

"We've no complaints," answered Robert.

"So you're off to seek the lives of sailors?"

"We are. With a bit of luck, we'll be meeting with Mr. Jameson this morning. I hear he's always looking for able hands."

She looked them over carefully and said, "And why would you be seeking a life on the sea?"

Johnny laughed and answered her, "Adventure. I want to see the world and meet her people. I've spent more than enough time following the back end of a horse up and down the furrows in my father's fields." His eyes sparkled. "It's a life of adventure for me!"

She patted his shoulder and said, "Then I hope you find what you seek. You have the advantage of youth. Go, and good luck to you!"

As they were about to go out the door, she called out, "Should I hold your room?"

Johnny looked back over his shoulder and grinned, "No need ma'am, tonight we'll be sleeping in a berth on a fine sailing ship."

She laughed and watched them go.

§§§§

Andrew Jameson's warehouses were indeed at the entrance to the largest wharf. As the boys hesitantly approached, they were amazed by the vitality of the place. Longshoremen hurried back and forth, carrying large wooden boxes, bales of exotic cloth, and a variety of other things. As Johnny stood watching, a large man yelled out at him, "Out of the way lad, there's work to be done here!"

He jumped back and called, "Do you know where we'd find Master Jameson?"

The man gave him a curious look and then asked, "That's a strange one you'll be asking for. Why'd you be seeking him?"

Robert stepped forward. "We were referred. My uncle sailed with him several years ago."

The man paused before he continued. "He did, did he?" Then he frowned. "See the blue doorway over there? Ask for him inside." He turned to go and then looked back over his shoulder, "And take care, lads. He's a strange one, he is."

Johnny shivered and said, "What an interesting warning. I wonder what he means."

"I suppose we'll find out soon enough," Robert replied as he strode purposefully toward the door. He looked back at Johnny standing where he'd left him, "You coming?"

Johnny snapped his head as if awakened and smiled. "Surely. On my way." He looked back at the longshoreman, now making his way down the wharf, "He's right, you know. Somehow I feel it."

# CHAPTER 18
## ANDREW JAMESON

The office inside the blue door was small and dark. An old, withered woman sat at a desk at one end of the room, reading what appeared to be a ship's manifest. She raised her brow when they entered, and then went back to her work.

Robert looked around. There was a grimy painting of a sailing ship battling through a stormy sea set above her desk. A brass ship's lamp hung from a beam in the ceiling. It provided more smoke than light, and added to the gloom of the room. He looked for a chair to sit in while he waited, but there were none, so he just stared at the woman, hoping that she would acknowledge them, but she continued to read the manifest. Finally, he cleared his throat. "Excuse me," he said politely, "We've come to see Mr. Jameson. Are we in the right place?"

She looked up at them. "You are." She had been marking a page with an old quill pen. Now she put it down and stared them up and down. "And why would he want to see you? Does he know you're coming?"

Robert stammered. "Uh, no, he does not. We've been referred to him."

"He's a very busy man," she said as she reached to pick up the pen again. She turned back to her papers.

Johnny put his hand down on her paper and said, "I should think that he'd want to know that we're waiting here."

She reached to flick his hand away and said, "As I told you, he's a very busy man."

"We truly are sorry to disturb you ma'am," he continued in a honeyed voice. When she looked back up at him, he drew her with his eyes and said, "but I do believe that he'll want to know that we're here."

She was about to snatch the paper back from his hand, when she relented. "All right. I suppose I can let him know you've arrived." She turned from her desk and disappeared through the door behind her.

As soon as she left, Robert grasped Johnny's sleeve. "What was that about?" he asked. "She wouldn't give me the time of day, but for you?"

Johnny shook his head. "I don't know. It just seemed the right thing to do." Then he smiled. "It worked though." He turned back to the sounds coming from beyond the door as Robert eyed him carefully, as if he was seeing a new side to his friend.

A moment later, the clerk reemerged from the office. She looked at Johnny. "He'll see you." She slipped back into her chair and then added almost as an afterthought, "Oh, and your friend as well."

Robert shook his head and smiled. There was more to Johnny than met the eye.

§§§§

Andrew Jameson was a tall, ascetic man. He regarded the boys with an appraising eye as they passed through the door, and then stood and offered his hand. "Margaret tells me I need to speak with you."

Robert took in the room about him. It was outfitted like a captain's cabin on a sailing ship, with tall windows in the rear, hanging brass oil lamps, and a large heavy oak desk, covered with neat stacks of papers. There was no clutter anywhere to be seen.

Everything was pigeonholed in its place. He spoke. "We were sent to you. We were told you could help us."

Jameson regarded him warily then grunted. "Help you? In what way?" He settled back into his chair and with a wave of his hand, motioned the boys into a pair of straight-backed wooden chairs facing the desk. "Do you seek employment? If that's what you want, you'll need to go to the guild hall and speak with the sailing master."

Shaking his head, Robert continued slowly. "My father was killed a few weeks ago. We've been in hiding. Johnny's father sent us to you. He said that you had been friends."

"Friends? It's possible. I meet many people in my business. His name?"

"Albert, and my father was Robert, like me. Robert of Masden."

Jameson shook his head. "No. I've had no dealings with anyone from Masden. It's what, two hundred miles inland?" He spread his arms and gestured about. "As you can see, I'm involved in maritime trade. I'd have no reason to go to Masden." Suddenly his head snapped to Johnny. "What are you doing, boy?" he asked harshly.

Johnny jumped with surprise. "Nothing sir, just waiting."

Jameson eyed him cautiously, as if looking for some kind of sign. After a moment, he shook his head and muttered, "Must be my imagination." He turned back to Robert. "I know no Robert of Masden. If you need work, you'll need to go to the guild hall."

His head downcast, Robert started to turn away. As he did so, Jameson shot another glance at Johnny. "Who taught you that boy?"

Johnny stammered, "I, I don't know what you're talking about."

Jameson stared hard at him and then shook his head again, as if clearing cobwebs. "An old man's imagination I suppose." Then he looked curiously at Johnny. "I could have sworn that you were trying to … but never mind." He turned back to Robert and spoke more softly. "I'm sorry about your father, but I didn't know him. I've never been to Masden. Has he had any dealings here?"

"No." He never left Masden that I can recall." He looked forlornly at Johnny. "We'll be going."

As he stepped slowly toward the door, Johnny grabbed insistently at his arm. "Show him," he hissed under his breath.

Robert regarded his friend with a puzzled look. He whispered, "Show him what?"

Johnny looked past him at Jameson and insistently tapped against his chest. "Show him!"

Robert shook his head. "We don't know this man."

"It's all right," Johnny said softly. "He's a friend, I can tell. And he'll help. He just needs to be prodded."

"But your father said to show it to no one except in times of great need."

Johnny stared at him, "And what time would this be?"

Robert glanced over his shoulder at Jameson, who was regarding the boys curiously. "What is it?" he asked.

"My friend suggests that I show you something. He thinks that might help our cause." He started to reach into his cloak, and then stopped, regarding the other two cautiously. Finally, with a shrug, he took hold of the leather cord and drew it out, carefully enclosing the ring in his hand.

Jameson stared intently at his hand, and then up at his face. "What do you have, boy?" he asked slowly.

Robert looked down at his fist, and then slowly opened his fingers. The ruby pulsed with a soft internal fire that lit his hand.

Jameson staggered back and grasped the back of his chair. "Put that away," he spat quickly. Then he looked up into Robert's eyes, "Where…how…where did you get that?" he whispered hoarsely.

Robert returned the ring to his cloak and looked about him. Jameson's whole attitude had changed. He studied his face for a moment and then said, "It belonged to my father. It's an ancestral ring. My mother told me that it's been passed from father to son in my family for many generations."

Jameson regarded them for some time, looking first at Johnny and then staring for a long time at Robert, as if trying to memorize his face. Finally, he nodded as if confirming some kind of assessment and whispering softly to himself, "It could be..." He motioned them back to the chairs. As Johnny was about to sit, he said, "You, before you sit. Set the bolt on the door. We want no interruptions."

After Johnny had latched the heavy wrought iron bolt, he came to his chair. He started to speak, but Jameson silenced him with a wave. "It may be that I can be of help," he said softly. "But not here." Making his decision, he rose and said, "Follow me."

He reached into the bookcase behind his desk and fumbled behind a book. A muted click sounded and he turned to the boys with a smile. "Sometimes I need to leave unobserved." He pushed on a section of wall that pivoted open and waved them forward.

Robert looked at Johnny, raised his eyebrows, and got up to follow. He stepped through the door, and looked back. Johnny was right behind him, looking about cautiously. They stepped into a small anteroom, and Jameson reached behind them to close the door. Then motioning with one hand, he led them down a dimly lit passage that curled gently into the depths of the building.

# CHAPTER 19
## SANDRA OF ABBYFIELD

Marie woke at daybreak. The canopy above her head glowed with the reds of the sunrise, and the whole room was bathed with a cheery light. She rose on one elbow and looked about. It was as she remembered. Her jailor, or keeper, or whatever she was, still slept on the small bed under the window. "I suppose to keep me from jumping out," Marie muttered ruefully. "Not that I'd have much chance there, it must be fifty feet to the ground."

She rose and walked to a basin against the back wall. The water in it was fresh, and she used it to wash the sleep out of her eyes. As she was drying her face, the woman in the bed said, "So you're awake are you?"

Marie turned and looked at her. In her nightgown, the woman looked far less imposing, and Marie estimated that she probably was only a couple of years older than she was. The woman rose, and then turned to Marie. "We'll be wanting to get cleaned up and dressed," she said. "Breakfast is served promptly at 7:00. We'll be eating with the servants behind the kitchen." Marie looked at her, and then at the room, and the woman added, "Get a move on girl. We've no time to waste."

§§§§

As they walked down the stairs with their ever-present guard behind them, Marie said softly, "I don't know your name."

"They call me Sandra. Sandra of Abbyfield."

"And how did you come to work here, for the Duke."

Sandra turned toward her and motioned with her head toward the soldier behind them. "It's a long story, too long for now. Perhaps later, after we've eaten. We're expected to spend our day in the room. We can talk then." Reaching the landing, she turned to into a long hallway on the right, toward the smell of baking bread.

§§§§

After eating, Marie and Sandra returned to the room. It had obviously been cleaned while they were out. The beds were crisply made, and the water in the basin was fresh. In addition, someone had placed a pitcher of water and a basket of fruit on the small table by the window. Noticing Marie survey the room, Sandra said, "It'll be like this every day. We're expected to stay here unless called for." As if to punctuate her words, the door behind them closed suddenly and they heard a bolt shoot across with a loud snap. "You're mighty important to the duke, for some reason. I've never known him to take such care over a prisoner." She walked to a small sofa and sat, and then patting the seat next to her motioned Marie to sit as well. "You had some questions?"

Marie looked at her and started toward the sofa, but then decided to remain standing. She needed to move. Thinking aloud, she asked, "Do you know why I'm here? And this?" She gestured to the luxuriously appointed room, "Why all this?"

Sandra just shook her head. "I know very little. I know that you arrived about three weeks ago and the duke ordered you jailed in the dungeon. He's a hard man. I think he thought he could break you." She looked at Marie. "You seem to have him confused. He's not quite sure what to do with you. Are you telling the truth and really have no idea why you're here? Are you hiding something? He's not sure. At least that's what little I've been told."

Marie paced the room for a while and then turned back to Sandra. "It seems to have something to do with my father and brother but what? We're simple people. My father is a stable master." She continued to pace and then muttered almost to herself, "He had us learn the old tongue. It never made sense."

Sandra's jaw dropped, "You speak the old tongue?"

"And read and write it," Marie mused.

"The language of court."

Marie shrugged, "I suppose. My father said that it would help us to communicate with the upper classes. I never saw the point, but he was so insistent and it came easily to me..." She looked over at Sandra, "But what could that have to do with this?"

Sandra looked down at the floor. "I don't know. But somehow it seems to be linked to your situation. Tell me, what was your father like?"

Smiling, Marie said, "He was a good man. A leader in the village; a demanding father, but a loving one too." Then she frowned. "He must be worried sick about me. He was always so protective of both of us."

Sandra brushed her chin and reflected, so she doesn't know he's dead. That could come in useful later.

She spoke to Marie, "You wanted to know where I came from. I was brought to the palace by my uncle after my parents died in a great sickness in the year I was born. He was a wool merchant. I suppose that I was part of a transaction. Maybe he paid the duke's clothier to take me, or maybe it was the other way around. Maybe the clothier paid to have me. I don't suppose I'll ever know. At any rate, I was raised as an only child in his home just outside the palace grounds. He and his wife were good people. When they passed, just before my fifteenth birthday, the duke brought me into the palace. I've been working here ever since."

"But what do you do?"

Sandra hesitated just long enough for Marie to notice her discomfort. "Mostly I care for guests, like I'm doing with you. When nobody is here, I help to clean the duke's chambers."

"So you're a servant."

Nodding, Sandra replied, "You might say that. I have certain favors that others lack, but yes, I'm a servant." She rose and looked out the window. "I have to wonder, why was your father so important, and why did a man like that live in Masden?"

# CHAPTER 20
## "THEY'VE ALL DISAPPEARED"

Duke Henry was in a rage. "You can't possibly be telling me that you have no idea where they've gone!" he howled.

"They're not in Masden sire. Of that we're certain." General Fictus was a proud man, but also a cautious one. He'd led the search himself. "We're scouring the neighboring villages now, but we've had no luck there either. And we've posted guards on all of the roads and bridges leaving the town. The boy and his mother seem to have vanished."

Duke Henry stroked his beard thoughtfully, "You had hostages?"

"As you ordered." He looked down. "I took three children. It made no difference. The townspeople don't know where they are. I'm certain of that."

"And where are the children now?"

The general gave him a startled look, "Sire?"

"I asked where the children are now!" the duke bellowed.

"You ordered me to hang them if nobody gave up the hiding place."

"And?"

The general looked down again and then answered in a near whisper, "I hanged them. Two boys and a little girl," and then added under his breath, "May God forgive me." He looked at the duke. "You've made no friends in Masden sire, and we still don't have the fugitives."

Duke Henry turned and paced back toward his throne, "Three peasant children won't be missed," he said dismissively. Then turning, he said, "They had to have help." He scratched his beard with one hand and added, "Was anyone else missing from the village?"

"We checked that out," the general added carefully. "One boy," he furrowed his brows in thought. "Johnny Tuppence, the son of a local farmer. His father'd sent him to Fairview to sell a goat."

"And did he return while you were there?"

The general shook his head, "No."

Duke Henry paced a while before asking, "And how old was this boy?"

"Nearly grown sire. About sixteen."

Henry looked over toward his son. "Well Frederick? What do you suggest we do?"

The young man jumped to his feet. "I think it's curious that two boys of the same age should be missing at once."

"Go on," the duke urged.

"The general needs to get back to Masden and bring the other boy here. And find out if he ever showed up in Fairview." Gaining confidence, he added, "If not, bring his father too."

General Fictus hesitated, looking from father to son. Finally inclining his head toward the duke, he said, "I already thought of that sire. There was no sign of him in Fairview."

Duke Henry raised a hand as if to strike him, and instead prodded him in the chest. "Then bring me his father!"

"That'll be a problem sire. It seems that after I questioned him, he and his family disappeared as well."

# CHAPTER 21
## ADDING FRIENDS

Kathryn stirred the porridge she was cooking over the fire. After a month in the hideout, she had grown accustomed to the confined space, and the constant dim light. When she grew too claustrophobic, she hiked down to the cave mouth where she could look through the concealing brush over the surrounding pastures and forest. Just seeing birds and other forest animals frolicking in the daylight encouraged her and gave her back her strength.

Once, while sitting at the entrance enjoying the warmth of the sun, she heard the metallic rustle of a soldier's chain mail nearby. Shrinking carefully back into the shadows of the entrance, she watched as three of the duke's men passed nearby. They'd been close, but not close enough to see her. That they'd still been in the area of Masden both frightened and encouraged her. Clearly, they were still searching for Robert, so at least he was safe.

Sound in the tunnel caught her attention and she shielded the light from the cook fire, and then settled quietly to wait. These times were the worst. She knew that she was well hidden; still it was unnerving any time that Albert came either to the gap at the top or as she hoped today, directly to the hideout. Some day, she feared, it would be the duke's men searching for her and Robert. As the sounds got close, she huddled further back in a corner, almost holding her breath. Finally, when she thought she could stand it no longer, she heard Albert's familiar voice, "Kathryn, I'm coming up."

Breathing a sigh of relief, she rose and walked across the room to the door. She opened it carefully and just made out Albert, his wife Elyssa, and their daughter Anna in the dim torch light. As the search for Robert had intensified, they'd started stockpiling additional food in the cavern and recently talked of joining her in her hideaway.

Albert swung his way through the door and dropped what appeared to be a heavy crate onto the floor. Elyssa and Anna joined him. After setting her canvas bag down, Elyssa breathed a heavy sigh. "Whew," she whistled, "that didn't seem so heavy when we left the village, but by the time we got here, wow!"

Albert sat at the table and said, "We're going to have to stay here for a while; no more visits to Fairview or any of the other villages. I stopped by the pub there and listened to the scuttlebutt. The Duke's men are looking for Johnny now. It's only a matter of time until they come after me and Elyssa and Anna. We've brought grains, vegetables, and smoked meats, enough for a few months anyway." He paused, and then looked knowingly at his wife. "I can keep them from looking here, but the chance they'll find us elsewhere when your defenses are down is just too great."

Elyssa nodded. She was a tiny woman, fair-haired and blue eyed. She brushed some dirt off of her dress and sat opposite him at the table, and then pulled her daughter into her lap, "Don't you worry honey, they'll give up eventually, and as long as they're looking, we know your brother's safe."

Anna looked from her mother to her father, worry plain on her eight-year old face. "I know, but I'm still scared for him."

Albert smiled and took her hand, "They were asking about Johnny in Fairview yesterday," he said soothingly. "They should be far from here by now, and the duke's still looking. That's a good sign." He turned his head toward the fire, "Kathryn, that porridge smells delicious and I'm hungry as a bear! When's dinner?"

# CHAPTER 22
## ESCAPE FROM WATERTON

Robert surveyed the small group of men arrayed around the room. There weren't many of them, but they looked dangerous, and he was glad that they were evidently on his side. He nudged Johnny and pointed toward their protector, Andrew Jameson. The man had risen from his seat and was making his way to the front of the room. As he walked, Robert cast a glance about the small chamber. The door to the dark passageway that led to Jameson's office was behind them, fitted carefully into a cabinet and hidden in the back wall of the room. He presumed that the other door led out to a bar, as he could hear the clanging of dish ware along with loud coarse voices. The light in this room was dim, but he could see that it was some kind of banquet hall behind the bar. Rough wooden tables were surrounded by a motley assortment of chairs and benches, all seemingly facing toward an empty area along the front. He looked back at Jameson who seemed about to speak.

Putting both hands down on the front table, Jameson leaned forward. "Thank you for coming. I'm going to need your help. These two boys wish to join our little group and I've assured them that I can make that happen."

One burly man looked back at Robert and Johnny and scowled. Then he turned toward Jameson. "I'm not turning down help," he said harshly, "But why these two?'

Andrew Jameson drew himself upright and looked at the man. "For now Walter, all you need to know is that they're joining us. I'm satisfied that they'll prove their worth."

The man named Walter looked back at the boys again and shook his head. "The big one; he looks like he could hold his own in a fight. That scrawny one though," he pointed at Johnny. "He looks like he'd blow over in a strong wind. Why him?"

Jameson was about to speak when Robert spoke up. "We've come together. Take us both or we'll be on our way."

Surprised, the big man looked back at Andrew Jameson. "Sassy pup! Well?"

"We take them both." Jameson looked at all of the men in the room. "I know that we've been very careful about adding new members, but I'll vouch for these two. We need to get them out of here and aboard the Starling before she sails tonight. They need to hide out for a while, and our base on Rocky Point Isle should be a good place."

One of the men shook his head, and then said, "Not sure how you're going to do it, Captain. The Duke's men have been swarming all over the docks the last few days. They're looking for something." He looked at the two boys, "or someone?"

Robert and Johnny just stared back at him, careful to hide any expression from their faces. Finally the man turned toward Andrew Jameson. "So how do you plan to do this?"

"I have a plan, but I'll need the help of every man here. Can I count on you?"

One by one, the men nodded their assent, and Jameson continued. "They don't seem to be challenging anyone before they get to the piers. Starling's berthed at Pier four. I figure a diversion on Pier 3 should draw any soldiers away from the Starling, so I'll be able to take these two aboard. Any ideas?"

One large gap toothed man with a scar running across his chin laughed, "Walter 'n' I haven' had a good dustup in ages." He looked over at the other man. "What do you say Walter? Bare knuckles? It'll give you a chance to get even over that drubbin' I gave you a couple of months ago."

"Bah," Walter spat but grinned. "If my memory serves me right Bill, you had another tooth before that fight." He tapped his teeth. "I've still got all of mine!" Then he laughed. "But sure. I'm always up for a good fistfight."

Nodding, Jameson looked out on the group and focused in on two other men sitting at one of the tables. "Joey, Tom, you go with 'em. If they need any help, you can jump in. Don't let anyone get hurt too badly, and let's not get anyone arrested. All I want is a diversion that lasts for a few minutes." He raised his gaze. "The rest of you will be with me. Here's what we're going to do."

§§§§

Dusk had started to set when the small group came out of the bar. The four men designated to fight had left a few minutes earlier. Before walking out, Walter splashed beer on his companions, so that they'd smell as if they'd been drinking even thought they hadn't. They were loud, obnoxious, and clearly spoiling for a fight as they made their way toward the piers. A number of townspeople, seeing them coming down the street, quietly slipped back inside their buildings and locked the doors. As they crossed the street, a pair of soldiers noticed them, and began to follow, hoping to prevent problems. It was just what they wanted.

Jameson watched from one of the windows of the bar. When he saw the soldiers turn to follow his decoys, he signaled to the back of the room. One of the other men opened the door and mouthed quietly, "Now."

Robert took a quick look out the door, and then motioning to Johnny, slipped quietly into the bar and strode across the room to the front. Once there, he joined Jameson and the others. He looked out the window just in time to see Walter push Bill against a warehouse door. Bill came back with a two handed shove of Walter and then howled something that Robert couldn't make out. Walter responded with a wildly thrown punch and an insult about Bill's parentage, and the fight was on. The soldiers hurried up the street to stop them and called for another pair who had been patrolling the entrance to Pier 4.

"That's our signal," Jameson said as he waved his hand toward the others. "Let's go. Walk quickly, but not so fast that we draw attention."

Cautiously, Jameson, Robert, Johnny, and the three others left the bar and headed toward the pier. Robert started to swivel his head toward the fight and Jameson said conversationally, "So how do you like our fair city?"

Startled, he looked at the man. "Huh?"

Jameson smiled. "Talk to me boy. We're just out for a walk, nothing's wrong, and we're minding our own business. Let's not draw any attention."

"It's a fine place," Johnny jumped in. "I only wish we'd had time for lunch. I'm starving!"

Robert looked at his friend and finally smiled. "Always hungry, that's what you are!"

"Of course," Johnny replied. "Those fellows in there thought I was a bit too skinny. I've got to keep in good fighting trim. He mugged and flexed his bicep. "See. These muscles just need a little nutrition. That's all."

Jameson patted him on the back as they walked along and chuckled to Robert, "I can see why you brought this one, quick as a whip and funny too. I'll bet he was quite a diversion on the trail."

Robert laughed, finally beginning to relax. "I'm not sure I'd call him that. A pest maybe…"

"Hey…" Johnny began.

"Better pick up the pace, Andrew," said one of the other men. "Looks like they've just about sorted out the little fight over there. Those two are looking our way."

Robert glanced to the side and could see that two of the soldiers had indeed taken notice of them. One looked back at the two fighters, now trying to argue their case with the other soldiers while avoiding their drawn swords. Seeing that everything was under control there, he nudged his partner and started back toward Pier 4.

Jameson's group had just reached the end of the pier and was starting toward the ship when one of the soldiers called out, "Hey you. Stop there. Nobody's allowed on that pier without my say so."

Jameson signaled the group to slow down, but kept moving toward the ship. "I own this ship," he yelled. "These men are part of the crew. I just hired them today. I'm taking them aboard."

The soldier hurried toward them and called out again. "Stop there! Nobody's to board any ship without talking to me first!"

Looking back at the quickly approaching soldiers, Jameson whispered, "Keep going. I'll hold them up here. Tell Captain Mizen to hide these boys. He'll know where." He then turned and walked back up the pier to the soldiers, his arms spread wide in exasperation. "What's the matter, gentlemen? I'm just going out to my ship. I'm the owner." He motioned toward the building they'd just left. "Let's go up to my office. You can check my papers."

The two soldiers surrounded him and the older one said, "Tell those men to come back now. I need to interview them as well."

Sighing, Jameson raised his hands in supplication and said, "I don't understand what the problem is here. I always escort my crews onto the ships. There's never been a problem before."

The soldier looked at him, and then at the others and yelled, "You men. Stop where you are!" He then called over to the soldiers who'd been dealing with Walter and Bill over on Pier 3. "Corporal, let those men go. They just had a little too much to drink. I need you over here."

One of the soldiers looked over and responded. "Sir. Right away." He then turned to Walter, and prodded him down the street using the flat of his sword. "You fellows move along. Looks like you get away this time. Don't let me see you fighting again." He and his partner then turned and jogged toward Pier 4.

As Jameson continued to argue, the older soldier drew his sword and yelled, "You men up there. Do not board that ship. Stop there!" He then waved his partner toward Robert's group and said, "Stop them."

The other man drew his sword as well and raced up the pier yelling, "Stop there!"

The older soldier used his sword to back Jameson against a wooden crate waiting loading and yelled, "Down on your knees! Hands on your head!"

Jameson chanced a quick look at the others and pushed his hands against the soldier's chest. "I'm just loading my crew," he said sharply. "I'll see that your captain hears about this."

Feeling threatened, the soldier lashed out with his sword, slashing Jameson across the upper arm and knocking him to the ground. Standing over him with his sword held against his throat he growled, "I said get down!"

Seeing the situation deteriorating, one of the men in Robert's group hissed, "Quick, get aboard!" He pushed Robert and Johnny toward the gangway and turned with the others and walked toward the onrushing soldier.

Robert took several steps forward, and then turned back and grabbed his friend's sleeve. "Johnny, we're not leaving Mr. Jameson out there." He looked back at the ship, and then up the pier. Jameson was lying against the wooden crates, clutching his wounded arm while the soldier who'd slashed him waved his sword, issuing orders to the two soldiers who'd been breaking up the fight. The other soldier had reached the three men from Robert's group and was facing them, his face red and his sword drawn. "We need to do something now."

"Right," Johnny said. "I'll take care of Jameson and get him on board. The others are yours."

He spun and walked purposefully past the soldier who'd chased them down the pier. The man glanced at him, and then thinking he was surrendering, nodded him down toward the entrance to the pier and turned back toward the others. "You heard the sergeant. Get down on your knees and put your hands on your heads."

Robert reached over to a tool bin and picked up a stout piece of wood and then walked slowly towards the soldier and said calmly. "We won't be doing that. We're boarding the ship. Now if you'll excuse me, we need to help our friend. As you can see, he's been hurt."

The soldier stared at him as he approached, and then turned his sword toward him. "Don't move! Get down!" he shouted.

None of the other men could tell exactly what happened next. Suddenly, Robert feinted left and then whirled to his right and brought the plank down with a heavy crack on the soldier's sword arm so rapidly that he had no time to react. The man howled and fell back in pain, his sword clattering to the ground. Robert quickly picked it up and turned to face the other two soldiers who were sprinting up the pier. Glancing back at the shocked men behind him, he said, "You'd better tell the captain to get ready to sail at once!"

Johnny had reached the entrance to the pier and walked calmly up to the sergeant. Using a honeyed voice, he said, "I just want to check his wound and make sure he's all right. I've some training as a healer."

The soldier looked up at Johnny and then pulled back his sword. "Fine, make it quick."

"Thank you," Johnny oozed. Then he turned and quickly assessed Jameson's wound. The cut was high on his left arm, deep, and bleeding profusely, but it would heal. He ripped a piece off of the man's shirt and bandaged his arm, all the while keeping up a soft monologue with the soldier. "You've allowed this situation to get out of control. It's time to get back under control and let me get this man some help. You can start by putting away your sword."

The man looked at Johnny, and then at Jameson, and then up the pier. Then seeming unsure of himself, he backed away and sheathed his sword. Johnny looked him in the eye for a long moment and said, "My friend out there is pretty upset right now and he's very dangerous with a sword. I'd suggest you call your soldiers back. Tell them that we're cleared to board."

The man looked at him, and then nodded. "Men," he shouted. "Stand down. Gather on me." He waved toward them and pointed to a gathering point at the entrance to the pier.

One glanced sharply back and then waved to his partner. Confused, the two soldiers facing Robert lowered their swords and started to back down the pier, taking their injured companion with them. Robert brandished his sword for a few more seconds, and then lowered it, grounding the point into the pier.

After taking a few deep breaths, he looked down the pier to see Johnny walking slowly toward him with one arm supporting Andrew Jameson. The sergeant was helping from the other side, all of his aggressiveness gone. When they passed the other soldiers coming back down the pier, he said, "As soon as I help this man get aboard, I'll meet you outside the pub. Oh, and corporal, tell those drunks back there that they're to board the ship too."

The man stared alternately at him and then at Johnny for several seconds before nodding, "Yes sir."

# CHAPTER 23
## MARIE BIDES HER TIME

Marie sat in the window seat, looking out through the wavy glass and musing quietly to herself. Granted, the suite was luxurious, but she'd been imprisoned here for a week now, and was desperate to be outside. She leaned her head out the open section and looked down, breathing in the fresh air. The walls were sheer, and so smooth that she couldn't possibly climb down. She'd thought of using the bedding to make a rope, but there wasn't nearly enough. And then there was the problem of what would happen if she was able to escape. She'd still be trapped inside the outer walls with no money, no contacts, and no idea of how to get home or even if she'd be safe there. Most likely, she'd be recaptured quickly and tossed back in the dungeon. No, that wouldn't work.

She returned to her book and was still reading when one of the servants came in to light the lamp. Looking out the window again, she was surprised to see that the sun was setting over the distant mountains. "The end of another day in paradise," she sighed sadly, "I wonder what's for dinner."

After the servant left, she turned back to the book and had read several pages when she heard the door open again. Looking up, she saw Sandra slip quietly into the room. She smiled. Sandra might be her jailor, but at least she was someone to talk to, and it turned out they had many similar interests.

She rose and started to greet Sandra when she noticed that the other woman was walking very gingerly toward the pitcher of water on the dresser. She poured herself a glass and winced as she lifted it to her lips.

"Sandra," Marie inquired, "are you all right?"

She held up her hand to wave off the question and then walked slowly over to her bed. Marie started over to help her and then gasped as she saw the back of her dress. The fabric was covered with a crisscross pattern of bloody red stripes. She raced to Sandra's side and helped lower her to the bed. "What happened to you?" she asked.

Raising her hand, Sandra squeezed her eyes as tears started to roll down her cheeks. "I've not pleased the duke today."

Marie cocked her head and said, "What do you mean?"

Sandra looked at her and said in a steely voice, "As you can see, I couldn't deliver what he wanted so he had me flogged." She sighed deeply and started to lie down. "Now I just want to sleep."

"No," Marie said. "Let me help you get that dress off. I need to clean those wounds."

"Just let me sleep," Sandra sighed. "It's all I want."

"No," Marie repeated forcefully. "You can sleep when I'm done. Now let's get that dress off."

Suddenly Sandra threw up her arm and batted Marie away. "Don't you understand?" she asked. "Don't you understand why he's mad at me?"

Marie took her arm and brought it down. "Of course I do," she whispered. "You can't tell him what I know, because there's nothing to tell. You've been assigned to befriend and spy on me."

Sandra's head snapped around and she looked into Marie's face. "You knew?"

Marie smiled ruefully, "Yes. I knew. I've known since the beginning. He tried the dungeon and that didn't work, so now he's trying this apartment. Your job was to get me to talk. Why else would you be here, asking me questions?" Using her thumb, she wiped the tears gently from Sandra's face and repeated softly, "Now let's get that dress off."

Quickly, she undid the buttons on the back of Sandra's dress and then very carefully peeled the fabric away from her torn skin. Once it was free, she used a towel and the water in the basin to dab at the wounds, cleaning out blood and tiny pieces of cloth. As she did so, she noted angrily that in addition to the three raw slashes in Sandra's pale flesh, there were several older healed scars. This was a message to me as well, she thought.

When she had finished bandaging the wounds, she drew Sandra to her and rocked her for a while, and then said softly, "When do you make your next report? Let's make sure you have something to say."

# CHAPTER 24
## ABOARD THE STARLING

"I tell you, I tried ta watch from Pier 3. Somethin's not right!" Bill slammed his mug onto the table in the ship's dayroom and glared at his companions. They'd managed to sail shortly after boarding the day before, and now were well clear of the outer harbor, heeling over in a steady wind toward Rocky Point Isle.

One of the others stood next to him, holding onto an overhead rail to balance against the steady rocking of the ship. "I can't say I disagree boys. That skinny one said something back there and all of a sudden the fight was over. It was the strangest thing I've ever seen. One minute the duke's man was full of bluster and ready to chop you all up. The next he was helping the old man to board the ship. Helping him! There was no way you were going to win that fight, but then they just gave up!"

"I don't know about that. Did you see how the other one took out that soldier? His sword was drawn; he was set for a fight; and then he was just laying there, and the boy was standing over him holding his own sword, and he used nothing but a hunk of wood. I'd hate to take him on in when he's properly armed."

One of his companions grunted. "We was just standing there," he said shaking his head. "I figured we was off to jail."

"Or worse," said the other.

"Right, or worse."

"We couldn't really see," Walter said. "What happened?"

96

"It's just like he said. The skinny one went walking back up to Jameson like he owned the place and then the other one grabbed a piece of wood and attacked the man who had the three of us pinned down there. If I'da blinked I woulda missed it."

"That's right. One minute he was holding his sword on us and the next he was on his back, holding his arm and squalling for his mama." He shook his head. "You're right about one thing Bill. Something's not right here. We need to talk with Jameson and find out who these two are."

§§§§

Johnny had been patching a hole in his spare shirt when heard a wince behind him. He looked over his shoulder and saw that Jameson was starting to stir in his berth. He stood and walked over to him and felt his forehead. The skin was cool, with no signs of fever, so the wound must be healing cleanly. Still, time would tell. No doubt the man was uncomfortable, but the herbs they'd found in the captain's locker should help him to sleep for a while. He looked around the room. The captain had insisted that Jameson take his cabin as soon as they boarded. The ship was small, but the cabin was relatively spacious, stretching from beam to beam and easily accommodating two wide bunks as well as a navigation desk. In the center of the room was a large plank table surrounded by six comfortable wooden chairs.

He started to sit again when Jameson said weakly, "How long have I been out?"

Johnny thought for a moment and then said, "Most of a day, sir. We boarded yesterday afternoon and you probably fell asleep before we raised anchor. We're well offshore now."

Jameson nodded, and then rose to a sitting position, grimacing against the pain in his arm. "Where's Robert?"

Johnny smiled and pointed over the man's head. "He's in the upper berth. He's been sleeping for the past couple of hours. Guess he was worn out."

The older man nodded and then looked at the bandage on his arm, "How bad is it?"

"It's deep, but it's starting to heal." He walked over and leaned over the wound, sniffing at the bandages. "There's no sign of mortification so it should heal cleanly. Captain Mizen helped me to pack it with healing herbs after we set sail. It'll leave a nasty scar, but you'll keep the arm."

"Well, thank goodness for that." He smiled. "I've grown rather attached to that arm. So, tell me…" He looked at Johnny, and then around the room, and then focused again on the young man. "What happened out there."

Johnny shrugged his shoulders. "Not much to tell, to be honest with you. Robert disarmed one of them and the others decided not to fight. I guess they took your word that you were simply escorting a crew to your ship." He looked back at the shirt he was mending, trying to look busy.

Jameson watched him for a few minutes, trying to sort his thoughts. His head was still fuzzy from the pain killing draft they'd given him but he could tell something just wasn't right. "Yeah," he said. "Well I think I'll get some more sleep. I'm still pretty woozy. Talk later." He lay back, gritting his teeth through the pain, and then rolled his head to the side and closed his eyes.

Johnny continued to stitch his patch on the shirt until he heard soft snoring coming from Jameson's bunk. Then he rose and walked to the large windows that filled the back of the room. The ship rose and fell easily with the swells, and he could see by the spray across the white caps and the wake behind the ship that they had a fair wind and were making good time. The captain had said that they should make port tomorrow or the next day, weather permitting. The sun was starting to set and a bright orange glow reflected off the water. He returned to the table and picked up his shirt and the needle. There was a lot to think about between now and then.

# CHAPTER 25
## ALBERT HITS THE ROAD

Albert shifted the heavy pack on his back and looked back at his wife and daughter. "Don't worry," he said softly, "I'll be fine." He could just make out their faces in the dim light of the tunnel. He looked toward the distant glow of the opening and then back again. As hard as it was to leave them, he knew it was time.

"Papa, when will you be back?" Anna asked tearfully.

He knelt and took his daughter's face in his hands. "I'll be back as soon as I can. It may be a while. I need to meet with some people. Johnny's going to need help."

He rose, and keeping one arm around his daughter, pulled Elyssa close with the other. Whispering, he said, "Take care of Kathryn and yourselves. I have a feeling you'll all have a role to play in this thing before it's over."

Elyssa nodded against his shoulder. "I wish you didn't have to go, but I understand. Take care and don't do anything foolish. Remember that you have a family here."

He kissed the top of her head; held them both for a long moment; and then pushed himself away. "You should have enough food to last for several weeks," he said hoarsely. "I know it'll be tempting, but don't go outside. The duke's men are still out there and they're looking for you now as well." He looked up the tunnel. "Especially you, Kathryn. He'll use you to draw in the boys if he can."

"But what about you, Papa, doesn't he want you too?" Anna asked tearfully.

He reached out and patted his daughter's head. "Don't you worry about me sweetheart. I've hunted these woods half my life. I'll blend right in. They'll walk right by and still not know I'm there."

They walked up to the tunnel entrance, where he surveyed the surrounding countryside for soldiers, and then with a wave stepped out and made his way cautiously into the forest. Almost before they knew it, he had vanished from sight.

# CHAPTER 26
## MARIE DROPS A HINT

Duke Henry looked down at the report he'd just been given by General Fictus. "So she's finally decided to talk," he said. "How do you know if this is true?"

The man stared warily at the duke. "I can't be certain sire, but Sandra swore that the girl had mentioned playing with her brother in a cave a couple of miles south of Masden when they were kids. It's a long shot, but it's the best information we've gotten so far. Evidently they fished the river not far from there and found the cave when they were still children."

"And how are you proposing to handle this?"

"I've dispatched a troop to Masden. I have a pair of scouts out looking for the cave. If they find it, they'll call in the troop. I've told them not to approach the cave themselves, simply to keep watch from a distance."

The duke nodded. "How large is the troop?"

"Twelve men sire. There will be no escape this time."

"Good," he said. "They understand that I want them all alive, don't they?"

"They'll do their best sire."

Duke Henry glared at his general. "Their best had better be good enough. Alive, do you understand. I don't care if you lose a hundred men bringing them to me. I want them alive." He rubbed his hands and smiled. "I've some questions to ask them." Then he turned and walked back to his throne. Almost as an afterthought, he waved his hand behind him and muttered, "Dismissed."

As he sat, Duke Henry speculated on the means he'd use to get the information he needed. It would be good to finally be rid of those pesky boys. Hopefully, they'd capture them at the cave. If not, he still held the sister to lure them out into the open.

# CHAPTER 27
## ROCKY POINT ISLE

Robert and Johnny crowded against the rail as the ship sailed around a spit of land that jutted out into the sea, protecting a small harbor. They could see a cluster of ramshackle buildings at the far end of the cove and noted that a group of people still the size of ants had wandered out to greet them. Johnny pointed, "Look, up there on the hillside, do you see the smoke? It must be a signal fire."

Captain Mizen joined them in the bow, "It is indeed. You have sharp eyes. That fire's been a tradition for as long as I've known of this place. Whenever a ship is sighted approaching the harbor, the fire is lit and people gather from all around the isle. This is the only safe landing spot and the only real town on the island."

Johnny frowned, "Is it a warning of some sort?"

"Nowadays it is," Mizen waved his hand toward the buildings. "This island is pretty remote. It started back when people first settled here. It used to be that a ship would come calling here just a couple of times each year, and they didn't stay long. If you lived on the far side of the island, as small as it is, you might not even know, so they started using the fires. As soon as they saw the smoke, people would gather up their wares and cart them into town. Also, if you wanted to leave, you'd best be on the lookout for a ship. If you missed it, you might not see another for months to come."

"How many people live here?" Robert asked.

"Not many, a few hundred maybe. There're more now that we're using it as a base than there were, but still," he chuckled, "is this where you'd choose to live?"

Johnny shook his head. He'd felt confined living in Masden. At least there though, he had his trips to the neighboring villages and a pretty large forest to wander through. He looked again at the desolate rocky shore. The few trees he saw were bent and grayed by the steady wind that blew off the sea. As they gradually drifted closer, he noted that the buildings all looked the same. It was as if they hadn't seen paint in years. "You say they bring their wares to this place. What could they possibly sell?"

Mizen looked at him and smiled. "Fish. Not much more. They grow just enough vegetables to fill their own bellies at dinnertime. They also mine a little tin. We'll take on a good load of salt fish and a few tin trinkets when we leave here." He pointed to a small inlet, hidden around a rocky breakwater. "Look there. It's just coming into view. You see the fishing boats?"

Both boys turned and followed his hand. At first all they saw were the rocks with a few scraggly pines behind. Gradually, as they sailed closer, Johnny made out the first of a cluster of masts sticking out above the rocks. "I see them," he shouted. "There must be what, half a dozen small boats?"

Robert stared and then finally smiled. "You're right." He scanned around the boats and was surprised to see a number of empty berths. He turned to Mizen. "Are there more?"

The older man nodded. "Most of the fleet is out at the south bank. They'll be coming in tonight with holds full of cod and haddock." He slapped Johnny on the back. "I'd better get back to the helmsman and check in. For you boys though, there'll be fresh fish for dinner tonight."

The two boys stayed in the bow, variously checking the shore and watching as the crewmen tied off the sails. Soon, they drifted to a stop a couple of hundred yards offshore. Robert was about to say something when he heard a loud clatter and noticed the anchors being dropped into the water. "Interesting. I guess we're too big to tie up," he said.

Johnny nodded and then pointed. A group of sailors was standing around a longboat lashed upside down on top of the captain's cabin at the rear of the ship. He and Robert watched in amazement as they ran a series of ropes through the block and tackle attached to the boom. After carefully lifting the small boat off the deck and righting it, a couple of sailors climbed in and directed the others to swing the boat out over the back end of the ship. As soon as it was clear, they started releasing the ropes and the boat lowered slowly down to the water.

"How do you suppose everyone else gets into the boat?" he asked. Just then, he noticed another man throw a rope ladder over the side of the ship. He ran to the side and looked down. Sure enough, the sailors in the longboat were rowing straight to the side of the ship. As soon as they reached the side, Captain Mizen strode up and announced, "Walter, Tom, Joseph, you come with me. I'm going ashore to check in. Mr. Harvey, lower two more boats and send them ashore with our guests. We'll want to load and unload quickly." Showing a lifetime spent at sea, he threw one leg over the side rail and grabbed the rope ladder, and then scrambled down until he could jump into the longboat. The three other men rushed to follow him, and once they reached the bottom, took up oars and pulled away to row to shore.

§§§§

Rocky Point Village was everything it appeared to be from the harbor, bleak, gray, and old. As the sun started to fall, the steady wind blowing off the sea turned brisk and people headed indoors to the warmth of a coal fire. Johnny and Robert hauled their packs to the island's only inn, where they were directed to a lean to behind the kitchen that they were to share with a pair of goats. "We're full up today," the innkeeper grinned. "You boys won't mind, will you? Anabelle and Mabel don't take up too much space."

Robert bent down and looked through the short door. The room was small and dim, but it was clean and well kept. A pair of small beds stood against opposite walls, blankets folded neatly at the foot of each. A half used candle stood in a battered tin cup on the short chest next to each bed. The only other furnishing was a three-legged stool just inside the door. Then he looked across at the goats. One of them bleated and stared back at him, nervously chewing some of the green grass it had taken from a bin in the corner. Their pen was separated from the bedroom by a short wooden fence. He could just see what appeared to be a rough hewn wooden door beyond the goats, obviously locked at night, but opened for them to exit into the yard during the daytime. He turned back and smiled at the innkeeper. "We've spent the past few weeks in the forest. This actually looks pretty cozy."

Their host just grunted and was about to turn away when he hesitated, "It gets a bit chilly at night when the wind starts whistling through the gaps in the walls. You'll find a couple of extra blankets in the chest out there."

"Thanks." Robert looked at Johnny and said, "Well, I guess this is home for a while," then he nodded toward the goats, "complete with roommates!"

"Like you told the man," Johnny said, "after sleeping out in the rain, this looks pretty good." He dropped his knapsack onto the floor, making sure it was out of the reach of the goats. "What do you suppose they're serving for dinner?"

Robert smiled, "I don't know. Fish? For once I'm probably just as hungry as you are!"

# CHAPTER 28
## THE CAVE

The two scouts huddled in a thicket behind a large boulder just off a narrow animal trail. They'd been exploring the area south of Masden for three days now, working ever farther away from the village. This was the first sign they'd had of a habitable cave, and aware of their orders, sent a third member back to the village to let the troop commander know where they were.

The taller man looked at his leader. Both were experienced hunters, dressed in forest green, their short swords and daggers sheathed in leather holsters. The soft-soled boots they wore were made for silent tracking and his whisper was as soft as a fluttering leaf. "You suppose we should hike on up there and check it out?"

The other man shook his head. "Don't forget what the Captain said. If we find a cave, we're to wait for reinforcements before closing in. He wants to surprise anyone there."

"Who do you suppose we're looking for?"

"Don't know, couple of boys, I hear. Maybe an old woman too."

"Why?"

"Duke wants them for something." He held up his hand for silence. "Someone's coming!"

Both men turned toward the animal path. They could just make out the sounds of footsteps on the trail, accompanied by a slight tinkling of metal. "Sounds like a small group. A dozen, maybe. You agree?" asked the taller man.

His partner nodded. He pointed toward the trail and silently drew his dagger. The footsteps got closer and he heard a whispered voice. "Over there, behind that big bush." The two men inched away from the opening in the brush and waited breathlessly until they heard, "Al, Jimmy, I'm coming in."

The leader nodded at his partner and signaled him to sheath his dagger. "In here," he replied softly.

The bushes parted and another green clad man came in, accompanied by six soldiers. One of the scouts raised his eyebrows and nodded toward the men. The new man looked back, then whispered, "I know. I told them that if they wanted any chance of surprising anyone, they couldn't come marching up here in full gear. Each man has a sword and a dagger. That's all.

The newcomers huddled in a circle, tightly filling the small opening. Now they looked toward their captain. One scout looked from face to face and started giving his report. "There's definitely someone up there; we've heard voices every once in a while." He pointed off beyond the cave. "We've checked out the area. There's a good ambush point just around the bend."

The captain nodded, asked a couple of questions, and then pointed to two men. "You two go with Al to the ambush point. It's a logical escape from the cave." He pointed to two others. "You two stay here. If they get past us and come running down the trail, you'll be in position to catch them." He looked at the remaining scout and soldiers. "We're going straight up to the cave." He motioned to one soldier's sword. "Can you keep that thing quiet or do you need to leave it behind?"

The man said softly, "You'll never know I'm behind you."

"Good," he said. "We're going to follow this trail. It winds up the hill and ends at the mouth of the cave. With any luck, we'll surprise whoever's there and take them without any struggle." He raised his voice just a little for emphasis, "Remember, we're to take them alive. If you do need to use a weapon, disable them with the flat side! Got it?"

He looked into each set of eyes and waited for every man to nod in agreement before motioning back toward the trail. "Let's go."

The men filtered out through the bushes, one group backtracking to another path that would take them to their ambush point, while others, led by the veteran scout, made their way silently up the trail.

As they came around the bend toward the mouth of the cave, the leader raised one hand and everyone stopped. Without turning his head, he gave a set of hand signals. Then he continued softly for a few more feet, before stretching his neck to look carefully through a bush at the mouth of the cave. Glancing back at his team, he gave a sharp nod and then strode deliberately into the cave.

The only inhabitants were four young boys, each about ten or eleven years old. They sat in the back, surrounding a small campfire in front of a narrow opening that appeared to lead further into the mountain. He called out, "You boys! Stay where you are!"

One of the boys took a panicked look toward the deeper part of the cave and started to spring up when the man yelled, "Stop!" and ran toward him. The other man had run directly to the inner cave opening and now blocked it with his dagger drawn.

The boy who'd started to rise looked at the four men, sat, and said in a quavering voice, "What do you want?"

The scout squatted in front of their fire and warmed his hands. Then he looked at the boys and said, "Who else is here?"

The boys looked at one another quizzically and one ventured, "Who else? We're the only ones here."

The scout looked up to the man at the inner cave. His partner shook his head and he scowled. All of this trouble to find a bunch of boys playing in a cave. Still, he asked, "Has anyone else been here?"

The boy who'd tried to run earlier seemed to have found his courage. "Sure," he said. Then he smiled, "But we chased 'em off."

The scout asked softly, "Who were they?"

"A couple of kids from the village," he said proudly, "This is our hideout."

"You haven't seen anybody else? Maybe some older boys? A woman?"

The boys shook their heads and then one, his eyes widening, said, "You looking for Robert and Johnny?"

"That's right," said the scout. "You know where they are?"

He shook his head, "I don't think anybody's seen them for weeks." Then he brightened up. "You think they're hiding in a cave? That'd be great!"

The other boys started to talk animatedly and the scout held up his hand. As if by magic, they quieted. "Do you know of any other caves around here?"

They talked together for a moment before one said, "What about Red Rock?"

Another boy said, "No, it's too far."

The scout stopped him. "What's Red Rock?"

The boys were enthusiastic now. "It's the only other cave like this, but it's over by Fairview. You think they'd be there?"

Standing, the scout said, "Can you boys show me how to get there?"

Sensing adventure, they all volunteered at once. "Sure," beamed one. Then he hesitated and looked at his friends. "We'll have to tell our mothers. We're supposed to be home for supper."

# CHAPTER 29
## THE MEETING

It had been a week since the Starling sailed away from the island, and she wasn't due back for at least another, so Robert and Johnny had had plenty of time to adjust to their new surroundings. They'd even grown accustomed to sleeping with goats.

During that time, their host Andrew Jameson, kept largely to his room, fighting the infection that eventually attacked his wounded arm. They discovered that like all villages, this one had a woman who was known as a healer. At first, Johnny was skeptical of Meghan's knowledge and use of herbs, having received some rudimentary training from his father. The more he watched though, the more impressed he became of her understanding of how to treat various illnesses and injuries using her herbs and her understanding of the body. Always curious, he became her willing pupil, and spent time every day helping her to treat Jameson's arm. She insisted on changing and boiling his cloth bandages every day, something Johnny wondered about at first. She also cleansed and retreated his arm each day with a salve that she made from the crushed extract of a cactus found on the other side of the island. As he watched the angry red swelling subside, Johnny became a believer that this woman truly knew what she was doing.

During the height of his infection, Jameson became so feverish that he spoke nonsense. Walter took charge of the two young men, but told them little, and left them largely free to roam the village and wander the surrounding hillsides. As his infection waned though, Jameson became more lucid and called Robert, Johnny, and Walter together for a meeting.

§§§§

Andrew Jameson was sitting up in his bed when they entered the room. Although Johnny spent time there each day, Robert had never been in this room before, and he looked around as he entered. Except for the absence of goats and their odor, it wasn't much different from their own. The walls and the furniture were all rough hewn, and he could see daylight through gaps in the boards of the exterior wall. It was small, though larger than theirs, and held two wooden chairs along with a small dresser topped by a rotating mirror. Walter dragged in two more chairs and motioned for them to sit. Jameson sat up in his bed, looking drawn, but alert.

"I understand that Walter's been looking after you for the past couple of weeks," he began and looked over at the big man. Walter nodded silently, and Jameson continued. "Well, what have you been up to?" He looked from Robert to Johnny, and back again, before finally, Johnny spoke.

"Not much sir. We've been wandering about, getting a feel for the island."

"Well then 'not much' describes it," he laughed. "There's not much here, is there?" He reached for his water and Walter rose to help him. Waving him back with one hand, he continued. "I feel weak as a kitten," he said, "but the arm's healing. Captain Mizen just sailed in last night, so it's time to get to work."

Robert cocked his head quizzically and Jameson nodded at him. "That's right, work. You didn't think we came here for a vacation did you. There's work to be done."

"I'm not sure what you want us to do," Robert answered him. "We don't know anything about fishing or mining."

Johnny looked at his friend, then smiled condescendingly. "It won't be fishing or mining we'll be doing, will it?" He looked over at Jameson. "I'm guessing this has something to do with the duke's men chasing us all over the countryside. Am I right?"

There was a knock on the door and he motioned Walter to answer it. When he swung it open, Albert strode in, nodded knowingly at Johnny, and took one of the chairs.

Robert was startled to see him. "When did you get here?" he asked, and then nodded his head. "On the ship last night, right." He looked over at Johnny. "You knew? Why didn't you tell me?"

"Let's say I knew, but I didn't really." He shared a look with his father.

Taking a deep breath and letting it out in a long sigh, Jameson nodded his head. "Well, we're all here. Walter, how secure is this room? Can we be heard outside?"

The big man shook his head. "You're at the end of the hall. Albert was in the room next door. I set Bill at the top of the stairs, carving on a piece of wood. He'll let us know if anybody comes up. We're secure."

Jameson nodded. "Good. We'll need to fill in the others soon enough, but I'd like to talk with these boys alone first." Seeing Walter step toward the door, he waved him back. "You too. Take a seat in that chair over there. I think you're going to be surprised with the story I've got to tell. I certainly was when Albert and I started putting it together last night."

Walter pulled his chair over toward the door so that he'd be in a position to block it if necessary, and then sat. He looked expectantly at Jameson.

Leaning back on his bed, Jameson seemed to close his eyes in thought. The room fell silent, all eyes on the older man. Finally, he began, "Robert, it's no surprise that your mother sent you to me. Way back before you were born, about twenty-five years ago, your father and I were good friends. My father, well, let me just say, he handled certain affairs for your grandfather."

Looking confused, Robert interrupted him. "But I thought you said you'd never been to Masden. Did your father help with the stable?"

Jameson laughed and shook his head wearily. "No, boy. Maybe as a child, but certainly not as a man. Now quiet down and listen for a while. There'll be time enough for questions later." He shook his head, chuckled again, and took a sip of water. "Albert, feel free to jump in and fill in the details if I leave out anything important. Anyway, as I was saying, your father and I were good friends; had been since we were small boys." He closed his eyes for a moment, as if seeing an earlier time, and then opened them and continued. "He and I used to spar together, not that I ever beat him. That boy was practically born with a sword in his hand." Seeing Robert's eyes go wide, he laughed again. "Ah, yes. Good times. This old body used to be pretty good with a sword. Too much work behind a desk, and I've gotten so soft you wouldn't believe it now, but it's true. I was trained by the best. Anyway, I was telling you a little bit about your ancestry." He looked over at Johnny, "And we'll be telling you a little bit about yours too, if you've a mind to listen."

Johnny nodded silently.

Albert interrupted with a look at Robert. "I think it's time to take out that ring and lay it on the dresser there, where we can all see it."

Robert looked at the others, and then slipped his hand into his tunic and withdrew the leather strap. He looked protectively at the ring, and then slid it over his head and untied the strap for only the second time since he'd put it on in the cave. Everyone watched as he set it on the table. The ruby showed a subtle sparkle as the light from the window hit it, and drew everyone's attention, eliciting a gasp from Walter. Jameson cast him a cautionary look and then leaned forward, picked up the ring, and rolled it around on his finger. "An interesting piece of jewelry, wouldn't you say?"

Robert nodded. "I've wondered where he got it."

"I'm sure you have," Jameson continued. And I think that's where I'll start my story."

# CHAPTER 30
## ANGERING THE DUKE

Duke Henry paced back and forth in front of his throne. He was alone in the room, puzzled and angry. General Fictus had returned the day before. Evidently the boys were not hiding out in the cave near Masden. A search of another, larger cave near Fairview had been equally unproductive. While he believed that it was possible that they had escaped his men and might be hiding somewhere in the forest, he couldn't imagine how they'd gotten out unseen by anyone. And the boy's mother was with them somewhere, and the other boy's whole family. Something wasn't right. Whole groups of people didn't just disappear. And from what he'd been able to find out, they'd been living in that little hole of a village for nearly twenty years. It was one thing to imagine that they'd run, but where would they have learned the skills to hide this long?

A small side table got his attention and he bounded angrily over to it and kicked it savagely, breaking one of the legs and scattering the contents. "Harrumph," he growled, and turned, the damage forgotten. He returned to his throne and sat, and then reaching for a bell, summoned a servant.

Almost immediately, a man poked his head through the door and asked nervously, "Sire? You need assistance?"

Duke Henry barked at him, "I need Fictus, NOW!" The servant jumped to go but he harshly called him back. Gesturing at the remnants of the table, he said, "And get somebody to clean up that mess!"

§§§§

Marie had been sitting in the window seat, looking out over the green valley below and thinking longingly of walking through the fields and hillsides, smelling the heady scents of spring grass and wildflowers when Sandra hustled into the room. She looked over to her, and raised her eyebrows when she saw the frightened look on her face. "What is it?"

Sandra looked at her despairingly, "The duke has summoned us. Together. Oh, I'm frightened."

Taking a deep breath, Marie walked over to Sandra and took her by the arm, guiding her to the window seat. "Tell me what's happening."

Sandra gritted her teeth. "The servants are talking. General Fictus returned last night. He didn't find your brother, and now the duke is stomping around like a madman. I don't know what he's going to do, but I…"

Marie nodded, and put her arm around Sandra's shoulder. "He wanted a place to look, and we gave him that. We'll have to give him another. I'm sure they've vanished by now." She smiled, thinking that the good news was that they still hadn't been found.

Shaking her head, Sandra sobbed. "You don't understand. The word he's using is deception. I don't think he'll believe you any more."

"That's a problem, but there's a way, I'm sure. We'll figure it out."

"No," Sandra wailed, "you don't understand. I've seen this happen before. If he doesn't think you'll be useful to him, he won't bother keeping you!"

Suddenly the door crashed open and two soldiers burst in. "You two, come with us. The duke wants to see you!"

Marie nodded calmly and rose, offering her hand to Sandra who clutched it and stood beside her. In a voice that she hoped masked her fear, she replied, "Well we mustn't keep him waiting."

# CHAPTER 31
## A HISTORY LESSON

Jameson picked up the ring, angling it so that the sunlight caught the red stone. "Many years ago, back in a time before men even kept track of time, King Ordel oversaw a great kingdom called Bonterra." He looked at the boys. "I'm sure you've heard of him." When they nodded, he went on. "He was a wise man, and a just king. His people loved him, for they were prosperous and happy. And so, on the twenty-fifth anniversary of his reign, they decided to repay his kindness with a gift." He glanced down at the ring. "The king's council invited the nobility and the wealthiest merchants to a secret meeting in order to consider an appropriate gift for their ruler. Some suggested that each man give the king the finest fruits of his harvest, or his greatest steer, or ram. Others disapproved of that, for the king did not seek wealth for its own sake, but merely to protect his people, so in the end it would be a gift that would enrich themselves. Others believed that they could best honor their king by offering to join him on a quest to expand his kingdom, but this idea was voted down as King Ordel was at peace with his neighbors, and none wished to disturb the harmony between their kingdoms. Finally, a man spoke up. He was a strange man with a strange name, Malovan, and new to the community. 'I will make him a ring,' he said." Jameson looked at the boys and then settled the ring on the dresser before continuing.

"Now this man was a stranger, but when he first came to the kingdom, he had set up a forge and was known to be quite cunning at his work, crafting beautifully decorated plates and cups of silver and gold. He also made intricately carved jewelry."

"And this..." Robert started but Jameson held up his hand.

"Many were nervous at the idea of hiring him to make a ring for the king, for his reputation was that he was also a practitioner of the magic arts." He looked around the room, letting his point sink in. "And some feared that he called upon dark forces in his work."

The boys were spellbound. Jameson tapped the ring. "After much discussion, it was reluctantly agreed that they would commission him to design and craft a ring." Taking the ring in his finger tips, he said, "It may not seem that way, but a ring such as this was very costly, and nearly every citizen of the kingdom gave freely from his own goods to help to pay for it." He paused and took a sip of water. "Albert, have you anything to add?"

"It's how I remember the story."

Jameson nodded. "The jeweler sent his employees to the farthest reaches of the known world to find gold, and even more important, to find this precious ruby. And when they returned, he locked himself in his shop for nearly a month, working on the ring in complete secret. Of course, people wondered what he was about for they heard strange otherworldly music and chanting at every hour of the day and night. Even the lowliest laborer knew that it should not take that long to craft a single ring. Some suspected that he had quietly snuck out of the kingdom, taking their wealth with him and leaving his workers to create a diversion. But that wasn't so. He was working," Jameson gave his audience a hard look before finishing his sentence, "And working his magic!"

He held up the ring again, so that it would catch the sunlight. The stone sparkled, and as he turned it, cast points of ruby light across the walls. "Remember, this ring was made for a king, and as such it had to be not only beautiful, but powerful!"

He put the ring back on the table again and adjusted his position on the bed. "I find that I get stiff, lying all day in this bed. It'll be a glad day when Meghan allows me to walk the hills again." He settled back with a sigh, and then smiled at them. "Our story. Finally, Malovan emerged from his secret forge and asked to see the king's council. All were excited. The same men who had come before, came again, and again in secret, to witness the unveiling of the ring. Once they had all gathered in the chamber, Malovan entered, carrying a beautiful wooden box, inlaid with silver. He lay the box on a table before the head of the council and then withdrew to a seat in the corner of the room. The head of the council opened the box and took out the ring for all to see."

Jameson took a breath and looked at each of them. "Now you have to understand, the men in this chamber were the wealthy elite of the kingdom, and they had given substantial gifts for the crafting of this ring. As the head of the council lifted the ring to the light, many were disappointed. One called out, 'fraud,' and then another and another. The head of the council, who had given the greatest gift toward the ring, was the most upset and immediately called for his guards to arrest Malovan and drag him to his dungeon, where he was to spend the rest of his days."

"But why?" Johnny asked.

Again Jameson held up the ring. "An excellent question. You have to remember that each had paid a substantial price to craft this ring, some would say enough to buy many rings such as this." He swiveled it around again, catching the ruby light. "And while it is beautiful, they felt that they had been cheated with a simple piece of jewelry."

"So what happened?"

Jameson sighed deeply. "I find that I am tired. So much talking. Perhaps Albert, you could continue for me?"

"Of course," he said. "They put the ring away for several months, while different men argued about whether it was a worthy gift for their king. Finally, they did decide to give the ring to the king, and he was pleased, but he was a good man, and would not have questioned even a lesser gift from his people, being honored merely that they had thought to recognize him. As I understand it, the gift was made in the king's largest audience chamber so that all of the notables of the kingdom could be there. And when he put the ring on, it lit the entire chamber with a soft red glow even though they had made their gift after the sun set. Many fell to their knees in fear, while others whispered among themselves about the treatment they had given Malovan. King Ordel was so surprised and impressed with the ring, that he ordered them to bring the jeweler to him so that he could personally thank him for his gift. At this point, the head of his council confirmed that Malovan had died just that morning, having left a note cursing the kingdom. The king, after questioning them on how it was that the jeweler had come to be in a dungeon, took off the ring and plunged the room back into shadows. He was so furious with their unjust treatment of the mysterious jeweler, and his fear over what the curse might mean, that he ordered his entire council arrested."

"What happened to them?" Robert asked.

"After they had spent some time in the royal dungeon, some say a few days, others a month, others a year or more, he relented. Nothing bad had happened, and his remaining advisors convinced him that there was nothing to the curse. So he took up the ring again, putting it on, and enjoying the light it cast whenever he wore it." He looked to the bed. "Andrew? Any more?"

"Just this," the man said. "Never doubt for a minute that the ring is magical." He took it and placed it onto his finger and then held it up to them. He looked around and summoned Walter. "Put this on and show us." The man wrinkled his forehead in confusion, but took the ring and slid it over his large finger. "Let us see it," he said, and Walter held it aloft. "Good. Give it to Albert, and then Johnny." Albert put on the ring and lifted it for the others to see how it sparkled in the light before handing it to his son who did the same. "Now Robert, you put on the ring."

Robert looked at it curiously. Johnny held it out and he took it. As it had before in his hand, the ring emitted a subtle glow.

He slid it over one finger and the glow increased until it bathed the room in light causing the others to gasp in awe. Robert stared down at the ring, trying to comprehend what was happening. When he slid it off, the glow diminished, and he turned to Jameson. "I don't understand," he said.

Jameson sat up in his bed and reached for the ring. Once Robert put it into his hand, the remaining glow vanished, and he continued with his story. "This ring has magical powers, but it is also cursed. The council were imprisoned, and their leader, the man who ordered Malovan to his dungeon, died a painful death shortly after his release. No member of the council or of those present when Malovan was arrested, survived that year, a great loss which nearly destroyed the kingdom. Only the leadership of King Ordel enabled them to survive, for he was a strong leader, a good administrator, a fearless warrior, an able diplomat, and a just king." He lifted the ring again to the light. "His son was also a good king but his grandson was not. He wore the ring, but he was jealous and petty, and it lost its luster while he lost his kingdom. There followed many generations of chaos, before finally, nearly one thousand years later, King Randall took the throne, restoring this land to greatness, and the ring to its originally glory."

He handed it back to Robert. "Put it on," he said. Robert slid the ring over his finger again, and and the soft red glow returned to the room. Jameson continued. "Duke Henry destroyed our greatness, our prosperity, and our freedom when he murdered King Stefan." His eyes bored into Robert's. "When he murdered your grandfather, that is. He only wore the ring for affairs of state, and your father managed to spirit out the ring before Henry could find it. He was, and now you sir," he said reverently as he bowed his head, "are our rightful king. The glow in that ring proves it."

Robert gazed about the room, unsure what to do or say. The ring continued to glow, softly, but steadily. He looked over at Johnny, who just grinned at him, and then to Walter, who nodded his head.

"But," he muttered.

# PART TWO
# BIRTH OF A KING

## CHAPTER 32
## "HE STOLE MY HONOR"

Robert was dumbfounded. He stared blankly at the ring for a long time, trying to sort out what he had heard. Finally, he lifted his head and said, "How can that be. I'm from Masden, a nobody."

"Not exactly," Albert said. "At least, not in the mind of Duke Henry. He killed your grandfather; he killed your father; and now he's after you."

"There's more to the story," Jameson added. "Much more." He looked around the room, gathering them all in his gaze. "And each of us here shall have a role to play before it's done."

He adjusted himself again in his bed before continuing. "When Henry stole power, we scattered, but did manage to keep in touch, at least for a little while. Your father and Albert, known then as Prince Gerald and Thomas, ran together, hiding in the forest. After some time, they decided that they should separate, and plan to meet later. Your father made his way west and eventually hid in Masden. He used his knowledge of horses and what little money he had with him to start a new business as a stable master. He was always a capable actor, and though he must have seemed better educated than others, he roughened himself so that he would fit into country life. Over the years, people forgot that he was a newcomer who had come to the village as a young man. And even those who remembered knew that the year after Henry took the throne was chaotic, with many people moving about the kingdom, and running from his forces. Albert disappeared into the forest and later emerged in Masden as a farmer. By coming separately, they were not associated with one another, and when they became friends, it was a natural piece of living together in the same village that nobody questioned."

"As boys," Albert said, "we were as close as you and Johnny here. My father was one of the king's chief advisors, and was slain with the king. Fortunately, he was able to elude Henry's henchmen just long enough to send me a message so that we could flee the capitol city before it was captured. As it was, they nearly caught us. Your father was injured escaping the duke's soldiers. We hid in a hayloft for a couple of days and I bound his wound."

"His leg," Robert said. "Right. It bothered him when it was overworked. It collapsed under him. It's why he was killed in the fight at the house."

Albert nodded. "We scrambled from place to place for weeks, hiding. I'm afraid I couldn't do much more than sew his leg up with twine and treat the infection that followed. Fortunately, we were young and he healed."

"I was young then, barely more than a boy," Jameson continued. "My father was the king's chancellor. We had a country house, and had traveled there for a few days of hunting and fishing while the king made his retreat, so we were spared for a time. When we learned of the king's death, I was sent with my sisters to live with a distant relative in Waterton, and warned never to speak of who I was. My parents hope was to hide us, and then to come for us when it became safe to do so. Sadly, they were captured and murdered, but I was considered unimportant enough that they never really looked for me. Of course, I was not of royal blood." He looked pointedly at Robert. "Henry searched for your father across the years, and now that he's found him, he's seeking you. Only when you're dead, can his family be secure enough to seek the throne."

"Meaning he'll declare himself king, something he's wanted for many years." Albert added. Then he chuckled. "Some part of him still knows that as long as you're alive, he can never be more than the duke, but when you're dead..."

Robert looked about the room, seeing the men around him in a new light. So many things that had made little sense to him before, started to come clear. He had always enjoyed the practice with swords and lance and bow, and it had come naturally to him, and as he understood now, most likely because his father had been trained by masters. Even though he knew that few of his friends had any experience with weapons, he had never really wondered about that. It was just a secret father-son activity that they enjoyed together. And there were the lessons in the old tongue, the language of court. Somehow he had never considered why his father should be able to speak it so fluently. It was just one of many things about him that were subtly different from the others in the village, but made perfect sense in this new context. His father was a prince. He shook his head, trying to settle these new thoughts. He himself was a prince but had never known it. And now that his father was dead, he supposed that he was a king. A king without a kingdom, he thought wryly. He noticed Walter now, still sitting by the door, guarding the room. "And you?" he asked. "Why are you here?"

Walter began opening his shirt as he spoke. "I was a member of the king's personal guard on the day that he was killed. It was a high honor, and a privilege to serve him in that way." He pulled aside the shirt now. He was creased with a thick scar that ran from his left shoulder down to the belt line of his pants and beyond. Another scar, the mark of an arrow, scored his abdomen, just beneath the ribs. He turned. Three more scars, puncture wounds, stood out on his back. "When they first attacked, we were ambushed from behind by a volley of arrows. The king went down and we formed a circle around him, all of us grievously wounded. We fought them off for a time, but there were too many of them and not enough of us. Once they had the king, they left the rest of us for dead. I should have died on that field, and would have, like the rest, had it not been for a young village girl who dragged me to her home after the battle was over. She hid me and treated me for a couple of months while I healed." He grinned. "She later became my wife, but that's beside the point." Scowling again, he added, "Duke Henry stole my honor when he murdered my king while he was under my protection. One day, I'll have my vengeance."

Robert looked down at the ring again. It lay heavily on his finger. It's soft glow could be mesmerizing if he let it, so he took it off and returned it to the leather thong. The others nodded approvingly as he slipped it over his head again. Something was missing in this story. He thought for a few moments before turning to Albert. "You said your father was murdered with the king. How did he get a message to you?"

Albert clapped Johnny on the shoulder. "Let us just say that the men of my family have inherited certain, ah, abilities and leave that conversation for another day." He nodded toward Jameson, who had sunk back into his bed, clearly exhausted by his earlier efforts. "We should let Andrew get his rest."

# CHAPTER 33
## A CHANGE IN STRATEGY

Duke Henry circled, wolflike, around the two young women. He'd forced them to sit on the floor, part of his effort to intimidate. It was clear that his chambermaid was terrified, but the young girl, the captive, seemed surprisingly composed. Still, she swiveled her head about as he paced, watching him. He was determined this time to play her differently. Slapping her had done nothing. Cold control might have a different effect.

"We checked the cave," he said. "We found a group of boys, playing." He continued to circle her, watching for her response. She had none. He raised his voice. "Well?"

She looked up at him. "I'm not sure that I understand. What cave?"

Momentarily confused, he looked to Sandra. Maybe it was as she had reported. The cave was mentioned in passing. Two women discussing childhood games. "I think you do. I'm looking for your brother. Sandra mentioned a cave."

She looked across, as if surprised that Sandra had shared a confidence and addressed her. "You mean the one we played in? Did I mention that?"

The woman nodded nervously.

Marie looked back up at the duke, disingenuous. "I didn't know she was reporting on me. Well, I guess I shouldn't be surprised." She cast Sandra a nasty glance, and then thought silently for a quick moment. "I suppose that would have been a good hiding place," she said, and then frowned, "well, maybe not since you checked it."

He leaned in. "Where is he? Where is your mother?"

She just shook her head. "The forest? He and my father used to hunt and fish there. They'd take off for a couple of days at a time." She paused. "But I didn't go, being a girl. In fact, other than trips to the market in Fairview or Tomton, I never traveled out of Masden."

Henry looked out at General Fictus. "Any sign in the forest?"

The man shook his head. "None. We've scoured the wood. There's nobody there."

He looked back at Marie, measuring her. She was nervous. He could tell. There was something she was still holding back. He contemplated his options. He had to tread softly with this one. A lash or two with his whip? Another spell in the dungeon? He walked back to his throne and stared at her for a long couple of minutes. She was starting to squirm. Good.

Finally, she spoke. "What do you want with me?"

She really didn't seem to know. Or maybe it was another front. Whatever, he'd break her. He leaned forward and hissed at her. "I want your brother. I want your mother. Why I want them is my business."

"I don't know. They'd be with my father, wherever he went."

Henry chuckled. He had a key that he hadn't even expected. "Your father is dead," he said flatly.

Her hand flew to her mouth, and her eyes widened. She sat like a stone, rocked with shock. He noted with satisfaction the tears that started to roll down her cheeks. "Why?" she moaned. "What have we done?" She looked up at him, unashamed in her grief. "One day I'm helping my mother make dinner and the next I'm here, my life upside down and my father..." She dropped her head and sobbed.

§§§§

In their room later, she looked at Sandra. "You knew." She said it without emotion and then sighed deeply. "I suppose I did too."

Sandra bit her lower lip, on the verge of tears herself. "I'm so sorry."

Marie squeezed her eyes shut, trying to focus her mind. There would be time for crying later. "What's going on?"

Shaking her head, Sandra said, "I wish I knew. For some reason, your family seems awfully important." And then she stared, as if trying to look through Marie. "Who are you?" she asked. "Not just who's the girl from Masden, but who are you really?"

Marie cocked her head to the side and Sandra continued. "It's more than just being here. It's more than the duke wanting your brother. You're," she paused, searching for words. "You're different. He doesn't intimidate you like he does everyone else. Why not?"

Marie was about to answer when the door flew open again. Two soldiers stood there as the tall man from the dungeon strode into the room. "Ah, ladies." He looked about the room. "So nice. Clean, comfortable, everything you could want. Oh well." He grabbed Marie by the arm. His grip was tight, painful, and she was repelled by the stale garlic odor of his breath. He smirked. "You're to come with me. New living arrangements." As he stepped out the door, he turned to one of the soldiers. "Get the other one too. It's back to the dungeon for both of them."

# CHAPTER 34
## SLEEPING WITH GOATS

Robert slept alone that night in the small room he shared with Johnny. His friend was enjoying a reunion with his father. It was just as well; he had a lot to think about, and needed time to sort everything out in his mind. The whole story Jameson told was just too big for him to wrap his head around somehow. In fact, if Albert hadn't been telling part of it, he'd have laughed it off as an old man's fantasy.

He rolled over on the cot and one of the goats bleated, causing him to laugh. First they tell him he was a king, and then they send him back to sleep with the goats. It seemed fitting. He'd earned nothing better so far.

He reflected back on what he knew. Arms training for a country boy who was destined to run a stable had made some sense, and he had never questioned it. After all, many boys served as soldiers for a time before returning to the countryside. Still, now that he thought about it, his father had been extraordinarily competent, an expert and a gifted teacher. He grimaced as he reflected back on the attacks at the house and pier. As a boy, he'd always thought they were simply playing with swords, but evidently, he had learned well enough to be able to overcome professional soldiers.

No doubt, the duke's men were hunting him, and this helped to explain that. He would be a threat as long as he lived.

He touched the ring against his chest. And of course, Henry would want the ring. With it, he could claim the throne as well as the power. His mind flashed on the title, "King Henry," and he growled.

He thought some more, and found his mind lapse into the old tongue. The language of court. He spoke it, as well as reading and writing it all because of his father's lessons. Now that he thought about it, he was certain that his mother had no knowledge of the language. But he did. And so did Marie.

And then he sat up. She was alive. Somehow he knew that, just as he knew that his mother was still in hiding. But she was in danger, mortal danger, and he needed to help her. He wasn't sure how, but that would come. He clenched his fist unconsciously. He would pull her free of Henry's grasp.

He lay back on the cot. There was much to do, and he knew that he needed his sleep. He knew too, that sleep wouldn't come easily. Not on this strangest of all nights.

# CHAPTER 35
## BACK TO THE DUNGEON

Marie winced and opened her eyes. Sitting carefully, she reached behind her and brushed away the pebbles that had been grinding into her back. After a several days on the floor of the dungeon, she definitely missed the bed upstairs in the palace. She could only think of one route back though, and that involved betraying her brother, something she wouldn't do even if she could.

She looked up to the high window. It was still dark out, and quiet except for Sandra's breathing next to her. Over the past couple of days, they'd formed the kind of bond both had wanted but been uncertain about while they passed their days looking out the window upstairs. Then, she suspected rightly that Sandra was a spy for the duke, and hadn't really opened up to her. Sandra, on the other hand, had said little to Marie for fear of punishment. Now that they shared a cell together, those barriers seemed to be breaking.

Living in Masden, they had been so far removed from the capitol city of Entaro, that little news filtered out to them. She had heard of the duke, of course, and occasionally seen his soldiers in the town. Still, she had expected to grow up, marry a local man, and have children, just like her mother. She had never imagined that she would one day meet Duke Henry, or that he would be angry with her. Now he was, and she found that the more she learned about him, the more she despised the man.

She looked over at Sandra. They had little to do in the dungeon other than talk, and had shared much about their lives. The story that Sandra told her earlier was repeated with more detail. She suspected that Henry had executed the people who had taken her from her uncle. She wasn't sure why, or even if that was true. She'd just heard strange things in her conversations with the other servants. Regardless of what had happened, she was clearly terrified of the man, and the scars across her back gave good reason for that.

Most interesting was the speculation among the servants that their guest, Marie, was actually a noblewoman, and that Henry was holding her as a hostage to lure in others. That made no sense, but whenever she tried to object, Sandra would simply say to her, "You speak the old tongue. Explain that." And that was the one thing that Marie simply could not do. She began to wonder increasingly where her father had learned it, and why he wanted his children to master it. None of it made sense to her. But then, she was sitting on the floor of a dungeon in the royal palace. That certainly made no sense either.

A dim light started to filter into the room as the sun rose. Marie stood, careful not to hit her head and started to move her limbs. It was cold, and she looked forward to the warmth the day would bring. Sandra woke and rolled over, "Morning."

Marie looked down at her. "Another day."

"I was hoping to sleep this one away. My dreams are ever so much more pleasant."

"Sorry. Was I making too much noise?"

"No. I've been awake for a while. I needed to move. Hard floor." She stood and stretched.

Marie watched for several minutes as the woman worked through a now familiar exercise routine, but could only make out shadows. She winked at her anyway. "I was thinking that pancakes would be good for breakfast this morning. And I'd like a little blueberry syrup and some bacon on the side. Maybe you can convince the guard to bring us the expanded menu. All I've noticed so far is the bowl of porridge, and that's getting a little old meal after meal."

Sandra grunted as she stretched her arms. "Well you certainly seem cheerful this morning. Did I miss something? Were you on the feather bed?"

Walking to the door, Marie peered out through the bars that stood out from the steel frame. There was no sign of their jailor. The men who rotated that duty usually sat in a small room behind another door, along the passageway up into the castle. They had beds in there, and the man on duty was probably still asleep. "I think we're alone today." Then she frowned, "Well, except for the folks in the common cells anyway. I don't hear the prisoner in the cell down the hall."

"Still asleep probably," Sandra said.

"Probably," Marie said softly. She hoped he was anyway. He hadn't sounded well, coughing and wheezing. She could remember him from when she did her first shift in the dungeon. She slid down along the metal of the door. It was cold against her back, but they had discovered that if they bunched their skirts under them, the floor was a bit softer, and the smooth surface of the door offered a reasonably comfortable surface to lean on.

A few minutes later, Sandra came over and joined her, sliding down along the door in much the same way Marie had. "I'm tired of the dark," she said. "I think that's the worst part."

Marie reflected on the dead woman she'd seen on her first visit to the dungeon, but decided not to mention her. "It's gloomy," was all she said. She leaned her head back against the door. "I keep thinking about what you said, about the old tongue." She turned her head toward the other woman. "And I can't figure out why I can speak it either. It's strange, but it's even stranger to imagine that my father was a nobleman." She laughed suddenly. We definitely didn't live that kind of lifestyle."

"You started to talk about your mother last night."

"She was a simple woman. My grandmother, her mother, as well."

"I would like to have known my grandparents. I guess they died with my parents. What was she like?"

Marie laughed. "Old. At least she seemed that way to me. She died when I was just a little girl. And my grandfather was killed in the chaos after the duke took over, before I was born." She sighed. "She missed him. She was kind, gentle, but strict. I can still see her chasing after Robert with a switch after he stole a hot bun she'd just cooked. She'd have smacked him good if she'd caught him, too." She looked over to Sandra with a smile. "And I remember sleeping in her lap. She had the softest woolen comforter, and I can remember snuggling up in that on cold days. She slept in the kitchen on a small cot in the corner. It was always the warmest room in the house." She mused for a minute or two, remembering good times before continuing. "It's funny what you remember."

They sat silently for a long time after that, quietly taking solace in one another's company. Finally, Marie said, "Are you sure about what you said last night?"

Sandra continued to stare straight ahead, finally answering, "What's that?"

"Rumors of rebellion?"

# CHAPTER 36
## THE STRANGE STORY OF JOHNNY TUPPENCE

After breakfast the following morning, Robert suggested to Johnny that they go for a walk. There was much to think about and he wanted Johnny's counsel. It was at the same time, exciting, confusing, and not a little bit frighting. They wandered the few streets of the village and then headed out of town on the only road. Several times, Johnny tried to start a conversation, but Robert silenced him with a wave, or a shake of the head. They'd been walking for nearly an hour when they reached the top of the highest point on the island. From there, they had a commanding view of both Rocky Point Village and the smaller communities to the north, as well as the dark blue-grey of the surrounding ocean. They settled down behind a stone outcropping that that blocked the wind that seemed to sweep its constant chill across the island. A few white dots on the ocean showed where the fishing fleet had centered.

Robert turned to his friend. He wasn't sure where to start, but knew there were things he needed to know. Johnny surprised him by asking the question that was foremost in his mind. "You want to know how I knew that my father was coming."

It was a statement, not a question. "Among other things. Did you plan it this way?" He looked out at the sea. He felt they were safe here, both in this spot and on the island. They'd spent so much time running for their lives that he had only begun to relax over the past few days. And then there was the turmoil of yesterday's meeting, with the stories about his supposed ancestors, and the ring. Everything seemed to swirl around him, creating a haze of confusion. "Did he know we were coming here?"

Johnny was silent for a while, staring along with Robert out at the sea. Finally he spoke. "How much do you want to know?"

"How much can you tell me?"

He chuckled. "I can tell you quite a bit, but there's a lot I'm still figuring out. I'd prefer to hold some of it to myself, at least until I understand it better."

Robert nodded, thinking. He'd feel the same if someone asked him to tell what he knew. "I can live with that."

They sat for a few more minutes before Johnny broke their silence by saying, "I'll tell you what I can now, and we can talk again later." When Robert looked over at him, he said, "Walter's on his way up here. He's taken over responsibility for guarding you. We have some time though."

He hadn't seen Walter this morning, but it made sense. "Fair enough."

Johnny started. "I can do things, see things, hear things, that most people can't."

"I know that," Robert responded. "Sharp eyes. You've always been able to see further than I can."

"It's more than that, and that's what I'm trying to understand myself." He looked at his friend. "Maybe an example. When you went fishing with others in Masden, and I wasn't there, how'd you do?"

Robert was a bit startled, but answered, "About the same as the rest. We all caught a couple of fish."

"And with me?"

"You caught more. No question."

"Why?"

Robert furrowed his brow as he looked looked at his friend. "I don't know. I always figured you were the best fisherman. Skill wins the fish."

"I'm good, but not that good. Think about it. I always caught more fish, no matter who I was with. Even if I was catching all of the fish in one spot and you all made me trade places with you, I continued catching fish, and you didn't. And it wasn't the bait, or the lures, or the cast."

"I'm not sure I understand, and what's this got to do with your father?"

"Give me a minute. I'm getting there." He paused. "Remember when we saw the riders coming?"

"Yeah," Robert said softly. "How could I forget?"

"You saw a smudge, right?"

"That was about it. A little dirt rising above the road."

"I knew how many there were, and that one of the horses was going lame."

Robert looked at him. "How? Your eyes aren't that good. They were miles away!"

Johnny shrugged his shoulders. "I just knew. Just like I just knew that Walter was on his way up here, or that my father was on the Starling. I just knew." He picked at a tall blade of grass, stripping down the worn dry leaves and sticking the rest in his mouth where he sucked on the sweet flavor. "And that's just the tip of it." He looked out again. "I was telling the truth about the fish. I really do tell them not to take your hook because mine is better. And those soldiers in the forest? I told them that the log would be a good place to sit down for a smoke. They faced away from us and then they left, thinking that they'd searched the area."

Robert shook his head at him. "Come on," he said. "They were just tired."

"Explain the captain of the guards on the pier. He wounded Jameson. He called over the guards from the fight. He sent others to arrest us. What happened there?"

"Well, that wasn't you. We put up pretty good resistance."

"You wounded one of his soldiers and he still let you go instead of arresting you. Does that make any sense?" He cocked an eyebrow toward Robert. "Well? And why release Jameson?

He'd taken him prisoner already. The man was injured and out of the fight. He not only released him, he escorted him up the pier and saw that he, and we, were safely on our way."

Now Robert stared at him. Everything he said was true. Why would the captain possibly have let them go. He had been ready for an all out fight with the soldiers, and then the captain just called them back. He'd been so busy that he hadn't really thought about it, but... He tilted his head to the side, looking at Johnny in a new light. "He helped you with Jameson, didn't he. You told him something."

"I told him to call off the soldiers. I told him to let us go. Just like I told the soldiers in the forest not to search any further or like I told Jameson's secretary to let us in to see him. Just like I told the fish not to take your hook."

"But how?"

"My father calls it 'the voice.' Evidently, I can make suggestions that people take for their own ideas. And the scary thing, is that when I try, I can do it without even speaking."

Robert looked at him for a while and then shook his head. "No. I don't believe it. We were lucky, that's all."

Johnny nodded. He'd expected as much. "How about this then." He stood and walked around the stone, into the wind, and then pointed back toward the village. "You see that tree down the trail? About a hundred yards from here?"

Robert looked. "I do."

"Walter's going to sit there. He'll smoke his pipe for a few minutes before coming the rest of the way up the hill. You'll know he's there when you smell his tobacco." He glanced over at Robert. "Good enough test?"

They both looked down at the tree. "Seems like a likely place to stop," Robert said uncertainly. "And I'm in no danger here. Maybe he'll just stop there to wait us out."

"All right." Johnny said. "Good point. So let's have him do something unexpected. You choose it. I'll send the message."

"Interesting." He thought for a minute. "How about this. Have him take of his hat."

"Ok."

"And his coat, and his shirt."

"A little cold for that, don't you think?"

Robert smiled. "And his boots. And have him hang the shirt and hat and sit on the coat."

Johnny laughed. "Any more, your majesty?"

Robert cringed. "Please don't say that." He watched the path from the village for a few seconds before saying, "That should be enough." He shivered. "Cold in the wind isn't it?" They walked back into the lee of the rocks and sat again. "So how did you know your father was coming?"

"Easy. He sent me a message from the Starling the day before they landed. He and I have always had that ability to communicate our thoughts."

Robert just snorted and shook his head.

"It's true. You want me to send him a message too?"

"Do you have any idea how completely outrageous this sounds?"

Johnny nodded. "Absolutely. Give him an instruction."

"All right," Robert said. He thought for a minute or so. "Tell him to meet us at the door to the inn with the ram."

"Interesting. That'll get him wondering."

"Can you do it?"

Johnny smiled at him for a few seconds. "I already have. He'll be there." He played a bit in the dirt between his legs. "It's an interesting gift, don't you think?"

"If it's there."

"Jameson has it too. He just doesn't understand how to use the power very well. To him, it's a set of feelings. He could sense it in me in his office, and it shook him. And he can use some of the abilities, but they're not very well refined. My father's very good, and can probably do things that I can't even imagine. I'm still learning, but he says I'm better than he was at this age."

"You said there were other things."

He grinned. "Starting to believe?"

Robert slapped his knee. "Let's just say I'm curious."

"There are some other things that I'd prefer to keep to myself for now. I'm not sure I understand them well enough yet. It's been helpful to talk to my father about it again, and I've already begun practicing a new skill that he taught me last night." He looked up, expectantly. "Is that enough?"

"It'll do, for now." He stared out over the grey ocean for a while. The wind had picked up and he was starting to lose the sails of the fishing fleet amongst the white caps. "Tell me, you were there last night. What would you do if you were me?"

Johnny laughed. "Easy. I'd get rid of that ring!" He paused and watched Robert's reaction. His friend looked thoughtful, and then shook his head, so he turned serious as well. "But you can't do that, can you?"

"No. I don't think so. The more I think about it, the more I feel like I've been chosen. For what, I'm not sure yet, but chosen to begin with, to bring the people together."

They talked for nearly thirty minutes, tossing around ideas and plans between them. Suddenly, Robert went still, sniffed, and lifted his hand. "Tobacco. Do you smell it?" He stood and peered around the rock. Walter was sitting under the tree below them. He gripped his pipe between his teeth so that he could beat his hands against his bare chest and shoulders in an attempt to ward off the cold. His shirt and hat hung on one of the lower branches and he appeared to be sitting on his coat. Johnny looked at him, and then smiled at Robert. "Well?" he asked. "Do you want to tell him to put his clothes back, on or shall I?"

§§§§

Robert showed very little surprise when Albert met him at the entrance to the inn. "Good afternoon," he said with a knowing grin. "I hear you wanted the ram."

# CHAPTER 37
## BREAKING OUT

During their weeks sharing the cavern, Kathryn, Elyssa, and Anna had become good friends. Their days had fallen into a type of pattern. They rose in the morning, had a simple breakfast of grains and dried fruit, and then as often as not, hiked down to the hidden entrance at the base of the hill. There, while Anna played in the tunnel, they would sit, chatting quietly, confident that the concealing brush and rocky slope would allow them to hear and see anyone else long before they got close enough to be discovered. Later, they would trudge back up the tunnel to their nest, waiting until full darkness before cooking dinner.

As time passed, their sightings of soldiers in the forest became less and less frequent. In fact, as they sat in the mouth of the cave one day, Elyssa remarked that it had been over a week since they had seen anyone at all. She'd brought a basket of rags when she came with Albert, and to pass the time, she and Kathryn started work on a quilt. Now they sat, stitching in companionable ease.

Kathryn drove her needle through a new piece of fabric, proud of the tiny stitches she was able to sew. "Has it been that long?" she asked.

"Nine days. Remember the men down by the creek?"

"You're right. I don't even know what day it is anymore. I've kept a calendar though, back in the cavern." She took another few stitches. "We could use some supplies. Isn't Wednesday market day in Fairview?"

"It is." Elyssa looked out through the branches. "Are you suggesting we escape from here?" She grinned. "Because if you are, count me in!"

"I know. I'm stir crazy myself." She looked up from her stitching. "It's about eight miles, and if we stick to the back trails, we shouldn't see anyone on the way." She thought for a moment. "We could leave before it's light out, do some quick shopping, and then hide in the forest on the way back until dark. Do you suppose it'll be safe?"

"They're looking for the boys," Elyssa said, and then added suddenly, "And Albert. Will anyone know you in Fairview?"

"I haven't been there for a while. Maybe, but probably not. I have cousins in Tomton," she continued, "so whenever we left Masden we usually went that way. Let me think. The last time we were in Fairview, we picked up a couple of horses and that's been at least three years."

Elyssa stared out into the forest, musing. "Albert and I went over there from time to time, but market day is big there, with lots of people. If we take care..." Then she grinned mischievously. "Maybe if we use disguises." She squared her jaw and lowered her voice. "I could be a man," she said gruffly. "Johnny left some of his clothes behind. They'll fit me. I can let my hair get dirty and scraggly; rub a little mud on my face; wear gloves to hide my hands..." She showed a wry wrinkle on her face and glanced downward. "I've never been what you'd call voluptuous; might as well take advantage of it." She looked over to Anna. "And she looks just like a boy in her overalls." She winked. "It could work. They're looking for men, not a family of farmers with a little boy."

Kathryn reflected, trying to foresee problems. "We'll need to get lost in the crowd. "I'll cut my hair."

"Are you sure you want to do that?"

She nodded slowly. "Absolutely. I've never worn it short. It'll change me in case there's anyone there who might recognize me." She toyed with a lock that hung down to her waist. "Besides, it was one thing to try to comb this out in front of the mirror at home. It's been a challenge in the cave. I don't think I'll miss it." She looked across at Elyssa. "We should probably cut yours too, a man's cut." The other woman scowled before sighing in agreement.

While Anna played with her doll, the two women scanned for intruders as they continued to plan their outing, their excitement growing as they spoke.

# CHAPTER 38
## THE VOICE

Protesting mightily, Meghan finally released Andrew Jameson from his room two days after Albert arrived at the inn. She and Johnny had been discussing his need to get out and exercise so that he could regain his strength. He'd avoided using his influence though, wanting her to make her own decision. Shaking her head, she finally relented. "He can walk, but not too far, and there should be someone with him wherever he goes, at least for a few days."

Johnny grinned. "I'll take care of him. Don't you worry."

"I'll worry," she said. "You see to it that he doesn't overdo. He had a nasty infection in that arm and he's weak as a baby."

"I'll be in good hands," Jameson protested, looking at Johnny. "And a little sun will do me good."

"Well," she demurred. "That part's true. But if you have any problems, you send this boy after me." She made one last check of the healing wound on his arm, and then frowning, left the room with a reminder that she'd be back the following day.

"Well," he said with a grin. "Where shall we go?"

"Down to the end of the street and then back to the pub?" Johnny asked. "A little porter might be good for your arm."

Jameson lifted his eyebrows in approval. "A very wise decision. That woman's kept me on a leash as sure as if she'd used a rope." He stood, and then slipped back down to the bed. Johnny started over but he lifted his hand in protest. "Just a little dizziness. It's passing." He took a deep breath and exhaled loudly. "Not too far," he said, "and then a chair in the pub." He stood again, wavering a bit, but gaining his balance. Johnny stretched out an arm and Jameson took hold.

§§§§

Their walk was largely uneventful. Jameson seemed to gain strength as they went along, and stopped several times along the way to talk with one or another of the shopkeepers they met. Still, by the time they returned to the inn, he was glad to step into the pub and relax at a table in front of the fire. Johnny brought over two tall mugs of porter and handed one to Jameson. "That was a good walk," he said, pleased with himself. "I missed people more than I'd imagined." Seeing Johnny's glance, he laughed. "Not that you haven't been fine company, but variety's what I've wanted, and movement. We'll walk a little farther tomorrow."

He tasted the brew and wiped the foam off of his upper lip. "For a little island pub, they do make a good porter," he said. Then he turned serious. "I was looking forward to a talk with Albert today. Where's he gotten off to?"

"He went hiking with Robert, and Walter of course."

"Ah yes. Robert's going to have to get used to a shadow. Walter's not likely to let anything happen to him, now that he knows who he is." He took another sip of the beer. "He's a good man, Walter. Loyal, trustworthy. Robert could do much worse."

"Which has me wondering," Johnny said softly. He looked around the room. They were sitting in a dark corner, lit only by the fireplace. The bartender/cook was the only other person in sight, and he was tending to a stew on the fire behind the bar. "Back in Waterton, you seemed to be expecting us."

"I was, but not two boys."

Johnny looked at him. "You were waiting for his father, the prince."

"Or yours." He set down his mug and leaned forward, beckoning Johnny toward him. "Don't worry about Jacob there. He's one of us. Still, it would be wise to be discreet." He glanced around. "We can talk here today, since it's empty, but never with anyone we don't know. Just saying these words is treason, and if word got back to the duke, it'd be the end of all of us."

"He's already chasing me."

"True enough, but the one he really wants is Robert, not you. If you can lead him to Robert, well enough. If not," he drew a finger across his throat and paused to let his point sink in. "Best not to draw attention to yourself, and believe me, he has eyes everywhere. We're safer on this island, but do I trust everyone? Not hardly." He took another draft of the beer before he continued. "As for expecting you, I was. I knew that one day the prince would come out of hiding, and that he'd come looking for me. And then you..." He laughed.

"What?" Johnny asked.

"You tried to use 'the voice' on me."

Johnny's eyes widened. "I didn't expect you to recognize it."

"Any more than I expected anyone to use it, especially on me. Tell me, is that how you got past my secretary?"

Johnny watched the other man for a moment before nodding slightly. "She was determined to keep us out. Robert tried to reason with her, but that wasn't working."

Jameson laughed. "No, I don't suppose it would. She can be amazingly stubborn." Then he laughed again. "I've used 'the voice' on her myself from time to time, though it hasn't always worked. Maybe I primed that pump for you." He stopped for a minute. When he spoke again, he was serious. "Even though I knew you were manipulating me, I had trouble resisting your voice. The power's strong in you." He stopped to drink. "I have to speak aloud, and then be well focused and even so, it doesn't always work if my target has a strong will, but I could feel your message well before you opened your mouth, and if I hadn't known your father, I would never have known that it wasn't coming from my own mind."

"Where did you learn it?" Johnny asked.

"Born with it, I suppose. Here's something I'll bet you didn't know." He smiled, as if discovering a secret. "Did you know why your father sent you to me?"

"Not at the time. Now I'm guessing it was because you were friends back in the old days."

"More than that," Jameson said softly. "Our grandmothers were sisters. 'The voice' was always stronger on his side of the family than mine."

Johnny should have been more shocked, but somehow he already knew. He just nodded, and then said, "That stew smells pretty good. You ready for a bowl after your walk?"

Jameson looked out the window. Dark as it was inside, it was still light out. "Jacob won't be serving yet. He's mulish on that. Waits until closer to supper time. I've never seen him bend. We'll have to wait."

Johnny just shrugged his shoulders before lowering his voice. "You said your father was the Chancellor?"

Jameson leaned back in his chair. He nodded slightly. "A powerful man. The king was a man of grand ideas, of leadership. His was the face that people saw when they thought of the kingdom. My father worked in the background, along with a number of others, but he and the rest were the doers. They translated the king's will into action."

"And my grandfather?"

"Now there was an interesting man." He mused for a moment, stroking his chin. "Remember, I was just a boy at the time, but I still heard things. They say he was like a ghost, always there, but never seen. My father said to me once that he could get lost in a crowd of one. I didn't understand him at the time, but looking back, it makes sense. I suppose it was his 'voice.' A man with that along with his other rather strange talents would want to work in the background, unseen, but influential. Too dangerous to let others know of something like that. They'd be a little frightened; might want him to really disappear." He dipped a finger into his mug, stirring contemplatively. "Your father was always the same, and I detect that in you. Does Robert know?"

"I told him yesterday."

"Everything?"

Johnny shook his head. "Just confirmed what he already suspected."

"Interesting." He was about to say more when Jacob interrupted.

"You two fellows look like you're hungry. I brought you a little something to eat." He took two bowls of stew and a basket of hot baked bread off of his platter and put them on the table in front of them. "Another porter?"

Jameson was too startled to speak. He looked across to Johnny who simply smiled at him. "Thank you Jacob. That sounds good."

When he left, Jameson leaned forward. "All right, you're good. Just remember what I said. Best to slide into the background and operate there."

§§§§

Marie had been leaning against the wall, dozing, when she heard the outer door open. She stretched and glanced at the window, trying to determine the time. The light was waning, so she guessed that it must be late afternoon, too early for supper. Probably a new prisoner, or a check. She glanced over at Sandra. She too was awake.

They heard footsteps come down the corridor and stop in front of their cell. A voice said, "Open it."

She looked up, preparing to stand, when the door swung open. In the dim light, she could make out a small group of men, led by a well dressed and armed man at the front. He was young; she could tell that from his voice. He stepped into the room and stared at her for a long minute before saying, "Are you enjoying my father's dungeon?"

Her eyes widened in surprise, but she sat quietly, unsure of herself. There had always been men in the chamber with the duke, but she had never paid them any attention.

"I don't hear you. Speak!" he commanded, and she could hear the same cruelty in his voice that she recognized in Henry's.

"I do not much care for the dungeon," she said softly.

He laughed roundly and turned to his followers. "She doesn't care for it. What a shame." They all laughed and he continued, saying harshly, "Then perhaps you should be more cooperative. We want your brother. We have no need for you. We'd just as soon set you loose, but until you give us your brother, you'll be here."

He stared at her malevolently, and she cringed back against the wall. Suddenly he stepped in and grabbed her by the hair, yanking her head painfully toward him. "It's only going to get worse!" he hissed.

He shoved her away and spun back to the door, wiping his hand on his pants. As he left, she heard him scowl, "Get me a rag, someone. I need to wipe away this filth."

§§§§

After he'd gone, Marie looked toward Sandra, "Who was that?"

"Frederick. He's the heir. He's a nasty one."

Marie felt her head, "I can tell."

"Oh, it's worse than that. Henry's a devil all right, but he's predictable. There's something wrong with Frederick. He can spin off with no reason, and when he's mad, he's brutal. Of course, being the duke's son, it's always someone else's fault."

"I guess I need to stay away from him then."

Sandra frowned toward the door. "It's a little late for that now."

# CHAPTER 39
## TROUBLE IN FAIRVIEW

Kathryn was waiting at the mouth of the tunnel when Elyssa and Anna settled next to her. "Anybody out there?" Elyssa whispered.

She shook her head. It was dark and she'd been searching for any points of light and listening for the rustle of armor, or the whicker of horses. "Nothing." She looked back. She could just make out Anna in the moonlight. Elyssa was right. At eight years old, dressed in overalls, people would likely mistake her for a boy. She reached up self-consciously and touched her hair. Cutting it had been harder than she'd supposed, but it would grow back. It was tied in a pony tail just below her shoulders now, hardly the waist length flowing locks she'd lived with her entire life.

Still, her hair was longer than the tattered mess they'd left of Elyssa's. After all, if Elyssa was to be the man, her hair should have the haphazard grooming that a man might tolerate. Elyssa seemed to be reading her mind. "Aren't we the pair," she said with a chuckle. Then she leaned down to Anna for one last reminder. "Now what did I tell you?"

"We're going to Fairview for food. I'm supposed to act like a boy and you're my dad and Kathryn's my mom."

"Great." She hugged her before asking, "And why is that important?"

Anna's face took on great seriousness. "Because bad men are looking for Johnny and Daddy, and we can't let them know who we are."

"That's my girl!"

"Boy," Anna said. "I'm your boy today."

§§§§

Their hike through the forest to Fairview was long, but quiet and uneventful. They had chosen to follow a series of winding pathways where possible, avoiding the road until sunrise, when they joined a few other travelers walking into town.

Within an hour, the stalls were open and the crowd had swelled with happy shoppers enjoying a carnival atmosphere, complete with games, children's laughter, and most intriguing of all to a group that had been living in a cave, the smells of roasting meat. Kathryn and Elyssa shopped quickly, selecting fruits and vegetables along with salt pork and dried beef. They even found a seller of smoked trout. After vigorously haggling with one vendor, they agreed on a price for a bag of beans which they added to a load that seemed to be growing heavier with every step.

Andy, as they called Anna, was perfect, staying close to her 'family,' and watching as they bargained for food. At one point, she was invited by a group of children to play a game where they kicked a ball about a field. When she looked to her mother and got an indulgent nod, along with instructions to meet them in front of one of the stalls, she ran off.

They'd picked up a few nuts and dried berries and were starting to think they'd overstayed their welcome. "What else do you think we need?" Elyssa asked, trying to stay consistent with her husky voice.

"We're running low on flour, and definitely need soap."

"Ah, that's right, soap. Making myself look like a dirty farmer was far too easy." They turned up another alleyway and she nodded approvingly. "There's a miller here."

Kathryn had been handling most of the bargaining chores, in part as the home maker of the little family, and in part to keep Elyssa from speaking. This vendor though, insisted on dealing only with Elyssa, and ignored Kathryn's attempts to divert his attention. Finally, Elyssa responded to him. "My wife's been doing the talking today because my throat's bothering me. You have a problem with that?"

The merchant puffed out his chest. "Like to barter with men, not women." He gave Kathryn a distasteful look. "What can I get you?"

Elyssa motioned toward a barrel full of wheat flour. "How much for five pounds?"

"Three-fifty," he said.

She turned away. "Too much."

"I can give you a better price on twenty pounds."

"I would hope so, but our wagon broke down and we had to walk the last few miles into town today. Give me your best price on five."

"I told you. Three-fifty." She gave him a withering look and he frowned, "Buy ten pounds and I'll sell it for five." Elyssa looked toward Kathryn who nodded slightly in agreement. She took out a small pouch, and dug through to find five coins.

While they waited, the man started scooping flour into a cloth sack. He filled it most of the way before carrying it to the scale in the measurement booth across from his stall. Selecting a ten pound weight, he hung it from one side of the scale, and then put the sack onto the tray on the other side. "Eight and a half pounds," he said. "I'll get some more." He brought a bucket and scoop from his stall and proceeded to sprinkle more flour into the sack. The tray slid down so that the scale balanced and he dropped the bag to the table when Elyssa grabbed his wrist. "I'll not be buying your thumb," she said.

The man went red in the face. "You calling me a cheat?"

"I'm calling you nothing, just asking for a fair measurement."

He shoved her and she stumbled, losing her hat as she fell against the man behind her. "Hey, watch out," he said, pushing her away. "Sorry," she mumbled in her normal voice and the man started, looking at her. She bent to pick up the hat and his eyes widened as he took in the swelling of her hips.

"What's the trouble here?" another voice called, and Elyssa's heart skipped a beat. The village constable came around the corner, followed by two of the duke's soldiers.

Before she could answer, the man she'd bumped into stepped forward, "It's the miller. He's got his thumb on the scale again."

The constable turned to him. "Fred, we've talked about this."

The miller blustered. "I give fair measure."

Now another voice rang out. "When you get caught you do. There's the sack of flour. Let's give it a fair measure now!"

The constable looked at him. "Good idea." He turned to Elyssa. "How much did he say it was?"

"Ten pounds," she whispered, and then louder and more hoarsely, "Ten pounds."

"Fred, what do you say to putting that bag back on the scale for everyone to see?"

"It's a fair measure," he blurted.

"Then it will show on the scale. Give it to me." The constable reached for the bag and the miller grabbed it back, spilling some onto the ground.

"Now see what you've done!" He threw up his hands and stomped away from the scale. "Ruining my product."

The constable lifted the sack and put it onto the scale. It measured just under nine pounds. "Bring me the bucket, Fred. Let's fill it up."

The miller stooped to scoop up the flour on the ground along with some loose dirt, but stopped when the constable grabbed him by the back of his shirt, standing him upright. "The bucket."

Grumbling, the man put the bucket onto the table so that the constable could fill the bag. He measured out ten pounds, and then put in another scoop. Looking harshly at the miller, he said, "For their trouble." He tied the string around the opening on the bag and handed it over to Elyssa.

She dropped the five coins into his palm and he passed them over to the angry merchant. "Thank you," she said. "And thank you too. I appreciate the help," she said to the man who'd called out the miller. He nodded to her, his slight smile confirming that he'd guessed her secret. Then she turned to Kathryn, suddenly all business again. "We should go. We've got a long walk ahead of us. Let's find Andy."

She knelt down to put the bag into her rucksack. As she tied it up, she heard the constable say in a loud voice, "Ok everyone, time to be on your way. Nothing more to see here. You can buy from Fred or not, it's up to you." He waved people away, and within seconds, the alleyway had returned to normal, except that others were staying well clear of the scowling miller. She stood and settled her rucksack onto her back, and then taking Kathryn's arm, headed for the end of the alleyway. Two soldiers blocked their way.

One stepped up toward them. "I haven't seen you here before," he said. "Where are you from?"

"Out toward Tomton," Elyssa said.

The man lifted his eyebrow. "That's clear across the valley. What are you doing here?"

"Just came for the market," she answered.

"Long trip for the market."

Now she smiled. "It was." She looked back at the vendor. "And unfriendly too. We'll stick to Tomton in the future."

"I think maybe you two should come back to the barracks with us. We have some questions for you."

Kathryn and Elyssa shared a frightened look. They were about to bolt when Anna came skipping toward them.

"Andy," Elyssa said.

"This your boy?" the soldier asked.  She nodded and he continued.  "Fine, bring him too."

He turned to go.  Anna, reading the panic in her mother's face, said, "Where are we going?"

The soldier looked down at her.  "Your folks don't come from here.  We're taking them in, checking them out."

"Oh, I'm sorry," she said, "but today's my birthday.  We can't go with you."

He laughed.  "Happy birthday."  Then he turned his look on Elyssa.  "Follow me."  He threw his head to the side, signaling the other solder to fall in behind them.

"Excuse me," Anna said pointedly, and pulled on his sleeve, drawing his eyes down to hers.  "We'll have to come back later.  My father promised to get me sweets today since it's my birthday.  That's why we came to the market."  She shook her head as she spoke to him, still holding her eye contact.  "You don't want to spoil my birthday surprise, do you?"

He looked at her for a long moment, and then rose.  "Of course not."  He focused again on Elyssa.  "Why don't you folks enjoy the rest of market day.  We'll see you over by the gate this afternoon."

§§§§

They were a mile out of town when Kathryn finally spoke.  "We forgot to get soap."

"You're right," Elyssa responded.  "I think we passed some soap weed on the trail.  We can dig up the roots."  And then squeezing Anna's hand, she turned into the forest.

# CHAPTER 40
## RUMORS

Marie watched as the guard closed the door into the hallway. Once she was sure they were alone, she picked up her bread and dipped it into the porridge that served as their meal before saying softly, "You said there was some talk among the servants in the palace?"

Sandra nodded slowly, reluctant to put a voice to what she'd heard. "There've been a couple of uprisings in outlying villages. The duke's army's put them down." She went quiet. "We shouldn't talk about this. It's dangerous."

"The men in the common cell won't hear us. We're the only ones in this section now."

"What about the man down the hall? He could be here to spy on us."

Moving closer, Marie said, "So whisper. What happened?"

"I heard that in Peltrose, a group of villagers chased he local garrison out of town and took over the barracks. The duke sent a force and arrested them all. Every one of the rebels was hanged. There's talk that he went after their families as well, but I don't know if that part's true."

"You said there'd been a couple of uprisings?"

Sandra nodded. "I don't know much more. From what I hear, they're still fighting in Branston."

Marie let the information sink in for a while. Finally, she asked, "What about the army? The palace staff? What side do they take?"

Sandra was about to speak when the door opened. She looked down and focused on her food.

§§§§

General Fictus stood nervously in front of Duke Henry. He had just delivered news that the missing fugitives were on the loose somewhere in the kingdom, but he had no idea where. What was increasingly clear, was that given the time they'd been gone, it was unlikely that they were anywhere near Masden.

"So you're telling me that despite the manpower I've given you, they've completely disappeared. You have no idea where they've gone."

The general squirmed. "I'm sorry, but that's about it. The boy and his mother vanished the first night. Obviously, they had a plan in place. We have to assume that the other boy and his family have either joined them, or run separately. And based upon what we've heard about their friendship, I'm not ruling out the possibility that the two boys left together."

The duke stroked his chin. This man had been his most effective military leader, but this was beyond acceptable. He'd been slapping his hand with a riding crop as he paced the room. Now he threw it against the throne. "You can't find a boy and his mother. You're telling me that they, along with another complete family have eluded your best soldiers. So be it. You can't find them. I'll get someone who will." He turned toward his son. "This man has failed us. What do you suggest I do?"

Frederick caught Fictus' eyes with his own, holding them securely while he said, "A demotion is not enough, and flogging not appropriate for one of his rank. Perhaps some time in chains?"

Henry grunted and slapped his hands. "So be it. Guards!" he bellowed. Two men ran to his side. "Take this man into custody.  Let's see if a little time in the dungeon might help him figure out his duty." He seemed to stare through Fictus.

The stunned guards glanced helplessly from their general, Fictus, to the Duke and back, until Fictus nodded slightly and held out his wrists for binding.  His initial impulse had been to protest, and just as quickly, he'd decided to hold his tongue.  However unpleasant it might be, he'd probably survive a few weeks in the dungeon, and maybe he should be thankful for his luck.  The last man to disappoint the duke had been publicly executed as example of what happens to those who can't follow a simple direction.

# CHAPTER 41
## THE KING'S FIRST COMMAND

When Robert returned from his walk with Albert, he sought out Johnny. They were still sleeping in the room with the goats, so they held a whispered conversation there after saying goodnight to the others. "Tomorrow you and I are going up to the hilltop. We need to talk some more. I can tell I'm going to need someone to advise me." When Johnny tried to protest, he continued, "I know your father, and I'm getting to know Jameson, but I know you better. What's more, I trust you. I always have."

Johnny started again to speak, but something in Robert's tone told him it wasn't the time for lightness. He bit his tongue and nodded his head seriously. "All right. Go on."

"To you, I'm Robert, son of Robert of Masden, the stable master, the kid you went fishing with, one of the boys in the village. To them, I'm some kind of royalty. They aren't sure what to do with me and I intimidate them. I can tell."

Johnny guffawed. "You intimidate my dad?" He shook his head. "Hard to believe."

Robert was serious. "I know, but I do. I guess my father must have too." He looked off toward the far window, as if he'd heard something. After a few seconds, he sighed. "And if everything they say is true, I think I'm beginning to understand why. They've hidden for so long that I don't think they ever expected this day to come and when I asked your father what we need to do next, it was like he didn't know, like he'd forgotten who he was. He told me just to bide my time, but that doesn't feel right."

Johnny fiddled with a piece of straw from the floor. Robert's serious mood had a chilling effect on him as well. He waited for him to finish speaking. When Robert looked over at him, he said, "Well then. A walk in the country. It'll be good for both of us." He waited a few seconds and then said, "You're right, you know. I'll call you 'your highness,' or whatever else I have to, but I don't feel it. It'll be a line for me, something to keep others happy. But they feel it. I could tell when they told the story of the ring, and again this afternoon when I was with Jameson." He started to say more, but could see that Robert understood him, so he ended on a lighter note, "It seems that I was raised to be your chief advisor, and I think I can handle that, but don't go getting all uppity with me. Like you said, you're still Robert."

Robert sighed and rolled into his blanket. "Good. I'll appreciate your candor. They're frightened, and a little confused, and we need to talk about that. I know one thing. The duke's holding Marie, and king or stable boy, I won't accept that. I'm not going to sit by forever. I will free her." He looked across at Johnny again, and his friend was struck by the look of absolute determination in his face. "So, with that in mind, I don't see staying here as much of an option." He sat up and laughed as he looked out across the pen. "Not that I mean to insult the goats, because I've certainly mucked a lot of stalls, but even in Masden I didn't sleep with the barnyard animals. Well then," he said, laying down again. "I'll sleep better tonight knowing that I'm not alone in this. Thanks."

That night, Robert slept deeply and only woke when daylight started to seep in through the window. By then, Johnny had been up for hours, pacing and fretting, lost in too many potential scenarios.

§§§§

After breakfast, they climbed to the hilltop again. Walter, Robert's new shadow, hiked up behind them, never in earshot, but rarely out of sight.

When they reached the peak, they sat quietly for a long time, looking out on the choppy grey sea, now empty since the fishing boats had sailed further in their ongoing search for the elusive schools of cod. Johnny broke the silence.

"What are you thinking?"

"Marie," Robert said, still looking forward. "She's alive, I know that. Don't ask me how, but each of us has always been attuned to the other. Part of being twins, I guess." He stared unseeing at the sea for a moment before looking in Johnny's direction, "But I can sense that she's in danger, and with each passing day, it's growing worse."

They sat for a while, both lost in thought. Finally, Johnny spoke. "Before my dad and I were able to get up to the hill fort, the duke's soldiers hanged three kids in the village because nobody could tell them where you were. They made everybody watch."

Robert winced. "I know."

But Johnny wasn't through. He paused for a moment to let this sink in. "Little Rachel. Will, the butcher's son. And Sammie. We used to go fishing with his brother Daniel. Sammie was only five. They didn't deserve that."

Robert squeezed his eyes shut. He couldn't tell whether the tears welling up were from anguish or rage, but they were real. Finally, he spoke, his voice husky. "No. They didn't. They absolutely didn't." He looked at Johnny. "And that won't stand. You can trust me on that." He gritted his teeth and repeated, "No, that can't be allowed. You asked what I've been thinking. Well thinking is just about all that I've been doing over the last couple of days. I feel like somebody just turned my life," he paused and nodded knowingly to Johnny, "I'm sorry, our lives, upside down." He shook his head, clearing his thoughts, and then added, "and the more I think about my father, the more I'm starting to believe what they're telling me. I can see now just how different he was from the other men in the village. He was wise beyond his station, and a leader without even trying. And it was effortless, like he was born to it, which I guess he was." He waited for a while before adding, "They're right. He was a prince."

Johnny started to say something else, but Robert was not listening, so he stopped. His friend continued to stare out at the sea, lost in thought. After a minute or so, he stood. "Walk with me for a while. I need to move. I think better when I'm moving." Johnny stood and they walked to the edge of the bluff where they could look down on green fields of barley where the island flattened out before reaching out to the rocky cliffs of the shoreline. Robert turned to him. "We start planning today. We may not get a lot done, and it may not make sense a week from now, or even tomorrow, but we need to start." He lifted a finger. "One. What do we do about Marie? If what they've told me is true, if what this ring is telling me is true," he reached into his shirt and held out the ring for both to see the glow, then she's a princess as well as my sister, and dukes don't kidnap princesses." He paused to think. "And two." Sure of himself now, he slid the thong from around his neck, untied it, and with great solemnity, slipped the ring onto his finger. Johnny cast him a nervous look and he chuckled. "Don't worry, I'll take it off later." He looked down at his hand. "I want the feel of it now though. Two," he repeated, "how do we get rid of the duke." He shook his head violently. "No," he said. "Not the duke. Never the duke." He turned so that he was staring directly into Johnny's face. "If I'm to be a king, then I'm going to have make some decisions and here's my first one." He fingered the ring, seeming to gain strength and a sense of command. "As of now, nobody is to use that title in my presence. Call him Henry, call him what you like, but nobody is to use that title. He is no longer a duke. He is the criminal who killed my father. Is that clear?"

Johnny nodded, a grin spreading on his face. "Crystal clear. Do you want me to tell the others?"

Robert mused for a moment before shaking his head. "No. It needs to come from me. They wanted a king. They may not like it once I get going, but they've got one, and that's my first command." Seeing the disappointment in Johnny's face, he consoled him. "Don't worry, once they get past the idea that I'm simply the mysterious grandson of a king and really hear my voice and begin to accept my authority, I'll let you start speaking for me." He smiled wryly, "though I've never known you to be quiet in the past and won't expect it now, especially given your own 'voice,' as you call it." He paused. "As for Henry, today he lost his title. Soon, he's going to lose his power. And before we're done, he'll lose his life."

He turned back from the sea and strode over to the rocky knoll where they could be sheltered from the wind. "So we have a lot to talk about today, including where and when you'll start using that 'voice' of yours for me. We'd better get started."

Johnny noted that the ring was glowing brightly.

# CHAPTER 42
# PLANNING


Marie was dozing against the wall of the dungeon when she heard the main door open. "In you go," the guard shouted, and pushed a new man ahead of him. The man was finely dressed, but stumbled awkwardly as he came through the door, and she heard the rattle of chains. She and Sandra were in the first cell, and when he passed them, she could see that he was finely dressed in a military tunic. She looked over at Sandra but got no response. As the man passed in front of her, she caught his eye. His face was bruised, as if he'd been beaten, but his back was straight and he remained proud. He stopped and stared at her for a moment before stumbling further down the hall. A few minutes later, the guards returned with the chains.

After they closed and bolted the outer door to the dungeon, she whispered to Sandra, "Do you know who that was?"

Her companion nodded. "Fictus."

Marie cocked her head to one side. "Who's that?"

Sandra sighed. "A bad omen for us. General Fictus. He was in charge of finding your brother."

Marie looked down the hall, toward the man's cell. She smiled inwardly. If the searcher was in chains, Robert must still be safe.

§§§§

Kathryn stirred the cooking pot back at the cavern. Night had fallen an hour or so earlier, so she felt it was safe to cook up a bean soup for diner.

The fact that the soldiers had been so determined to question them led her to the conclusion that they hadn't found the boys, or for that matter, Albert. But that had underscored just how dangerous it still was for them on the outside. She looked over to Elyssa, who was sitting on one of the cots, reading to Anna. "I've been thinking," she said.

Elyssa looked up. "Yes?"

"About the market." She continued to stir the broth. "We should have enough to last here for a few more weeks, but we're going to have to go back again for supplies if we're still here after that."

"I know. I've thought about that too."

Kathryn looked over at her. "I have to think that we got lucky this time. If we have to go back," She let the thought dangle for a few seconds. "I'm not sure what'll happen. They may be looking or us too."

"It sounds like you have a suggestion."

Kathryn grinned. "I do. An idea anyway. Remember when we were girls? I didn't have any brothers, so my father taught me about farming, and took me hunting with him from time to time. I got to where I was pretty good, at least with traps and snares." She checked the others.

Elyssa was nodding thoughtfully. "So you want to hunt for our meat?"

"We have everything we need here, and if we do it right, it'll keep us out of town for a while at least. We'll still need grains and other things."

"Maybe. It's an idea. Let me think about it." She went quiet for a few minutes and Kathryn returned to the soup. Finally, she said, "I think it'd be safe enough, especially if you were to go out in the early morning or late evening when anyone out there is at home." She stood up, and handing Anna the book, took down some bowls for dinner and started to set the table. "I never learned to hunt, but I can pick berries, and I know where there's a patch of wild onions in the forest." She paused. "Potatoes and grapes, and a few other things too."

"So we could support ourselves," Kathryn said.

Elyssa nodded, still thinking of what would need to be done. "We'd have to be careful, but yes, we could. And if worst comes to worst, we might raid a barn or two for grains, but I'd prefer not to. If we take enough to last for any length of time, the farmers are sure to notice. We should have enough to last us until winter anyway, and if we plan, we'll be able to put away a pretty good cellar. Hopefully, we'll be out of here before then anyway."

Kathryn lifted the pot off of the fire and set it on the table so that she could ladle soup into their bowls. "I like that idea a lot better than chancing another trip into town. At least for now."

§§§§

Robert put his mug down and looked around him. Jacob had roasted a lamb for their dinner meal, and he was feeling well satisfied. Albert, Jameson, Johnny, and Walter sat with him at one of the large round tables by the fire. They had asked Jacob to close the inn after dinner, so that they could meet, and now the rest of the chairs were empty and the shutters on the two small windows closed. Even the barmaid had gone home for the night. He looked around the group and said softly. "Thanks for agreeing to meet with me tonight. I've been thinking a lot about what you've said over the past couple of days, and what that means for the future." He touched his chest, where the ring hung, and then deliberately made eye contact with each. "For me, and for us. Every one of us is going to have a role to play in this little drama that's been set in motion. Last night, while I was laying in bed, I started to think of this as a soccer match. So far, we've been running, trying to stay free of Henry's forces, just like a soccer team defending their goal, but that needs to change." He glanced over at Johnny. "When we win at soccer, it's because we force our opponent to react to us, right? And that's what we need to do here. We'll be the ones who set the rules of the game, and we'll force Henry to react to us." He let that sink in for a moment before focusing on Jameson. "You mentioned that Jacob was 'one of us.' I've been wondering exactly what that means."

The man hesitated, as if unwilling to give up a secret. Finally, he said, "We call ourselves the family." Seeing Robert's arched eyebrow, he clarified himself. "Not literally. We're not related. We're part of a group. But if others overhear us and we're talking about the family, they form their own opinions. Really, we all have a similar goal."

"And what's that?"

"Get rid of the duke."

He nodded. "That's what I suspected." He looked over at the man, washing mugs and generally cleaning up for the next day. "How much does he know?"

"Not everything. He knows who I am, and that I'm part of the resistance, and has helped to plan a couple of events."

"He could hang for that."

"So could we all."

"Ok. Anyone else in this group?"

"Captain Mizen, a handful of people scattered on the mainland." He looked across at Albert. "I'd have included you if I'd known where you were."

"Just as well." Albert said. "We didn't need the attention."

Robert continued his questioning. "You mention events. What kinds of things have you done?"

"This and that. A little sabotage, we broke into an armory and stole some weapons. We've supported a couple of uprisings."

"Really? Uprisings?" He looked around the group. "Masden's pretty isolated and I wasn't paying much attention anyway."

"There've been a few but they haven't accomplished much other than to cause some havoc. At least not yet. Still, we're working on that."

"And Jacob knows of this?"

"Some of it."

Robert scanned the faces. "Anyone else who's here in town?"

Jameson started to shake his head when Walter said, "Bill, the others you met in Waterton. They've been involved a bit. Mostly just Bill though."

"Hmm. That's right."

Robert looked at Walter quizzically and he explained, "The one I had that little dust up with back in Waterton. He's my brother-in-law."

"Ah yes," he chuckled. "That was a nice diversion. Gave us just enough time." He looked back to Jameson. "Let's expand our group then. Call Bill and Jacob over."

Walter rose. "I'll have to go get Bill. He's across the street." He grinned. "Has a lady friend."

"Tell him we're sorry to disturb him."

He laughed. "I'm not." He left.

Jameson had called for Jacob while they spoke, and he left the bar and came over to them, still holding his rag. He looked at them questioningly. "Something else I can get you fellows?"

"No." Robert said. "Pull up a chair. I'd like you to join us." The man frowned and he gestured toward the glasses. "Actually, there is something you can get us. Let's refill these mugs and draw two new ones. One for you and one for Bill."

Jacob looked at him for a moment, and then glanced at Jameson, who nodded. He left. By the time he returned with filled glasses, Walter had come back with Bill. He sat in one of the empty chairs. "Family business?" he asked, clearly uncomfortable with the idea that the two boys were present.

Jameson inclined his head in the affirmative and looked over to Robert. "I'd suggest you start by introducing yourselves."

Robert snuck a glance at Johnny. They had discussed a number of things during their meeting on the hilltop and how to manage this meeting had been one of their most pressing concerns. He took out the ring and set it on the table in front of him. It glowed softly in the muted light of the fire. Jacob's eyes widened and Bill's jaw dropped. "My Pa told me about that," he said. "But I never..." He looked at Robert in disbelief.

Robert picked up the ring, untied the leather thong, and slid it onto his finger. The glow increased and he slowly panned it around the room for all to see. "I am Robert, and I have been known as Robert of Masden, the son of Robert of Masden. And I wish you to refer to me simply as Robert, at least for now." He looked down at the ring. "But with this, everyone here knows who I really am." He looked directly at the two new men. "I am the grandson of the late King Stefan, and his only rightful heir. When I take my throne, I will be called King Robert."

He waited for his message to be received. Johnny was grinning widely as he watched the others bend to Robert's will.

When he was satisfied that he had their attention, he went on. "It's time we start planning not how we're going to annoy and inconvenience Henry, but how we're going to strip him of his power. We all know he's a murderer and a thief, and I plan to end his reign of terror." The others were nodding now. It was nothing they didn't all agree with.

Jameson whistled softly, "It's going to be some work, going after the duke, but you can count on us."

Robert turned to him and smiled. "Thank you Andrew, for so perfectly setting up my first command as king." The man frowned in confusion and he continued. "I told Johnny this afternoon, and I'll repeat it to you now. "As of today, I, King Robert, am officially stripping Henry of his title. He is no longer a duke and nobody is to use that title in my presence." He looked around the group and their grins told him that he had their agreement along with their growing admiration. "Today we take his title. Later we'll take his power and then his life." He raised his mug. "To the end of Henry!"

Once all of the mugs were down, he lifted the ring once more. "Every time we meet, if it is possible, I intend to wear this ring as a visible reminder to each of us, and that includes me, that we are conducting affairs of state." He paused for a moment and then said, "So, gentlemen, every king has his council and you have become mine tonight. Where do we stand now? What do we need? And what do we do first?"

They talked for over an hour, agreeing to meet the following evening after the normal closing of the inn. Jameson, still weak, had wanted to meet earlier, but Jacob objected. "We closed early tonight, and that's fine. I do close early from time to time. Once is a party, and people understand. Twice is an inconvenience. More than that and people will start to talk."

"Agreed," Robert said. "Tomorrow after closing." He looked over to Jameson. "How long until you can make it up to the top of the hill?"

"Give me a week."

"And until the Starling is back?"

"At least another week. Maybe two."

"So we have some planning time." He looked about the group. "Well. Everyone has an assignment. "Walter?"

"Bill and I are in charge of security."

"Albert?"

"I'm going to work on organization and planning with Andrew and Jacob."

"And Johnny and I will come up with some ideas for letting the people know that they have a king."

# CHAPTER 43
## MISSING GOLD

The last patrons left the inn and Jacob locked up and secured the windows before gathering the group. It had been agreed that if people routinely saw them meeting or even eating together, questions might be asked, so they were scattered about the inn, or in Bill's case, across the street. Once they were all together, Robert opened the meeting.

"I know that you haven't had much time. Johnny and I weren't able to do much more than brainstorm ourselves. Still, it seems like a good idea to meet frequently if for no other reason than to get to know one another better." He looked around the group as he took out the ring and slid it onto his finger, noticing that they seemed captivated by its glow. "Well, who's first?"

Walter glanced over at Bill. "We, uh, came up with a few initial ideas. We've some friends back in Waterton, mostly old soldiers who hate the duke," he grimaced, "excuse me, this'll take a bit of getting used to. Men who hate Henry, and who would be willing to help out, forming a guard. We obviously can't walk around armed without attracting attention, but we can hide some weapons under our cloaks, enough to cause a lot of trouble anyway. We figure to start with a team of two to four on you at all times when you return to the mainland."

Robert nodded, cringing inwardly at the loss of privacy. "Will they be reliable?"

"The best," Bill added. "I'll vouch for them."

"All right then. I'll take your word for it. Anything else?"

The two men shared a look before Walter said, "We'd want to run an advance team to check out spots you plan to visit, just to make sure we don't walk into a hornet's nest. It's going to take some training. Between that and the start up, about a month after we get back to Waterton. Until then, we'll ask you to be invisible." Johnny frowned and he continued. "I know you want to get the word out soon, but give us time to be safe. We'll train as quickly as we can, I promise that."

Robert looked around the group. Others were nodding. He felt the urge to move rapidly, especially given his concern for Marie, but they were urging caution. He sighed deeply. It was the right decision even if it wasn't what he wanted, and some inner voice was telling him that showing that he honored the advice that this group gave was a goal in itself. "All right." He turned to Jameson. "Any progress?"

"Some," he said.

Albert spoke. "You have two organizational needs. First, how do we form a resistance that can overthrow Henry. Second, how do we turn that group into a government that can start on their first day."

"As to the first," he continued, "the biggest need will probably be propaganda. It's one thing to talk about who you are, but once you show your face, you'll be branded as a dangerous criminal, with a reward on your head. We'll need to convince people that you really are the legitimate king because Henry will be denying it. The good news is that he has been brutal, so he has little support in the populace. If we can offer a legitimate alternative, the resistance should swell." He looked to Jameson.

"My father was chancellor, and he was training me to follow him, so I was pretty familiar with how things worked under King Stefan. We'll split the government into three basic divisions." He held up one finger, "The military. Some of the best will come from the many professional soldiers who are unhappy with Henry and will defect to the legitimate king. Others will be our own forces, among them, the ones that Walter and Bill recruit. We'll find leaders as we go." He held up another finger. "Second, we'll need competent and fair administrators. Henry has neither. I'll be contacting people I knew as a boy. Many of them are like me. Their fathers served King Stefan, and they have some training. I also have contacts with a number of successful people who have always been outside of government. I'm sure quite a few would be willing to serve." He frowned and held up a third finger. "The third comes down to money, and the sad fact is that we have none. That will cause problems."

"How about Henry's treasury?" Johnny asked. "Can we rely on that after Robert take control?"

"What treasury? That's why Henry levies so many taxes. The man's spent too much and has to steal from the people for that."

"But you said King Stefan was a good administrator. Wasn't there money there? Did Henry spend it all?"

"Ah, good question," Albert said. "I asked Jacob about that earlier. There was very little gold in the treasury when he seized power." He looked over to the bartender.

The man looked down, not wanting to speak, but when Albert continued to stare at him, he suddenly relented and Robert wondered if Albert was using the voice. "All right. Before I came to Rocky Point Village, I lived in Entaro. I was a boy then, about the same age as you fellows. My mother worked as a clerk in the Office of the Lord High Treasurer. After he took over, Henry had her arrested and threw her into the dungeon for several months. He arrested everyone in the treasury department, not just her, and flogged them all trying to get information. She was just a clerk though. She didn't know anything." He squeezed his eyes shut, not wanting to show his emotion. "Anyway, my father had died when I was young, so while she was gone, my brothers and sisters and I ended up living with our cousins. And then Ma died shortly after she got out of prison." Clearly angry now, he spat. "She was too badly beaten up and never really had a chance to heal. That's how I ended up on the island, and at this meeting, I suppose." He was about to say more, but then took a deep breath and refocused. "Sorry. That's another story, even if it is why I'm here. Anyway, according to what she said when she got out, the gold deposits had disappeared completely." He looked around the room. "Stolen, they said."

"Stolen?" Robert said suddenly. "But how?"

"She didn't know. She took in bills, authorized payments, that sort of thing. She never even knew where the gold was kept." He shrugged his shoulders and stopped talking. "It's all I know."

Everyone was silent for a moment until Jameson picked up the story. "He's right. I'd completely forgotten this until Jacob brought it up today. There was a fortress several miles from the palace, on Blue Lake. To anyone who visited, it just seemed like a well fortified manor house that the king and his family used as a vacation home, and they did spend time there, but that was all a fraud. The gold vault was hidden behind a secret door in the basement. My father told me that the idea was that if anyone captured the palace, the gold would be safe because nobody knew where it was. I don't think even the guards there knew about the treasury, and I'll bet that when word got out that all of the palace guards had been killed, they figured they were next in line and abandoned their posts."

Johnny looked from man to man. "So how did Henry find out about the gold?"

"You have to remember that his hooligans were busy grabbing power and rounding up all of the officials loyal to King Stefan. According to rumors, it was a week or so before they finally sent a force out to secure the palace on blue lake. They got there only to find that it was abandoned. The staff and the guards had all disappeared. When they searched the building, they found the vault. The hidden door was open, but the chamber itself was empty."

"So they interrogated everyone in the treasury department."

"Not everyone," Jacob said softly. They looked at him and he continued. "The Lord High Treasurer was gone too."

Johnny gasped and his eyes went wide. "The brooch."

§§§§

Jameson stared at him. "Go on," he said finally. "What brooch?"

Robert held up a finger and said, "I'll be right back." He backed away from the table and hurried down to the small room that he and Johnny shared. He'd hidden the brooch down at the bottom of his backpack. Now he took it out and walked back into the dining area. Once there, he slapped it down on the table in front of him.

Jameson reached out his hand and picked it up. He turned it over and over in his hand, reading the lettering that encircled the front rim. "Where did you get this?" he asked.

"We found it."

"Do you know what this is?"

Robert chuckled and looked at Johnny. "We figured we'd save it and if we were ever desperate for money, we could try and sell the metal, but now I'm wondering."

Handing the piece to Jacob, he said, "Did you ever see this? Do you know what it is?"

The man studied it for a minute before shaking his head and handing it back. "No, but I'm guessing you do?"

Jameson held up the brooch for all to see. He shook his head in wonder. "My father wore one just like this, only in his case it identified him as the Lord High Chancellor. This one is the official seal of the Lord High Treasurer. It was his badge of office, awarded by the king himself." He set the pin against his right shoulder. "He wore it above his right breast like this, and whenever he needed to sign an official document, he would take it off and guarantee his signature by pressing it into sealing wax."

Albert looked closely at his son. "Where did you get this?"

Johnny smiled, pleased with himself. "Now there's an interesting story." He looked at Robert who bade him continue. "After we crossed the Founderie River, we walked for several miles before we came across a cabin. It was well off the main road, and we were cold, and wet, and tired of sleeping in the forest, so we decided it would be a good place to hide out for a couple of days." He went on, telling them about finding the skeleton in the bed, drying in front of the fire, and their exploration of the area. "And then Robert found this out in the woodlot, right?"

He nodded. "It was half buried. I noticed it when it caught the sunlight. I dug it out and brought it back to the cabin where I cleaned it up." He took it from Jameson and held it up so that the fire reflected light off of the gold and silver. "We wondered at the time how it got there and what it was. Do you suppose this could have been from the missing treasurer?"

"No doubt." Jameson said. "The question is how it got there." He looked around the group. "And whether you two stumbled across the missing treasury." He paused for a moment, thinking. "Tell me, you say the man you found was a mere skeleton. Did you find anything else that might have identified him?"

Robert shook his head. "No, just his bones."

"Clothing, anything?"

"He'd hung his some things on nails on the walls, but it was what any peasant might wear, nothing special."

"So maybe he simply found the pin and then lost it again. Maybe somebody dropped it there. Maybe..." he started, but stopped when he saw Johnny's grin. "What?" he asked.

Johnny stood. "There was one other thing." He cast Robert a look of chagrin. "Sorry, but it seemed kind of ghoulish, so I didn't tell you. I must have lost some weight hiking out of Masden, because I was having trouble keeping my pants up."

"You were using a rope, right?"

"It was coming apart before we left and the swim pretty well finished it." He lifted his shirt and held it away so that they could see his belt. "It was hanging with his pants."

"An expensive belt," Jameson noted.

Johnny shrugged his shoulders. "Like I said, I needed something to hold my pants up, and couldn't see wasting it. We burned most of the rest."

"So we're left with a few possibilities," Jameson said. "Either this man stole those things, or he found them..."

He paused and Albert finished. "Or he was the treasurer."

"You're right. Or he was the treasurer."

"So what's next?" Robert asked.

"Easy," Johnny blurted. "We'll go back and find it. You know where the brooch was. We dig up the area and see if we can find any gold."

Albert shook his head. "No, not Robert. He stays in hiding for now. We can't put him at risk. What I'd recommend is that you and I go look." He nodded pointedly at Johnny. "If anyone can find the gold, we can." Then he looked at Robert. "Did you show Johnny where you found this?"

"Generally," he said. "We went back up to the woodlot together and I showed him what I'd seen. We even found an axe. It was pretty rusty, but I took it back and cleaned it up so that we could chop some firewood."

"Then we're settled. Once we get back to Waterton, we'll hire a cart and a couple of horses and go hunting." He looked at the others before focusing on Robert. "That is, with your approval."

"Hmm." He shook his head unhappily. "As much as I'd like to be with you, I can't. I understand that. All right. Sounds like we've got a couple of weeks anyway."

§§§§

Later that night, Robert lay in his bed, his mind fighting to make order out of all of the different things they'd discussed during the day. After a long time, he sat. "You awake?"

It was silent for so long that he had rolled back over in search of sleep, when he heard, "Yeah."

"Hard to sleep?"

"A lot to think about."

"Me too." He sat up, hugging his knees in the dark. "So why didn't you tell me about the belt?" he asked.

He heard movement from across the room and imagined Johnny squirming. "I don't know. I guess I didn't really feel right about stealing from a dead man. But then, he didn't need it any more." He repeated himself. "I don't know. Once I had it, it never seemed like the right time, and the longer I waited, the less I thought about it."

"You think there's gold there?"

"Who knows. If there is, we'll find it."

Robert sighed. "This being king, it's harder than it looks. Lots of things to think about."

"Yeah," Johnny laughed softly. "And to think that a month ago your biggest problem was that I always caught more fish."

"Good times," Robert said with a chuckle. He lay back down. "I'll see you in the morning."

# CHAPTER 44
## THE OPEN DOOR

Marie was just finishing up her morning exercise routine. Though athletic, she hadn't much cause for exercise back home in Masden. Here though, where she missed her opportunity to walk around the village, or the berry gathering trips into the woods with her mother, she found that she needed a disciplined routine to keep her muscles toned. Besides, there wasn't much else to do, locked in the dungeon day after day. She wished she at least had some books to read, but given the dim light from their high window, would have had trouble with that.

She and Sandra had begun exercising together, pushing one another to just one more push up, or taking turns protecting the one climbing the wall, from a fall. This morning, they were running in place when they heard the rustle of footsteps outside their door.

Panting, Sandra gasped, "I think it's time for breakfast." She stopped and swiped a hand across the sweat on her forehead.

Marie nodded, slowing her pace, but still jogging. After another few seconds, she stopped, hands on her knees, breathing heavily as the door opened. Their guard motioned them toward the back wall with a nod of his head, and then set their bowls on the floor. Without saying a word, he left, leaving the door partially open behind him.

Both young women watched for nearly a minute before approaching the opening. They heard the door to the exit open, and then close and latch, and when they peeked out into the hallway, could see that he'd left. Cautiously, Marie ventured out of the cell, breakfast forgotten. "Do you think he's coming back?"

Sandra stepped up next to her, and shrugged her shoulders. "Probably."

Marie looked up the hallway. She had taken the opportunity to peek into the other cells, when she'd been brought back to the dungeon. From what she knew, four of the six were occupied. She and Sandra had one of the small ones. Another, a large one down the hall, housed several men, and the one next to it seemed to be where most of the women were kept. The occupants of those cells seemed to turn over frequently, often accompanied by loud wailing. When she commented on that to Sandra, and asked why they weren't in with the other women, she'd learned that they were political prisoners, unlike the others who were criminals. "Be glad you're here," Sandra had told her. "Once they get to the duke's dungeon, the only way out for the criminals is to the gallows."

She eased cautiously down the hall, her ears attuned to the sound of the door that led to the guard's chamber. She peeked through the window of the cell next door. It was empty, as they had suspected. The same was true of the next one on their side of the hallway. The final cell, the one at the end of the hall furthest from the guard's room, was where the mystery prisoner had been locked up. Now, evidently, it was where the general was. Whereas the doors to the other cells were locked tight, his was also open.

She looked back at Sandra, who was several feet behind her and pointed toward the door. Sandra shook her head violently and motioned that they return to their cell. She stood for another moment, trying to decide what to do, when she heard a deep voice from inside the cell. "No point in standing outside there all morning ladies, come on in."

# CHAPTER 45
## A CURIOUS TEA PARTY

Marie looked back at Sandra. The other woman had slid down the hallway back toward the relative safety of their cell. She gestured for her to join her, but Sandra silently shook her head and eased back behind the door.

Turning, Marie considered her options. The cell was safe, and she could always return, but something was calling her, telling her to take a chance with this stranger. She lifted her head high and strode the remaining distance to his doorway.

What she saw startled her. The man sat on the edge of a wood framed cot. He looked out at her as she scanned the room, and smiled. "I asked Eric to leave me some tea. Would you like a cup?"

She nodded silently. Whereas the cell she shared with Sandra was completely empty, except for the pebbles on the floor, this one was furnished. It was not elaborate, more likely the kind of furnishings that one might see in a peasant's home, but nonetheless, it was furnished with a simple cot and blankets, a table with a bowl of water and a tea service with three cups, and a chair. A lantern glowed from a shelf on the back wall, a book next to it. She glanced down. The floor seemed to be smooth finished stone and to have been swept clean. And then she glanced at his door. It was the same as the one on her cell, solid, with a gap that allowed in a little light. She nodded again, and moved nervously toward the chair.

"Sit, sit," he said as he poured tea into her cup. "I'm sorry I can't offer you any sugar or cream, but we are after all, in the dungeon. I have some tea cakes though. would you like one?"

She nodded, still unwilling to speak, and he lifted the cloth cover off of a basket. Immediately, the room was filled with the scent of fresh baked pastries and her mouth flooded with juices. He held the basket out to her, and she took one of the cakes, forcing herself not to immediately cram it into her mouth. She snuck a furtive glance around the cell again before asking, "Who are you?"

He laughed. "Not quite what you expected in the dungeon? Rank does have certain privileges, and Eric used to be one of my orderlies. He's been taking good care of me." He stood. "Fictus," he said. "General Odell Fictus." And then he frowned. "Well, I was a general. Who knows now. As you can see, the duke's rather angry with me. The problems of command." He shrugged his shoulders. "You haven't tasted your tea. Go ahead."

She lifted the cup to her lips. The tea was hot, and pungent, and after nothing but water, wonderful. She sipped slowly. "Why are you here?"

"Your brother," he said. "I couldn't deliver him to the duke." He lifted his own cup to his lips and drank. "It's been what, two months since he disappeared? No telling where he is now. I certainly don't know. He and your mother vanished well."

She leaned back in the chair, delighting in the feel of something other than the hard floor against her body. "What do you want with us?"

"Good question," he answered. "I wondered if you knew." He drank, silently, waiting for her discomfort to build. She sat as well, accustomed by now to extended silences, knowing that she'd asked the last question. After a minute, she tasted the tea cake, looking over at him, judging him with her eyes. Several more minutes passed without a word spoken.

Finally, he took a sip of tea and the put down the cup, looking over at her. "You're tough, I'll give you that. Not many of my officers would have been able to hold out like that. They'd have been singing by now." He reached for the basket. "Another cake?"

She shook her head and he said, "One for Sandra, I should think, even if you don't want one."

Marie nodded subtly and grasped one of the pastries. "Why are we here?"

"What has Sandra told you?"

"I'm important for some reason. She's not sure. She thinks my family was noble because I can speak the old tongue, but that's hardly the case. We weren't poor, but we certainly weren't nobility." She wrinkled her brow in confusion. "Duke Henry seems to think I know something."

"And do you?"

"You mean where my family is?" She dropped her head and whispered. "No."

He stared at her for a while, drank some more of the tea, and then sat quietly. After a while, he said, "No, I don't believe you do. No matter. He'll show up, and then the duke'll use you as a hostage."

"A hostage? For what?"

"Your brother. He'll want to rescue you, of course."

She looked at him, "And the duke will capture him as well."

"Or kill him. I don't think it much matters to Duke Henry so long as he gets what he wants."

She stared hard, trying to look straight through him. "But why us? What have we done?"

Fictus took a cake and broke off a piece. He placed it on his tongue, savoring the lemony flavor. He hadn't often been present when the girl had been interrogated, but his spies had reported just what he was hearing now. She really seemed to have no idea why she was here, or where any of her family had hidden after they'd gone to ground.

"Don't you think it curious that Duke Henry's entire army has been searching for your brother and your mother and haven't been able to find them?"

"He spent a lot of time hunting in the forest as a boy. I'm sure he'd be able to live there now."

"We scoured the forest. There was no sign of Robert, or of your mother, or of Johnny and his family for that matter."

"Johnny? You're looking for him too?"

Interesting. He changed the subject. "I asked Eric to leave the cell doors open this morning. I thought you might want to talk. I thought also that you might enjoy a little tea and something other than the gruel you've been getting."

She didn't flinch. "It's a nice diversion, and I thank you for the tea and the cakes. I do appreciate them." She continued to sit silently across from him, waiting for him to direct the conversation back to what he wanted.

"Well," he stated abruptly and stood. He offered his hand. "I've enjoyed our little talk. I get rather bored in here all by myself. I'm sure you understand. If there's anything I can get for you..." He let the sentence dangle in the silence.

She looked around his cell. The chair, the cot, the lantern, the table, the blanket, they all seemed to call to her. And then she shook her head. He wanted something and she had nothing she wished to give. She took his hand politely, just as she'd been taught by her mother. "No, but thank you again for your hospitality."

Laughing, he squeezed her hand just enough to express his amusement. "In that case, I'll let you go. We don't want to be caught out of our cells. Do come back tomorrow though."

Just after Marie stepped back into her cell with Sandra, she heard Fictus repeat, "Tomorrow." Then he closed his door.

# CHAPTER 46
## RETURN OF THE STARLING

Captain Mizen brought the Starling into the harbor at Rocky Point Village ahead of schedule. It was a foggy day, but Robert and Johnny had decided to hike up to the hilltop for another private conversation. Midway up the ridge that lead to the rocky outcropping they used as a wind break, Walter strode ahead of them to the top of the hill. The two boys had been so immersed in their conversation that they had failed to notice that others were already there on the hilltop. They continued up, following Walter.

When they got to the top, they noticed two of the village men working a fire. One glanced over at them while the other dropped a green pine bough onto the flames. The needles smoked for a minute before catching fire and Robert was reminded of the signal fire they'd seen when they first approached the island. One of the men pointed out to sea, and when they looked, they could see a sailing ship approaching the island.

"Looks like the Starling," Walter declared, watching over the two men. "Shall we start back down?"

Robert took a long look at the ship beating against the waves. "She won't make landfall for some time yet. We'll stay here for a while." He looked over to Johnny who was watching the fire keepers and then back at Walter. "You can go back if you want."

The man just scowled. "I'll stay." Robert noted with a smile that he'd placed himself between his youthful king and the two villagers.

"Johnny," he said. "How about that grove of trees we passed on the way up. It's pretty well protected from the wind. We can talk there."

The two young men hiked down the hill to the forest, and then followed a footpath until they found a comfortable glen. Two dense trees blocked the wind from reaching them, and hid them from the view of any passersby. They watched as Walter settled himself at the entrance to their trail. He huddled his coat around him, trying to cut the wind. Robert watched him for a moment before calling him over.

"Sir?" he asked as he walked up to them.

"Come join us. Get out of the wind."

"I thought you wanted to talk."

Johnny looked up at the big man. "Nothing that you can't hear." He motioned a spot against one of the trees. "You should be able to see anyone coming from there."

The man looked behind them, and then certain that they were safe from any approach through the forest, sat on a stump.

"So," Robert turned to Johnny. "You said you'd thought you might have a plan for enlisting recruits."

"I've been thinking about it." He picked up a small stick, and started turning it around in his hands. "Here's my idea." He drew a circle in the dust between them and wrote, 'S.' "We go to the schools, looking for older kids. We can tell them about the resistance, and gather some that way." He drew another circle, and wrote 'C.' As we visit the village schools, we can also go to the churches and speak there. We'll gather recruits from the village leaders that way as well." He drew another circle and wrote 'B.' "Finally, and I'm not quite sure how we'll accomplish this, we work on encouraging soldiers to come over to our side. They'll be trained fighters, and according to Jameson, there's already some dissatisfaction in the ranks."

Robert looked down at the circles and weighed what he'd heard. Each idea presented its own challenges. Would school boys follow them? And if they did, how much training would they need, and how long would that take? Most important, would they stick, or would they drift in and out. Could they speak in churches? If they did, would they be able to convince people to overturn their lives just to go up against Henry's army? Finally, how would they even get into the barracks? He was about to speak when Walter interrupted.

"May I speak sir?"

He looked over at him and nodded, noting as he did, that Walter's eyes never stopped scanning the forest.

"Begging your pardon. Those are good ideas for later, but they won't work for now. You're after the gentle people, the ones who are doing well enough to go to school, or to church. They'll never join you. At least not until it's safe. They're not ready; not convinced that they need to put their lives at risk to get rid of Henry. After all, they're comfortable."

"So what do you suggest?"

"Pubs."

Robert wrinkled his brow. "Why there?"

"Couple of reasons. First, you don't want boys. Not yet. You want men who can fight. The boys'll follow. Girls too, for that matter. And word'll spread from there. You'll get workers from around the village and they'll talk to others. Travelers will tell the story of a budding revolt when they get to the next pub." He nodded as if confirming this to himself. "Pubs are the key."

Robert leaned back against the tree, lifting his hand to his jaw, which he massaged contemplatively. It could work, he thought. The men could spread out and visit several pubs, dropping hints that the king had returned. It would certainly generate interest, and get Henry's attention. But would it be enough? "So we get the word out. What gets them to join us? For that matter, how do we get past the rumor stage and even get them to believe us?"

Walter shook his head. "Don't know. But I still think it has to start in the pubs."

"I don't disagree with you there." He looked over at Johnny. "And the schools, and the churches, and certainly the barracks. It's just getting them to believe. How do we convince a man to toss aside his security to join a revolution?" He looked from face to face. "Are they that unhappy? Or are we unhappy and projecting that onto others?"

"Ooh, good question," Johnny said. He glanced over at Walter. "I do think you're onto something about the pubs though. That's where people get together to talk, to gripe about the boss, to laugh and play. A few hints there might take off like a wild fire."

Suddenly his face lit up. "I've got it." He turned to Robert. "What do you suppose will happen after Walter and his men go from pub to pub spreading word that the king is back and he's looking for help to overthrow the duke. Henry." Then, despite their skepticism, Johnny started to lay out a plan that looked more and more like it might just work.

# CHAPTER 47
## A NEW FRIEND, OR…

The following morning, their jailor left the door open again after he'd brought their breakfast. Marie waited for him to return to his quarters, and then walked out into the hall. Fictus' door was also open. She motioned for Sandra to join her, but the other woman shook her head and refused to move. They had talked about her visit with the general the previous day, after she'd returned from his cell, and Sandra had been insistent that it must be some kind of trick. Despite Marie's entreaties, she shook her head, complaining that she was in enough trouble already without being caught out of her cell.

Marie shrugged, and walked down the hall. She stopped when she reached the doorway and looked in. The man was folding his blanket. Once done, he placed it neatly at the foot of the bed, and then, as if he sensed her presence, looked up. "Good morning," he said, and motioned her into the room. "I trust you slept well?"

"The floor is hard," she said.

"It is. I'm glad to have this cot. An accommodation for an old man."

"But you're not that old," she said.

He smiled and touched his hair. "Thank you for your kindness, but I've had this grey for some time. I'll be forty-five next year. That's a bit too old to sleep on the floor." Then he shook his head. "But where are my manners. Sit." As she moved toward the chair, he held up his hand. "No. Wait." He reached back to the bed and unfolded the blanket enough to make a pad for the chair. "I hope you'll be a bit more comfortable with this." He noted the surprise on her face and waved toward the chair. "Go ahead. Sit."

Marie sat in the chair, marveling at how comfortable it felt with the addition of the padding. "Thank you," she said.

He busied himself with the teapot, and after pouring two cups, reached one out to her. "I assume you'd like a cup of tea this morning?"

She nodded and took the offered cup. He settled on the edge of the cot just like he had the day before and tasted his tea. "It is nice to have a warm beverage in the morning. The dungeon can be chilly over night" He took another sip and then set the cup on the table between them. "Tell me, where's Sandra?"

"You frighten her. She's afraid coming here will get her into more trouble."

He thought about that for a moment. "But I don't frighten you?"

"No," she said, and sipped at her tea.

"You're an interesting girl." He reached for his cup and drank again. "Apple?" he asked, and lifted the cloth off of the basket.

Marie's eyes widened at the pile of bright red apples in the basket. She reached out and took one, and as she had the day before with the cakes, resisted the urge to shove it whole into her mouth. She knew it was a bribe, but she was hungry enough for the taste of fresh fruit that she didn't care. She tasted it daintily, and closed her eyes with the pleasure of it. After a moment, she said, "What do you want from me?"

"Why do you ask that?"

She groaned at him. "Come on. The tea, the apples, the cakes, just having the door left open so that I can wander. What do you want?"

He took an apple and tasted it. "Well, as far as the tea and the food, I have some, and I might as well share. As I told you yesterday, Eric is taking good care of me." He looked around the cell. "And I'm bored in here all day. I enjoyed our talk yesterday."

"But you're not sharing with the others. Why me?"

"I'd just like to talk really. And," He sipped the tea again. "Information, I suppose." He waited for her to respond, but when she sat still, he continued. "You do come from a rather interesting family, after all, and..."

She interrupted him. "Everyone says that. Believe me. My family was anything but interesting. We lived in a small house in a small village far from anywhere." She was about to say more, but then contained her frustration and settled her hands on her lap. "We were not that interesting."

He smiled at her. "Tell me about your parents. How did they meet?"

She shrugged. "I don't know. They lived in the village. I suppose they must have known each other for years. Maybe their families were friends." He sat silently, and she continued. "I don't remember ever hearing actually. Why do you ask?"

"Conversation," he replied. "Just making conversation. As long as you and I are here, we might as well get to know one another. My parents had an arranged marriage. I believe it was set up when they were children." He gestured toward the basket. "You will take the rest of these to Sandra, won't you?"

Marie was startled by his sudden change of topic. "Yes," stuttered. "Yes, and she thanks you for the cake yesterday. It was a special treat."

He beamed. "I'm glad I could be of assistance." He settled back onto his cot so that he could lean against the wall. "May I ask more questions? I really am just trying to get to know you, not to offend."

She shrugged and he went on. "Tell me about your parents."

She tasted her tea again, framing her answer. She'd been asked this often enough, that she had begun to wonder. What was it that she didn't know about them? What was it that she'd never been told about their past. Where did they meet? She started cautiously, "My mother was a simple woman. She kept the house, cooked our meals, cleaned our clothes, and made sure that Robert and I were well taken care of." She smiled at an old memory. "She was warm and soft, and always there when we needed her."

"Did she do anything outside of the house? Anything to bring in some income?"

Marie thought for a moment. "We had chickens. She was constantly scolding them, as if they were her unruly children. She sold eggs in the market, and the occasional rooster. And she was a seamstress. Women used to come to her for help with their sewing. I don't think that she was paid for that though. She enjoyed helping them. It was kind of a social thing, a reason to visit." She grinned and pointed to the tea. "A little like this."

"And your father?"

"He was a stable master. He took in the horses when travelers stayed at the inn, repaired their tack, that sort of thing." She hesitated for a moment. "Oh, and he was the one people called on when a horse or a cow was sick." She looked up at him.

"I guess I'm asking what he was like as a man. You described your mother as warm and soft, loving. How about your father?"

"Not warm and soft." She laughed. "No. Definitely not warm and soft, but he loved us, in his own way." She reflected for a while. "He was demanding." She scowled. "Really demanding, but patient too. I remember a time when he was teaching us cyphering. Robert seemed to have figured it out, but I was stuck. I just couldn't grasp the idea of subtracting one number from the other. I was taking something like eight from thirty-one, and the idea of taking eight from one just didn't make any sense to me. I can still see it. We were in the kitchen, and he reached into a bag of beans and took out thirty-one of them. He made me lay them out, and said, take eight. I did, and he made me lay them out again, only in rows of ten and put a straw between the rows so that I had a two rows of ten on one side and one row of ten with the single bean on the other. He told me to take eight from the side with eleven beans. I did and he asked how many beans I had left. I showed him the three and he reminded me that I still had the original twenty, so I had twenty-three. And suddenly it made sense to me. I wasn't subtracting from thirty-one, I was reaching over to get eleven, subtracting from that, and adding the twenty back in." She shook her head and chuckled. "Lots of things like that. He didn't get frustrated when we didn't understand something. He just found a different way of saying it so that we could understand." She put on a serious face again. "But there was no quitting. He kept going, and so did we, until we mastered whatever he wanted us to learn. It was the same with Robert and the practice sword. I think he really wanted Robert to be good enough to beat him one day, and he wasn't going to let up until he did."

Fictus raised an eyebrow at the comment about the sword, but decided not to follow it. "So you learned to work with numbers," he said. "Was that common for girls in your village?"

She shook her head. "Not at all. But father wanted me to be able to help with that part of the business. That was why he sent me to school."

"Were there many girls at your school?"

"A few. Most stayed home with their mothers and helped around the house. But then lots of the boys stayed home so that they could help out in the fields. Probably only about half of the kids in the village even went to school."

"Your parents believed in education?"

"My mother thought I'd be better off at home, helping her and making a little money for the family."

"So your father was the one who insisted that you and your brother both go to school."

"Yes." She took another taste of the apple. "I hadn't really thought about it that way, but it was his idea. In fact, I think he's the one who taught mother to read."

"Really. An interesting man. How did he get along with the other men of the village?"

"I'm not sure I understand."

"Was he friendly? Aloof?"

She cocked her head to one side, thinking. "Respected, I think would be the best way to describe him." She thought for a moment. "Yes. People used to come to our house just to talk to him, to get advice." She laughed. "I can remember Robert asking him one time how he had learned so much."

"And what did he say?"

"Work hard and listen."

Fictus lifted up the tea pot. "I think there's a little left. Would you like some more?"

She was about to say no, but was feeling far more comfortable than she had the day before. "All right," she said.

He poured, and then tasted the hot beverage. "I understand that you speak the old tongue," he said in that other language.

She was startled, and immediately her defenses went up. She nodded slowly, carefully. He noted her alarm and backed away, but continued to speak in the language of court. "Did you like the apples?" She nodded again, silently. "I'm glad. I'll speak with Eric later. Some other fruit tomorrow? Oranges? Grapes? Perhaps some melon?"

"That would be nice," she replied, reverting to the common language.

"What's that?" he asked again in the old tongue. "Please. I hear it so infrequently now and I do need to practice. Indulge me."

She started slowly, practicing the words she'd learned. "An orange tomorrow would be wonderful."

"Well then," he grinned at her. "I've made you nervous, and I just heard Eric's door open, but I do thank you for the conversation." He stood. "Don't forget the apples."

Marie stood as well, and when he reached out his hand, she took it this time without hesitation. "Tomorrow," she said.

§§§§

Elyssa spooned the last of the warm soup into Anna's bowl. "There," she smiled. That's it. We'll have to make some more tomorrow."

Anna dipped her spoon into the soup and lifted it to her mouth. "I like the vegetable soup better."

"I know, honey," her mother said, "but we're out of vegetables. Just beans and carrots for now." She shrugged her shoulders. She'd lost weight during her time in the cavern, and between that, and the fact that they hadn't been able to get out into the sunshine, she'd begun to take on a gaunt appearance.

They had spent much of this day, as they did most days, sitting in the entrance to the tunnel, watching the birds flying over the forest and envying them their freedom. That, and their need for fresh vegetables, had led them to consider another trip out of their hiding place. Now she looked across the table at Kathryn. She raised her eyebrows and Kathryn frowned.

"Still no soldiers around here," she said. "I think if we're careful..."

Kathryn was less sure. "We have enough to last for another couple of weeks."

"But nothing fresh. In an hour in the forest, we can fill our pantry. Our bodies are craving the nutrition they'd get from fresh greens. Look at yourself. Look at me. Look at Anna." She cast a hopeful look at the other woman.

"I don't like it," Kathryn responded, "but you're probably right. We have to go."

"Good," Elyssa said, clapping her hands. "Where, and when, and what are we looking for?" She got up and took the plates over to the wash tub that served as their sink and started to scrub them. "Tomorrow? We're going to have to go during the day if we're going to look for greens. Night's too dark for that."

"I know," Kathryn said slowly. "That's what worries me."

"I could go alone."

Kathryn considered the idea for a while before rejecting it. "No. We'll be faster if we go together."

# CHAPTER 48
## BACK TO THE MAINLAND

"Enjoying the view?"

Robert turned around. Johnny was walking up the deck to the fore rail where he'd been watching as they approached Waterton. He turned back toward the approaching city. "More than last time," he said.

Johnny settled his arms on the rail next to him. "I'll be glad to get back onto dry land. That storm was something else. I never imagined we'd be tossed around like that. I'm not sure I got any sleep; too busy just trying not to get tossed out of bed."

Robert just nodded and Johnny too went serious. "There's a lot to do in the next few weeks. You worried?"

"About Marie, yes. Very. About the rest, not yet."

Johnny laid his arm over his friend's shoulders. If Robert noticed, he didn't let on. "She's all right for now. I can feel it."

Robert looked at him. "I know. Me too. But not forever. We need to pull her out; send her someplace safe."

They turned back toward the approaching harbor. They could make out individual buildings now. Johnny looked down at the wave breaking against the fore hull. They were making good time, still on the outer edge of the storm that had made the middle of their journey so miserable. Somehow he thought Marie might have a lot to say about his friend's idea of sending her someplace safe.

# CHAPTER 49
## A SECRET

As soon as the door to the hallway closed, Marie hurried down to Fictus' cell. It was the eighth time she was to visit him, and she was surprised by how much she had come to look forward to their visits. Sandra had started venturing out of the cell, but only as far as a bench across from their doorway. She was still terrified of being caught out of the cell itself, and figured that if she was alert to signs of the exit door being opened, she could bolt back without being seen. Marie, on the other hand, disregarded the danger, figuring that at worst, they'd simply lock the cell doors again, so she might as well enjoy her limited freedom while she had it. Of course, she hadn't been whipped, and Sandra had.

"Some tea?" Fictus asked when she looked in.

"Yes, please." She looked over to the water basin in his room, and he nodded at her before pouring the tea. She had begun washing as soon as she arrived in his room. Just cleaning her face and hands with the warm water had an amazing effect on her morale. Her jailers brought a bucket of cold water to each cell once a week for washing, and she and Sandra did what they could with that, but when Fictus suggested that she take advantage of the warm water he received every morning, she jumped at the chance. Still drying her face, she thanked him again, and sat down. As usual, he'd draped the blanket over the wooden chair to make it a bit more comfortable. "Sandra doesn't know what she's missing," she said as he handed her the cup of tea. "Thanks."

He sat on the edge of his cot. "Still afraid to come out?"

"She thinks this is a trap."

"And you?"

"I'll take my chances," she said.

He laughed. "We seem to have been forgotten. Eric's the only one who's been here in the past few days." While she sipped her tea, he took the cloth cover off what she now recognized as the food basket. It was full of grapes, and her mouth watered imagining their sweet juice. He held out the basket to her. "Help yourself."

She took out a small bunch and pulled out one of the grapes. "How do you get all this?"

"Like I said. Eric takes care of me. And, of course, I can afford to buy certain comforts."

She scowled. "Unlike us."

Shrugging his shoulders, he said, "It pleases me to be able to share with you. I enjoy the conversation. It helps the time pass." He took a grape and put it into his mouth. "It's interesting. I was so busy being the general, supporting the duke, and doing my job, that I lost track of the simple pleasures in life. Being in here really has helped me to focus on what's really important."

"And what's that?" she asked.

He held up a grape. "Enjoying the tangy sweetness in a piece of fruit, for one. A good conversation with an interesting person. I especially like being able to think, reflect on things I would do again and things I might do differently."

"If you get out."

"Well there's always that," he chuckled. "But we will. You and I are survivors. I can tell." He looked at her. "You know there's not one single time that you've been here when you've complained about your situation."

"Oh, I don't know about that," she said.

"You've been confused, certainly, wondering why you're here in the first place, and that's not surprising, but you haven't taken on the attitude that I might have expected." When she cocked her head at him questioningly, he added, "You're not mad at the world; beating your head against the wall; wondering why you've been selected for this special torture; basically feeling sorry for yourself."

"Believe me, I'm angry enough."

"But at who? What?"

"That's easy. Duke Henry. Don't ask me what I think of the man. I might scorch your ears."

He chuckled. "Don't forget that I've spent my life in military service. I've probably heard, and used, any words you might be thinking." Then he looked at her more closely and grinned. "All right. You might at that. But you have a target. You're not mad about everything, like the poor fellows across the hall, wondering who turned them in, and if they'll see the next morning. You're," he paused, thinking. "Different. Strong. And in some ways, wise beyond your years."

She shrugged her shoulders and took some tea. While she was pleased with the compliment, she still didn't know him very well.

"Tell me," he continued, "is your brother like you?" She bristled, and he backed away. "Sorry. Sensitive topic?"

"Everyone wants to know about my brother. And I still don't know if you're reporting everything I say back to the duke. You could be his spy. He tried hitting me, jailing me, starving me, even pampering me. Maybe this is just another tactic."

"Fair enough," he said. He drank his tea and ate a few grapes, all the while watching her. After a minute, he asked, "Have you discussed this with Sandra?"

She was surprised by his question. "What do you mean?"

"I think you know. Have you discussed our conversations with Sandra?" She nodded cautiously, and he added, "And what did she say?"

"That you are who you say you are, for one thing." He sat still, letting her work through her thoughts. "And that she's not really surprised that you're here."

"And why is that?"

"Well, she's here because she couldn't get information out of me. And you evidently couldn't find Robert."

"We both failed the duke."

"Essentially."

"And do you believe that?"

"I don't know." She put the tea on the table and placed her hands in her lap. It was a defensive gesture he'd grown to recognize.

"I'm not reporting back to the duke. Of course, you'll have to decide whether I'm lying to you or telling you the truth. The fact is, I'm interested."

She shook her head. "But why?"

He looked at her for a long time, as if thinking of how to explain himself. Finally, he said, "You're not supposed to know this, so I'll thank you in advance for keeping it to yourself. I'd prefer not to end up in the cell across the hall. Can I count on you?"

She pursed her eyebrows. Was it one more ploy on his part, or was he genuinely going to say something that could put himself at risk, and give her some leverage over him in the future. She stared at him for a moment before saying, "All right."

"Fine. I'll accept that." He poured himself some more tea, as much to buy time as anything else. When he offered to refill her cup, she nodded silently. He settled back on the cot. "Many years ago, before you were born, I counted your father among my friends."

# CHAPTER 50
## DANGER IN MASDEN

Kathryn reached through the green bramble, careful to avoid the thorns, and plucked a ripe blackberry from the bush. She'd nearly filled her basket, and figured she'd be finished in just a few more minutes. After that, she planned to go directly back to their hiding place beneath the old hill fort. She looked up at the sun. It was hovering just above the western horizon. It would be setting soon and she wanted to be back before dark.

She'd been listening carefully for any signs of human activity. Not only was she worried about being away from the relative safety of the cavern, she was also growing increasingly concerned about Elyssa and Anna. After picking a few berries themselves, Elyssa had decided to take Anna deeper into the forest to the site of an abandoned vegetable patch. The farmer who had owned it died without any family, and since it was relatively far from town, nobody had taken it over. Over the years, much of the plot had overgrown with weeds, but many of the vegetables seeded and came up every year. Elyssa was hoping to fill their bags with string beans and onions and squash.

She turned back to picking and soon filled the basket. She had just covered it and started for home, when she heard the sound of someone racing toward her. She stepped off the trail, hiding quickly in a dense thicket. Within seconds, Elyssa came into sight, balancing her bag over one shoulder and pulling Anna by the hand. Kathryn stepped out. "What's wrong," she called softly.

Elyssa didn't slow. She answered breathlessly, "Soldiers. Don't know if they're still following."

Kathryn jumped in line behind Anna, carefully protecting her basket of berries as she hurried up the trail and across the creek that separated their hill from the forest.

§§§§

The light was fading by the time they made it back into the cavern. Kathryn lit a candle, and then stuffed a blanket into the shaft in the ceiling to keep the light inside. Only when she was finished, did she whisper, "What happened?"

Elyssa was unloading some potatoes onto the table, brushing the dirt off of each one as she did so. "Soldiers. We were gathering vegetables when we heard the rattling of chain mail. Anna was working the opposite side of the field, nearest the forest. She'd found some peas and wanted to gather as many as possible. I don't think they expected to see us. She had just started running back to me when they stepped out of the forest, right between us. One yelled, and the other took off after her. He grabbed her and I went after him. Fortunately, he slipped and fell down, and we managed to get away."

"And keep your sacks."

Elyssa smiled grimly. "I don't know why. I suppose we never thought to leave them." She went back to unloading the vegetables. Anna stood next to her. She'd dumped her load on the table and after husking several, hummed to herself as she plopped the dark green peas into her mouth.

"And how are you?" Kathryn asked Anna.

The girl just smiled. "I'm fine," she said, shucking another handful of pees.

"Not scared?"

She shook her head. "I knew we'd get away."

Kathryn watched the others for a few minutes. They had a good cache of vegetables that would last them for several more days, but she had a feeling that their days of hiding in the cavern had come to an end.

§§§§

"Now tell me what happened again. I want to be sure I understand you."

The soldier remained at attention, but shifted uneasily in front of his commander. "Like I said sir. We were on a routine patrol out in the forest. We come on that old abandoned farmstead when we saw them."

"The woman and the girl."

"Right. They was pickin' vegetables."

The commander stroked his beard. "You see anyone else there?"

"No sir."

"Where are they now?"

"Don't know suh. Took off. Not far, I'd wager."

"They ran back into the forest, toward the creek."

The commander stared at the two men. Something was wrong here. Why couldn't two trained soldiers capture a woman and a girl? Or if not the woman, at least the girl. "How old did you say you thought she was?"

"Don't know. 'Bout eight or so."

"We had the girl. Fred did."

"So how'd she get away?"

"Woman come runnin'. Fought like a wildcat."

"Still, one woman and one girl against two trained soldiers in chain mail."

"'Twas the bees, suh."

"So you said before. What bees?"

"Don know. Stranges' thing. Wasn't there, then was. Hundreds of 'em. A stingin' and a swarmin'. All over us."

"And the woman and the girl?"

"Did'n seem to bother them."

The other soldier added, "Bees didn't seem to want them at all. Stayed on us, even when they ran."

The commander looked them over closely. The two men claimed to have been attacked by a swarm of bees, but neither showed any welts on their faces or hands. "So where were you stung?"

"Tha's whats so strange. Felt like we was bein' stung all over, even through the mail." He looked down at his hands, "But nothin." He looked back up at the commander. "Can' splain no better'n that."

The commander shook his head. If he hadn't know these men so well, he'd wonder if they'd been drunk, but they were among the most responsible of his troop. "All right, dismissed." They turned and left, muttering to themselves.

So, he thought. A woman and a girl in the forest. Nobody in Masden would dare run from his soldiers, and it was a long way out to that abandoned farm just to go for vegetables. No, it had to be someone else. The girl was the right age, and he couldn't think of any others in the area who might be out there. It was just too far from any of the neighboring villages.

He made a decision and stepped into the outer office. "Sergeant?"

"Sir?"

"You hear that?"

"Yes Sir."

"Let's double the patrols. I want a special focus on that area of the forest, and the creek. Somebody's out there. I want them caught."

"Yes Sir."

"One more thing. I'm going to write this up. Get a messenger ready. I want this to go to Entaro first thing in the morning."

"Consider it done, Sir."

## CHAPTER 51
## HUNTING FOR GOLD

Robert watched as Johnny and Albert loaded the last of their supplies into the heavy wagon and climbed on board. It had turned out that Jameson, through his freight business, had ready access to wagons and teams of horses. Even better, since they often were heavily laden with boxes of goods from one of his ships, the wagons were of sturdy construction, certainly much heavier than they needed to be for the bales of wool they carried now, but perfect for the gold that they hoped to hide under the wool on their trip back.

Johnny took the reins and turned back. "We should be back in a week. Wish us luck!" He tipped his hat and looked to his father. "Ready?"

Albert rolled his eyes as he shook his head at Jameson. "He thinks this is just another part of some grand adventure." He turned to Robert then. "You keep safe. Remember, don't leave Andrew's place. He can protect you there." He glanced over at his son and nodded.

Johnny slapped the reins and the horses started forward, out of the warehouse and onto the street.

Robert stood there for a few more minutes, until they turned around a corner onto the road that led out of town. He felt lonely all of a sudden, and knew that despite his meetings with Jameson and Walter, the next weeks would be long. For the first time in his life, he felt alone, without his family and without the friend who had become so important to him over the past months.

He walked over to Jameson. "Let's talk about Marie. You said you'd heard something?"

§§§§

Johnny squirmed uncomfortably on the hard wooden seat. They'd been traveling all day without more than a break to water the horses and eat a small lunch, and he was stiff and sore from the jostling on the rutted dirt road. The roadway had been busy for the first hour or so, but as they got further from Waterton, the traffic dropped off to just the occasional farmer hauling grain to market. They had passed one armed patrol, but the men ignored them. "Not too much farther now. I remember that little hill over there. We talked about the rundown fort on top; wondered if there was a crypt under it like the one by Masden."

Albert looked at the fort on the hilltop. "Don't know," he said. He'd taken over driving the team at the last stop. "I'll be ready to stop. Horses too, I'd wager. They're starting to struggle, especially after that long uphill climb they had." He looked around. "Was there a good place to pull the wagon off the trail?"

"We'll have to cover it later, but yes. Whoever was there cut a forest trail through the trees."

They traveled alone in silence for the next hour before Johnny stood, looking closely at the forest to their left. "There," he suddenly said, pointing to a barely visible opening in the trees. "I think that's it."

"You think?"

"It's been a while," he explained. "And we covered it pretty well, but yes. I think that's it."

Albert directed the wagon to the side of the road and reined in the horses. "Why don't you go check before we pull this wagon off the road. It looks a little muddy and I don't want to get stuck here if it's the wrong place."

"Right," Johnny said. He jumped off the wagon and jogged across the road to the opening. Albert got down from the wagon seat. After stretching his cramped muscles, he walked up to the horses. They were quiet, grazing in their traces while they waited. He checked each one, noting the sweat rising off of their necks and backs. If this was the right place, it would be good to get them unhitched so that they could loosen up a bit as well. It had been a long day.

Suddenly, he was alerted to the sound of another vehicle approaching from the west. He looked over his shoulder and then walked out to the edge of the roadway. Half a dozen men in chain mail were riding in protection of a heavy wagon. He nodded to their commander as he approached, wondering what kind of cargo they might be carrying.

The man held up his hand, and the group stopped, and then he spurred his horse over to Albert in a slow trot. "What brings you out here?"

Albert smiled up at him. "We're on our way to Middlefield. Carrying wool to the spinners there."

The man looked over the wagon. "Pretty heavy wagon for a load of wool."

"I'm planning to pick up a cargo of grain for the return trip. I'll need this one for that." He reached up to the buckboard and took out a bag of apples and then held one out to the soldier. "Apple? We picked these a few miles up the road. They're good on a hot day."

The soldier nodded and Albert put an apple in his hand before taking a bite of his own. "So why'd you stop here?"

"Nature called," Albert chuckled, chewing on his apple. My son's off in those trees right now."

The soldier looked over Albert's head into the forest just in time to see Johnny come up the rough trail.

"Ah," Albert said pointedly. "Feeling better?"

Johnny grinned at him. "Like a new man."

"Well then," Albert said. He looked up at the sun, hanging low in the west. "We'd best be on our way." Almost as an afterthought, he looked back at the soldier. "Say, we've got plenty of apples. Would you like a few to take back to your men?"

The soldier was about to answer when suddenly he turned to Johnny. "Why'd you run across that way? Why not here?"

As if he'd expected the question, Johnny said, "See that big old oak over there? It just looked like a good spot." He climbed up on the wagon and picked up the reins. "I'll drive for a while."

The soldier wasn't finished with him though. "Where are you going," he asked Johnny.

"Middlefield. Taking a load of wool there."

He nodded, satisfied. "Good trip then." And then he spurred his horse around and trotted back to his troop. Albert climbed aboard and Johnny flicked the reins, guiding the horses back onto the road. As they passed the soldiers, he waved, and then hunched over, concentrating on the road ahead. A few hundred yards later, he pulled the wagon over to the side, and said, "I think I'll run back and see if they've moved on. That's definitely where we want to be."

"Good, I could stand a break," Albert said. He leaned back on the seat, contemplating his apple, before taking another bite.

Just a couple of minutes later, Johnny came jogging back up the road. He hopped back aboard and turned the horses, leading the wagon back up to the side road, and then carefully guided them into the forest. Ten minutes later, they pulled up in front of the abandoned cabin. He jumped down and checked the inside. "Just like we left it," he said. And then he headed back down the trail. "Why don't you make yourself at home. I'm going back out to the road to cover our tracks."

# CHAPTER 52
## NEW CHALLENGES

Marie stood and walked over to the door. She stared outside for a moment, trying to make sense of what she'd just heard. Before he began, Fictus had made her promise not to interrupt him until he finished. His story was so outrageous, and she had so many questions now that she could hardly contain herself. She looked back at him, started to speak, and then held herself, looking at him from across the cell.

"Anyway," he went on, after she settled again in her chair, "When the duke took control of the palace, my unit was out on the border, on a training mission. It's probably what saved us. When we got back, we ran into a real mess. He was consolidating his power, and there were only a few of us. The senior officers had all been executed. The rest of us were given two choices. We could either join with him, forming his new army, or we could join the others at the bottom of a trench. Fortunately, I was a foot soldier then, and I'd always done my best to be anonymous. I think a few of the men in the barracks knew my mother was a maid in the palace, but I had wanted to rise on my own merit, and could never see any point in telling anyone that I'd known your father for years, or been his sparring partner. It turned out to be a good thing. So far as Henry knows to this day, I was just one of many poor foot soldiers." He looked over at her. "Anyway, that's my story."

Marie stared at him. She decided to start at the end of his tale, the rest so unbelievable that she didn't want to touch it for a while. "But you rose to become his general."

"For a time." He chuckled and waved his arms to take in the cell. "Not much of a general now, am I." He offered to refill her cup, and she nodded absently. While he poured, he said, "It's a lot to absorb, I know."

"It doesn't make any sense."

He inclined his head to the side. "It's a wild story to be sure, and yet you're here. You may be in the dungeon now, but how about earlier? He had you tucked up in one of the guest suites. Those are reserved for nobility. How about that? Have you a better explanation?"

"But you say my father was a prince!" It was so outrageous that she had trouble even forming the words. "No. He owned a stable in Masden."

Fictus bit his apple, chewed for a moment, and said, "He was a leader in the village, right? You said yourself that others seemed to defer to him." She nodded and he continued, "And he taught you to speak the old tongue. Where would a stable master even learn that and why would he consider it important for his children to speak it?"

She just shook her head in confusion. "I don't know. It just doesn't make any sense."

"Then think about this," he said. "Why was he killed, and why is the duke so interested in finding your brother if he was just a simple stable master?"

She stared at him, thinking that what he'd said was just too outrageous. But he was right. She was here, that much was true, and this made as much sense as any other reason she'd been able to think of. She sipped her tea. "Tell me," she began, and then stopped, wondering how she could test his story. "Tell me how he hurt his leg."

He cocked his head to the side and shrugged. "I don't know. The last I saw him, his leg was fine."

She sat there, thinking that could well have been the case. She could ask what he had looked like, but what would that prove twenty years later. Besides, if it was all a lie, and he was trying to trap her, wouldn't he know what her father had looked like? After all, she'd described him to the duke. She searched her brain for something unique to her father, and suddenly she had it. It was a saying that he repeated to them often as she and Robert were growing up, one that she had never heard from anyone else, and one that she was certain was his alone. "Set your goals... he used to say," and then waited to see if he could complete the rest.

Fictus looked at her for a long couple of minutes. "Set your goals," he muttered to himself. "I've heard that." He squeezed his brows together and looked around the room, as if searching for an answer, and then suddenly he smiled. "He said it. When we were sparring with the wooden practice swords, and I was exhausted and wanted to quit, he'd say it. It was his way to push on when every muscle was screaming for a rest." He looked across at her. "Set your goals high, and let your effort define your character."

Marie squeezed her eyes tightly and still the tears escaped to roll down her cheeks. It was one of her father's favorite sayings, and hearing it from this man simply reminded her of how much she missed him. Fictus handed her his handkerchief and she wiped her eyes. When she handed it back, he was smiling nervously. "Well," he asked, "did I pass?"

§§§§

Kathryn glanced nervously back down the tunnel. She felt like she was leaving behind her safe haven, but couldn't see any alternative. The soldiers, missing from the forest for so long, had returned. Each of the past few days, she'd hidden behind the heavy bushes at the end of the tunnel, watching them march up and down the creek bed, looking for any trace of the woman and child they'd found in the farmer's field. The day before had been particularly harrowing. For some reason, the duke's forces had focused in on the hill fort for the first time in several weeks. They'd been able to hear them digging around in the crypt, and hiking across the top, just above their hiding place. It was definitely time to move on.

Now, everything in their hiding place was carefully stashed, and they'd worked hard to hide any evidence that it had been occupied at any time in the recent past. Hopefully, if the soldiers did find their cavern, it would appear to be an old hideout, abandoned many years earlier. She looked back up the tunnel. Elyssa was whispering encouragingly to Anna while she tightened her backpack, ensuring that she was ready to carry her share of the load. They'd packed little other than a stash of food, hoping to dash as quickly as possible to Waterton and Andrew Jameson. At least, that was the plan. Hopefully they'd find the others safe there. "Well, are you ready?" Elyssa asked.

Kathryn took a deep breath. "As ready as I'll ever be. It's getting pretty dark out. You sure they're going back to the barracks at night?"

Nodding her head, Elyssa said, "I can't think of anywhere else they might be. They're certainly not here, or at least, not within earshot. I sat up for several hours after sunset last night. I didn't hear any sounds or see any sign of campfires. I'm guessing that they know somebody was out in that field, but they don't know who, and they don't know where, or even if they're still in the area. It seems they don't want to give up the comfort of a warm bed on a strange guess."

"Well then," Kathryn said. "We might as well get started. She looked down at Anna, "You ready for a walk in the forest?"

When the girl nodded, she made her way out from behind the bushes and climbed slowly down the hillside, careful not to dislodge any of the rocks in her path. The moonlight provided just enough light for her to pick out her way. Anna followed shortly behind her, and then came Elyssa, doing her best to hide their trail as she climbed. She turned down the trail that led to a shallow crossing in the creek, and waded silently upstream for several minutes before crossing into the underbrush on the other side. Within minutes, they had all disappeared into the forest.

§§§§

Johnny woke as the sun started to rise in the east. The cabin was as he remembered it, small and primitive, but safe. He looked over at his father, still sleeping soundly on the bed, and grimaced. The idea of sleeping in a dead man's bed still bothered him, but evidently his father found nothing wrong with it.

After checking in on the horses, he hiked out to the road. There was no sign of anyone out there, and when he tried to see traces of the heavy wagon plowing its way up the trail, he was pleased that his work in concealing their passage the night before had been so good.

He walked back through the forest to the side road, and climbed up to the old wood lot. Again, everything was the same except for one thing. They were here this time in search of treasure that they hadn't been aware of before. He crossed to the middle of the lot and sat on one of the stumps, facing out away from the path. Slowly and carefully, he scanned the forest in a circle from left to right, and then right to left. From what he could tell, there were no disturbances indicating another path anywhere. Of course, if they were right, it had been nearly twenty years since the gold had disappeared. Any pathway would have been completely overgrown by now. He changed his plan, and started looking higher, hoping to find an area where the trees seemed thinner and shorter, as if an ancient path had been cut through them, but again, there was nothing. Groaning, he trudged back to the cabin.

By the time he got back, his father was up. He'd lit a smokeless fire, but still, Johnny could smell the aroma of bacon and hotcakes heating up in the pan. He walked through the door. "Good morning. Smells good."

Albert had his back to the door, and now turned around. He stretched out his hand, palm up, but fingers closed. "I found something you might be interested in."

As Johnny came closer, he opened his hand. He was holding a gold coin, larger than anything Johnny had ever seen before. "What's that?" he asked.

"It's a danae," he said. "Here, feel it."

Johnny reached over and his father dropped the coin into his hand. It was surprisingly heavy. He looked up at him curiously. "I've never seen one of these."

"No, you wouldn't in Masden. They're used more for larger scale commerce than for local trade. Had anyone tried to buy a beer at the pub with one of these, it would have been all the brewmaster could do to find him change." He sniffed and then looked toward the pan. "Enough for now. I think I'd better attend to our breakfast." He strode over to the fire and flipped the pancakes out onto a plate. "Put it here, on the table."

Johnny put the coin next to the plate and asked, "Where did you find it? I thought we'd done a pretty good job of searching the place earlier."

"Not everywhere."

Johnny looked at him for a moment before his face brightened. "The bed." When his father nodded, he went on, "We got the old man out of the bed and buried him as fast as we could, and then stayed away from that whole corner." He looked over toward the bed his father had slept in the night before, only now noticing that it was pulled away from the wall. "Behind the bed? Is there a hiding place there?"

Albert shook his head. "No. I thought there might be a trapdoor, or something like that, but there's not. I think this one simply dropped by accident." Seeing Johnny's confusion, he pointed to the open window behind him. "When the sun hit that window, I caught a sparkle down in a crack in the floor."

"But we didn't see anything."

"No, I wouldn't suppose that you did with the bed in the way." He picked up the coin and walked to the corner where the head of the bed had been, before dropping to his knees and wedging the danae between two of the rotting boards. When he stood, the coin was effectively invisible. "The sun had to hit it just right." He bent down, retrieved the coin, and said, "No woodcutter would have use for a coin of this value, but somebody here did." He flipped the coin in the air and caught it in his other hand. "Let's eat. Then we can work on figuring out where there might be more."

§§§§

Robert found that Jameson's library was his favorite place to rest. His morning had been busy. He'd sparred with Walter's fledgling protective force, helping train the men in sword techniques, and then met with Jameson to discuss the differences between the tax policies of King Stefan and Duke Henry. The first wore out his body in a good, wholesome way. The second seemed to tax his brain almost more than he could bear.

The essential difference, as he understood it, was that his grandfather employed an army of tax collectors, who worked under the strict supervision of Jameson's father, the Lord High Chancellor. Their charge was to tax every member of the populace enough to support the nation, and not a penny more. Henry's policy was entirely different. He taxed the great nobles, who collected from the lesser nobles, who collected from the merchants and the peasants and the artisans, and each member of the nobility considered taxation as a personal revenue stream, keeping much of what they raised, and sending only what they had to on to the duke. No wonder his father had often complained when the local sheriff came to Masden. All of his hard work went to enrich the nobility.

He was picking from the hundreds of volumes on the shelves in the library when Jameson came in carrying two mugs of hot tea. He sat opposite Robert's place at the heavy wooden table in the center of the room and sipped, waiting for him to settle.

Robert had watched him enter, and made his selection. "Which one this time?" Jameson asked.

Robert showed him the cover and Jameson arched his eyebrows. "You planning to care for my horses?" he asked.

Chuckling, Robert said, "You never know when it might come in handy." He tapped the mug. "Thanks for the tea. I was thinking something warm might be good." Then he held up the book. "The Anatomy Of The Horse. We could have used this back in Masden."

Jameson settled back in his leather chair. "Well, if all goes well, you'll be able to hire stable hands."

"Just being prepared. Just in case I need a fall back profession. I'm already pretty well versed in managing a stable, but might want to understand how to treat a sick horse."

Jameson demurred for while, drinking his tea. If they challenged the duke and failed, it was unlikely that Robert would be able to find work running a stable. They'd all likely hang. He changed the topic. "There's someone I think you should meet."

Robert arched his eyebrows. "A visitor? Today?"

"Not here," Jameson said. "Histon." When Robert looked confused, he added, "A small town about twenty-five miles north of here. Actually, he lives a little beyond there, but it's far enough that we'll need to stay at the village inn."

"An overnight trip! You've got my attention!"

Jameson laughed aloud. "Tired of my hospitality already?"

"Never," Robert said. "I'm just used to being outside, moving about. I didn't even want to stay abed when I was sick as a child. This is worse because I'm healthy." He drank from his cup and said, "Who am I to meet?"

"His name is Emmon of Histon."

"And he's a supporter?"

"Oh, I should think he will be. He's retired now, but he used to be your grandfather's armorer."

"What do you mean armorer? Did he make armor?"

"No." Jameson chuckled. "Though it would sound like he did. No. He was in charge of all of the arms as well as the training for the king. It's the training part I'm interested in."

"For Walter's force."

"And anyone in the future. He was the best."

Then Robert hesitated. "Wait, Walter's been pretty firm about keeping me inside. What's he going to say about a trip to Histon? Why not bring this Emmon here?"

"Well, there's the problem. Emmon's kind of a funny guy. I doubt he'll come just because I invite him, and he'll definitely want to meet you before joining us."

"So we need to talk to Walter."

# CHAPTER 53
## "BE DONE WITH YOU THEN!"

Marie was napping when she heard the keys rattling in her door. She opened her eyes. The light coming from the window told her that it was still daytime, but little else. She stretched, but remained where she was, huddled in a corner on the back wall of the cell. A guard she hadn't seen before poked his head through the door, and then pointing at Sandra, said, "You, come with me."

Sandra cast Marie a frightened look and then rose. She walked, head down, to the door. Marie watched silently as the door was slammed shut again and the lock secured. She closed her eyes and tried to go back to sleep, but found her head spinning with thoughts and worries.

§§§§

Four days after arriving at the cabin in the forest, Johnny and Albert had made no progress in finding any trace of the gold they'd been seeking. True, Albert had found the one coin, but they were beginning to believe that had simply been an accident. The only thing that they wondered about was why the man had even had a coin of that size. He certainly wouldn't find it easy to use. It was much too valuable for that.

They'd trapped a pair of quail earlier in the day, and after pulling the feathers and cleaning them, Johnny speared each onto a stick and was roasting them over the fireplace. He turned to his father. "Well?" he asked. "Any more ideas?"

Albert shook his head slowly back and forth. "We've been over this place with a fine toothed comb. Nothing in the wood lot. No sign of any burial vaults, or hidden stashes back in the trees. Nothing around the cabin."

He looked around the tiny room. It was in much more disarray than before. After searching the outside areas, they'd carefully pulled up the flooring on the chance that there was a hidden cellar down below. There was nothing but dirt.

"I keep thinking we've missed something," Johnny said.

"Well, if anything is here, we have." He looked out the window, thinking. "Could it be that he hid the gold somewhere else and then came here to hide himself?" Then he shook his head. "No. If whoever was here hid that gold, he'd want to keep it close." He snorted to himself. "It's either here, or we're completely wrong."

"But the coin," Johnny mused softly.

"That's right, how did that get here? And in my experience, anyone who can afford to deal with that kind of coin doesn't have just one." He looked over at his son. "That quail's starting to smell pretty good. Didn't realize how hungry I was until just now. Gold hunting must be hungry business. Think I'll head out to the outhouse before dinner."

And then suddenly he and Johnny stared at one another. "The outhouse," Johnny said.

Albert nodded. "It's the only place we haven't looked. But would he..." he started.

Johnny continued his thought. "He had to dig a hole anyway. He could have dug a little deeper. How much was there?"

"Well, I'm hoping there were a couple of wagon loads, at least."

"Ok," Johnny sighed. "A lot deeper."

"Well, I'm going to use it anyway. We can dig it up tomorrow." Albert opened the door and went out, leaving Johnny to tend to the quail.

§§§§

Sandra didn't come back that night, and the next morning the guard dropped off breakfast and then closed the door. So Marie was isolated again.

She brushed away a few pebbles, bunched her skirt under her, and settled down against the cell door. Already, after just a few hours, she missed Sandra's voice. The fact that the door had been locked and she was shut off from Fictus only made it worse.

She looked down at the bowl of porridge she'd set next to her on the floor. It was funny. She had always loved her mother's porridge. As she stared at the bowl, she imagined sitting at the kitchen table back in Masden. She closed her eyes, and let her mind wander. It was a sunny spring day, the light pouring through the kitchen window, warming the room and bathing everyone in the cozy glow that was so different from the damp cold she'd grown accustomed to in this cell. She smiled. Warmth was part of what she equated with home. Her mother, wearing a simple dress covered by an apron, worked at the counter, mixing oatmeal, raisins, and a finely diced fresh apple. She sprinkled a few grains of sugar onto the mixture, just enough to give it a sweet flavor. After blending the ingredients, she took a pot of hot water from the fire and poured it into the bowl, stopping frequently to stir, making sure that she kept the oatmeal thick. She drifted further. She could hear her father in the back of the house, his boots loud on the wooden floor. Robert was back there with him, and she could hear the two of them arguing. Robert wanted to help in the stable instead of going off to school. She'd heard the argument before, and laughed to herself because it ended so easily, Robert knowing that he'd be going to school, her father knowing not to push too hard, and to offer something in return, in this case, an afternoon fishing expedition. The two men came into the kitchen and took their seats just as her mother put the oatmeal onto the kitchen table and took her own chair. They bantered lightly. What are your plans for today; did you remember to pack your homework; and other topics like that. She poured some milk onto her porridge and smiled. She'd milked the cow just minutes earlier, and it was creamy and warm and frothy and blended perfectly with the hot oatmeal. Robert reached for the pitcher and started pouring his own milk, laughing about something her father had said.

Suddenly, the hallway door banged open, startling Marie out of her reverie. She shot a glance down at her bowl of porridge. No apples, no raisins, no sugar, and certainly no warm milk, but it was food. She grabbed it and hustled away from the door just as she heard the keys turn in the latch.

It was the guard, the same one she'd seen take Sandra away the day before. Behind him, she saw the duke, scowling and looking vastly out of place in the dreariness of the dungeon. His fist was entwined tightly Sandra's hair, holding her head up so that her neck stretched out and she looked up almost toward the ceiling. He made eye contact with Marie, glowered evilly, and yelled, "Be done with you then! Get used to it here. It'll be a nice slow death." Marie shrank back against the wall of the cell just as he jerked Sandra up by her hair and cast her into the cell. The woman landed awkwardly, stumbling and falling before sliding across the floor and coming to a rest just in front of her. Sandra tried to rise, but her arms refused to support her weight and she crumpled back to the floor. Marie rushed to her just as the door slammed shut and the cell was plunged back into the dreary half light. Sandra's back was crisscrossed once again with bloody stripes.

# CHAPTER 54
## DIGGING UP TREASURE

Johnny wiped his brow with the back of his hand. Leaves had started to fall with the season, but the morning was already unseasonably hot. They'd been digging for two hours, having spent more than half of that time simply dragging the outhouse away and cleaning out the pit underneath. It was a dirty, smelly job, and he was glad that the cabin had been abandoned for so long. At least there wasn't too much fresh sewage underneath. He thrust his shovel back into the heavy clay they'd found at the bottom of the pit. It was thick and hard, and more work than they'd anticipated. Still, they were making steady progress.

"You want some water?"

He looked up at his father and smiled. "That'd be good." He had to reach up to grasp the cup that the man offered, careful not to spill too much as he took it. He drank thirstily, and before finishing, poured the last of the cup over his head. Reaching up again, he handed the cup back to his father. "Thanks."

He was about to take up the shovel again when Albert said, "Let's go down another foot or so. He wouldn't have dug any deeper than that. You need me to spell you for a while?"

"I'm all right for now," Johnny said. He took up the shovel, thankful for his heavy leather gloves. He thought he could feel a blister forming on one hand, but the gloves had protected him from more than that. "Another foot." He thrust the shovel into the clay in the center of the pit. It went down about four inches before he jammed his boot onto it and pushed it that much further. Straining, he pulled back on the handle of the shovel and lifted out another small load of dirt. He flung it up and over his head, out of the hole and then repeated the whole process again, and again, and yet again.

About twenty minutes later, he called up to his father. "I think you're going to have to help me out of the hole this time. You got the rope?"

In response, a length of heavy sisal rope came sailing down into the hole. Johnny grabbed it. He was about to try pulling himself up when Albert poked his head over the edge. He looked down. "Dig out a couple of footholds in the side. It'll make it easier to pull you out."

"Good idea, he responded. He jammed the shovel into the side at head level and pulled out a hunk of clay, leaving a firm base to stand on. He repeated the action at stomach level, and again at thigh level. He tried stepping into the lower slot while hanging onto the rope, and decided he needed one more hole, so he took aim at a spot just below his knee. Holding the shovel against the side of the hole, he lifted his foot and pushed it against the top of the blade. It went in just an inch, before hitting something hard. He frowned. Most likely, it was another of the many rocks he'd been struggling with all morning. He was going to move to the side, when he decided first to try prying the rock loose. He set the shovel blade just a few inches higher and jammed it into the earth. This time it slid in easily, surprising him, and he wedged it upward, trying to loosen the rock. Loose dirt tumbled out, and he bent down to look into the hole. There was something there, but he couldn't tell what.

Curious now, he took the shovel and started carefully scraping the dirt away from the hole, widening it to the point where he could tell that he'd hit a metal box. "Got something!" he yelled.

Evidently, Albert had returned to the cabin, for it was a minute before he heard his footsteps above. "What's that?" he yelled and poked his head over the edge of the hole.

"I've got something. I'm trying to pry it out now." He continued working the shovel around the box until he was able to reach in and grasp either side of it. He shoved it from side to side, loosening it, and finally was able to pull it out. "Got it," he yelled. "You ready to help me up?"

"Give me a minute," Albert said. He backed up a few feet, wrapped the rope around his waist, and leaned away from the hole. "Ready," he said.

Within seconds, Johnny scrambled up the side, tossing a small metal box out ahead of him as he rose, and then picking it up when he stood. It was flat, about four to six inches on a side, and made of of rusty iron. He shook the box as he got to his father, and grinned at the rattle inside.

"Let's clean it off, see what you've got," Albert said, and pulled a rag out of his back pocket. He gave it a few cursory swipes to remove much of the dirt, and discovered a clasp on one side. "Water," he said.

They carried the box over to the cabin, where Albert poured water over his rag. He wiped it over the box, cleaned it, and repeated the process until the box was nearly free of dirt. The front was secured with a small, rusty padlock. "I packed a few tools in the wagon. Go see what we can find to get into this." He inspected the lock. The ring on the top was nearly rusted through.

Johnny jumped up and returned with the heavy wooden toolbox. He dug through it until he found a crowbar and a wrench. "Let me try this. I should be able to break it open." While Albert held the box, he slipped the crowbar into the ring on the top of the lock. Then, grabbing the lock firmly with the wrench, he began to pry. Suddenly, the ring snapped through. He looked up at his father, his eyes bright.

"Shall we see what we have?" Albert asked. He tried lifting the top, but the metal had rusted together, so he wedged the blade of the crowbar through a narrow rusted opening, and lifted it. The top snapped up. Eagerly, both looked inside. Laying on top of what appeared to be an oil cloth wrapper, they found a single gold coin, similar to the one they'd found in the cabin. Johnny lifted it out. He stared at the coin for a moment, and then said, "You suppose this is it?"

Albert had taken out the oilcloth and was busy unwrapping it onto the table. Inside, he found a rolled up piece of leather. "It's vellum," he said softly.

Johnny looked at him curiously and he continued. "Leather. High quality calfskin, to be exact. It's used like paper, for writing. Very expensive though. Carefully, he unrolled the vellum until it was flat on the oilskin, and smiled. "Interesting."

Johnny looked down at the vellum on the table. The inside was covered with letters and numbers, but they weren't organized to look like any language he'd ever seen before. He looked up at his father. "What do you suppose it means?"

# CHAPTER 55
## JOURNEY TO HISTON

Walter hadn't been happy about leaving Jameson's compound before he could train a large enough force to protect his young charge, but after much discussion, grudgingly agreed that adding an armorer to his team could only help. Still, he would have preferred to wait for either Johnny or Albert to return, just to enlist the skills they brought. In the end, it was Robert's decision, and he wouldn't let go of the idea of the trip.

Not wanting to attract attention, they agreed to travel in a small group. Jameson and Robert would travel at the front, as father and son, while Walter and Bill accompanied them as their guards. It would deter outlaws, but be common enough not to attract the attention of the roving groups of soldiers.

They stopped in Histon on their first night, and Jameson booked two adjoining rooms at the inn, a secure facility that occupied an abandoned manor house, complete with walls and a strong gate.

They were up early the next morning. After a hearty breakfast, they mounted their horses and headed out of town. The Histon countryside was different from any that Robert had seen before, sparse and dry, its grey trees shriveled and twisted by the constant wind that blew in from the sea just a few miles away. "Why would anyone live here?" he asked, as they plodded on, mile after mile.

"Salt," Jameson said. "They mine it here and ship it throughout Bonterra. I carry loads overseas as well. It may not look like much on the surface, but they're rich mines below."

They rode on in silence for another mile before Jameson stopped and pointed to a building on a knoll in the distance. "That's where we're going. He'll have seen us by now, and wonder who's wandering onto his lands, so leave the talking to me. He's wary, and as you might imagine, very dangerous with a sword."

"He doesn't know we're coming?" Robert asked.

"No." Jameson spurred his horse forward. After sharing awkward glances, the others followed.

§§§§

The men who met them at the gate were grizzled with long straggly grey hair, but they'd seen them ride up, and they had the horsemanship of men accustomed to the saddle. The taller of the two raised his hand as they approached. "Private property here. You'd best be on your way."

"I'm here to see Emmon of Histon," Jameson called. "Tell him my name is Andrew Jameson."

The men appeared to be startled by the name, and after a short, quiet conference, one approached midway and said, "How would I know that?"

Jameson rode a couple of steps closer and the man said, "Stop there."

He stopped his horse and opened his cloak to show a dagger. Using just two fingers, he carefully pulled it from his belt and dropped it onto the rocky path. "This belonged to my father. Emmon will recognize it." Then he backed his horse away, returning to the group.

The lead horseman ambled up to the dagger, and then cautiously dismounted, and picked it up, never taking his eyes from the group. "Harrumph," he snorted, looking over at Jameson. "And what would you be wanting with me?"

"A few minutes of your time is all," Jameson called, "to talk about a proposition."

"House is up ahead," Emmon said, waving them to pass him. "We'll follow behind." Then he remounted his horse. As they passed, he stared at each, trying to measure this strange group that dared ride through his lands. When his eyes passed over Robert, they widened, and then almost instantly, faded back to their wary look.

§§§§

The house was a low, rambling structure, built of sod and stone, and finished with gnarled branches from the local timber. Robert dismounted out front, tied his horse to the post, and looked back to their host.

Emmon followed them, and before dropping from his horse, waved one arm in a circle over his head. Instantly, two men popped up out of the grass and trotted down to the farm.

He stared at Jameson. "Interesting introduction, but ya look like him." He handed back the dagger. "There's coffee on the fire. Come on in." And with that said, he turned and strode through the front door. His men, three of them now, and all ancient just like their leader, stopped behind the group, waiting for them to enter, and Robert could see now, that all were well armed, especially the two who'd been hiding in the grass. Each carried a quiver full of arrows, and had hooked a bow over his back. They were obviously trained archers.

The inside of the house was lighter and more spacious than Robert had expected. It was a man's place, furnished in heavy leather pieces made from the local wood, and decorated with old armaments and hunting trophies. Emmon was at the fireplace, pouring black liquid from a huge battered pot. He motioned toward the mugs hanging on hooks on the mantle. "Ya want coffee, pour it." Then he sat in one of the large chairs and lifted the mug to his lips. "What brings Andrew Jameson to Histon?"

"Perhaps if we could speak in private," Jameson said, motioning toward the other men.

"I got no secrets from my brothers. Anything you say, you can say to all of us." Then he pointed to the table and the benches. "Sit. Talk. Ain't got all day."

Robert move to a bench, and Jameson took a chair, and the man who'd ridden out with Emmon pulled out another, sitting between them. The others remained standing, nervous and uncomfortable, and ready to fight if needed.

Jameson began, "I was hoping that I might convince you to come out of retirement."

"Ta train this pup like I did his pa?" Emmon said.

Robert's jaw dropped and Jameson sputtered.

"What, ya think I wouldn't recognize him. Made my living noticin' things. Never forget a face, and he's the spittin' image. Walks like 'im. Suppose he'll sound like 'im too when he opens 'is mouth." He stared at Robert now. "That bump on your chest, that where yer carryin' the ring?"

Robert nodded slowly and started to reach for it, but Emmon stopped him. "Don' need ta see it. Yer face is good enough fer me." He looked to the other sitting man. "Danny, ya agree?"

The other man nodded sharply and he said, "Well, I figured this day was a comin'. We'll start soon as he finishes his coffee. You can meet me out in the barn." And with that, he rose, and followed by his brothers, left the house.

§§§§

An hour later, breathing heavily, Emmon said, "Enough for now." He reached out and took Robert's wooden practice sword and racked it alongside his own. Then he took two rags, dipped them in water, and tossed one to Robert. After wiping the sweat from his face and drinking some water, he said, "Yer good. Yer pa teach ya?"

"Yes sir," Robert replied.

"Well, I suppose if yer here with Jameson, he must be dead, am I right?"

When Robert nodded, he shook his head. "Gerald was a good one. That's a shame. The duke?" Again, Robert nodded, and he said, "Well, can't change that. Ya favor yer right, don't ya."

"Sorry," Robert said, trying to follow the conversation.

"Yer right side. Ya favor it. Not much, but a little bit. Leaves the left open. Coulda split ya wide open with a real sword a couple a times. We'll start with that."

"Actually," Robert said, "We'll be leaving before dark. We were hoping to have you join us in Waterton, mostly to work with the force Walter's assembling."

Emmon looked over at Walter, sizing him up, and said, "Figured that. Be followin' in a week. Gotta settle some business first. Danny'll come with me. The others'll watch the farm." Then he tossed Robert a practice sword and said, "Left handed now." Then he took up his own in his left hand and before Robert was fully ready, lunged at him.

§§§§

Walter sat on a bar stool back at the inn at Hinston, slowly nursing a mug of apple cider. For what he figured must be the hundredth time, he scanned the room, spending a little extra time looking through the front windows and checking out the street, beyond the gate. Everything was peaceful, and he saw no danger, but he sensed trouble ahead. He glanced over to Bill, sitting at the other end of the bar, also drinking cider. Each of them had a different vantage point, hopefully covering all possible problems. Bill tapped his glass softly, and stared out the window, their pre-arranged signal that all was well. Better, he thought, but still, his nerves were on edge.

Robert sat with Andrew Jameson at a table in the back corner of the bar. "Tell me about Emmon," he said.

"Interesting man, wasn't he?"

"Short on words, but amazing with a sword for a man his age."

Jameson picked up a piece of cheese, popped it into his mouth, and wiped his upper lip with his sleeve, before saying, "An expert, like any good armorer, and not just with a sword. Not many could take him on with any kind of weapon."

"And he recognized me."

Jameson chuckled softly. "And me. I figured he'd know the knife. It was his design, and had my father's crest on it. Still, after all these years…" He sighed. "I'd forgotten that about him. They used to say that he could tell you what he had for breakfast on any given date years past, who else was there, and what they ate. Amazing memory. I remember him saying once that he could see the past just like today."

"He'll be useful." Robert rubbed his sore ribs, where he'd taken a hit from the wooden sword. The ones on his left side, he mused. He recounted their sparring matches and he realized that he'd never been close to touching the older man. Not even once. He was remarkable. He was about to add more, when a rowdy and obviously drunken group of men clamored through the swinging doors at the front of the bar. He glanced across at Walter, who was already off his stool, scowling.

One of the men yelled at the bartender, "Beers all around for my friends."

They pushed toward the back, jostling a few other patrons out of their way, and most settled at a couple of tables next to Robert and Jameson. It was a small bar though, and four were left without seats. Two took the extra chairs from Robert's table, leaving two others staring at Robert and Jameson. "We'll be havin' them chairs too," one said, reaching for Jameson's chair.

Jameson was about to rise when Robert put his hand on the older man's arm. "We'll be leaving shortly," he said. "You'll be welcome to them then." He turned back to Jameson. "Ignore …" he started. Suddenly, one of the men, a brute who towered over his companions, grabbed Robert by the collar of his jacket and yanked him up and out of the chair.

"Said we'd be havin' them too." He tossed Robert to the side, as easily as he might have a rag doll and reached for the chair.

As soon as he touched it, Walter appeared at his side, his hand an iron band on the man's arm. "You'll get the chairs when they're ready to leave," he hissed.

The man turned, looking down on Walter. "Who 'r you ta tell me what I git?"

"A friend. I heard him say they'd be leaving soon. You're welcome to my barstool."

"Mine too," Bill said, appearing at Walter's side.

The stranger was swaying on his feet, and smelled of dirt, sweat, and alcohol. Faced now with two men, albeit both smaller than he was, he hesitated. His friend broke the stalemate, throwing a drunken roundhouse punch from behind that caught Bill in the back and slammed him into the table.

The big man bull rushed Walter, who sprang to the side, kicking out his foot and tripping him. Suddenly, others jumped out of their chairs, and joined their companions, throwing wild punches.

As soon as Robert went down, Jameson had rushed to his side. Before he could even get there though, Robert was up, using one arm to push the older man protectively behind him. "Stay," he ordered. He then threw the table to the side so that he could grab one of the men who was grappling with Walter. Flinging him back against the bar, he opened space.

Just then the big man rose, lifting a chair over his head. Walter yelled, and Robert ducked, just in time, as the man smashed the chair down, splintering the wood, but missing his target. His movement had knocked him off balance though, and as he stumbled, Robert swung a punch that caught him just beneath the chin, crumpling him to the floor.

"Quick.  Let's get out of here," Walter yelled, backing toward a rear entrance.  Bill grabbed Jameson and pushed him toward the exit.  Walter tried to do the same with Robert, who shrugged him off, while using one of the splintered chair legs to advance toward two men who were crowding in on them.  "We've got to go now," Walter yelled.

"Behind you," Robert said, holding his ground.

Suddenly, one of the men hurled a heavy glass mug.  Robert saw it coming, and ducked left just in time to hear it shatter against the wall behind him.  That move allowed his attackers to gain though, and one of them smashed a heavy stave against his sore ribs.  Robert stumbled, and another grabbed him by the front of his tunic, slammed his head back against the wall, and then kicked him in the knee.  Robert slumped to the floor, his body screaming in pain, and his head fuzzy.

Walter managed to pull the man off, flinging him to the side.  Then, pulling his sword, he stepped between Robert and his attackers.  Faced with an armed man, the others backed away, looking at one another and trying to gather the courage to rush their battered foes one more time.  It was clear though, that the terms had changed, and their barroom brawl looked like it might turn deadly.  None was interested in using fists against a man who clearly knew how to use a sword.

Just then, the front door to the bar smashed open and four soldiers rushed into the room, swords drawn.  "You there," one yelled, pointing at Walter, "Put that weapon down!"

Seeing his attackers back away, Walter slowly lay his sword on the floor and raised his hands in the air.  Bill, protecting Jameson behind him, lifted his hands as well.  Robert was kneeling on the floor, and could only look up blearily as the soldiers marched deliberately between the two fighting factions.  Two of them, using the flats of their blades to slap anyone not moving fast enough, forced the larger group of men into one corner, while the other two disarmed Walter and forced his group into the exit opening.

Their leader turned to the barman. "What happened?"

"Harold's group come in, drunk as skunks again, makin' trouble," he said.

The man shook his head. "Well, they got some." He looked to his soldiers. Tie 'em all up, hands behind their backs. We'll take 'em to the garrison."

Several of the men grumbled, and resisted when the soldiers approached with short lengths of rope. Their complaints faded away when another troop of four soldiers ran through the front doors.

"With your permission, we'll be going, officer," Jameson said. "We were just having a quiet meal. We didn't want any trouble."

The captain stared at him for a moment, uncertain, and then motioned toward one of his soldiers. "Bind them too. We'll settle this out in the fort."

"But," Jameson said, "We need to be on our way."

"In time. Ya don' go fightin' in my town and walk away." Jameson tried to protest again but the man said, "Enough. We'll put you all behind bars and then settle this out." He scanned the room then. The big man who'd started the fight was just rising, trying to shake the cobwebs from his head, but when the soldiers approached him, he growled and tried to fight them off. Finally, one poked a knife against his belly, just enough to get his attention. He snarled, but reached his hands behind his back.

The soldier who came to Robert hesitated when he saw the blood on the side of his head. "Looks like you got the worst of it, boy," he said. He gently pulled him to his feet, but when Robert tried to put weight onto his knee, he nearly crumpled. "I'll tie yours in front, just in case you need 'em."

"Thanks," Robert said grimly. The soldiers were busy tying up the others, so he tried stretching to a full standing position, but his ribs screamed in pain, so he remained partially huddled over. His sternum hurt too, and he reached up to massage the spot in the middle of his chest. Suddenly, his eyes widened and despite the robe binding his wrists, he ran both hands frantically against his chest. The ruby ring was gone.

# ABOUT THE AUTHOR

I hope that you've taken as much pleasure in reading this story as I took in writing it.

I retired a few years ago from a career that started with stints as a businessman and salesman in Northern California before entering public education. For the next twenty some years, I worked as an elementary school teacher and later, as a school principal.

Even while I worked, I enjoyed writing, and now that I am retired, I spend some time every day recording the stories that I've accumulated over a lifetime. When I am not writing, I enjoy traveling and spending time with my new grand daughter.

Other books I've published include:
The Santa Hat, a short story about the challenges a boy faces when moving to a new community.

Coming soon:
The Ruby Ring, Fight for the Crown, The sequel to this story. I've included a short excerpt below.
The Ruby Crown, an adult novel about a jewel heist
The Prompter, an adult science fiction story that mixes time travel, adventure, and romance
Uncle Albert, a children's story about a 6th grade boy who is suddenly cast into the role as the school principal

# The Ruby Ring

## Fight For The Crown

### Stephen Gilbert

The crashing of the door woke Duke Henry out of his slumber. Surprised and disoriented, he snapped his head around. What he saw woke him instantly. "What's the meaning of this!" he yelled, trying to recognize the man who stood in the shadows.

He was met with a single cry. "I've come for you. Your time is over."

The man rushed into the room as Henry, startled now at the sight of the raised blade, shouted, "Guards!"

And then he jumped back, grabbing his coffee and flinging the cup into the face of his attacker, but the man ducked easily aside and continued to advance. Henry was up now though, and tipped his chair, throwing it in the man's path. That gained him only a couple of seconds, but it was enough, as the man had to jump back out of the way and he was able to grasp at the handle of the decorative sword, the one his men had brought back from the cavern, that he'd hung on the wall of his library. He turned and faced the man, his own blade spinning loosely in the emerging sunlight. "Drop your weapon," he warned, and shouted again, "Guards!"

He glared at the man, trying to recognize him in the faint light, but his face was still masked by shadows. Both had stopped in place now, warily circling one another, knowing that there could be only one end to this battle. "Drop your sword and live," Henry said darkly, "or fight me and die."

As he circled, he worked his opponent toward the window, so that he could better see him. He was a large man, powerfully built, handling his sword with the practiced ease of one who'd spent many hours on the training field. Still though, it was too dark in the room to make out his face, though he swore the bone structure was familiar.

They circled, and then Henry feinted left before swinging low to the right, hoping to take his opponent's legs out from under him. The man leapt back at the last minute, and his sword swung free. He recovered quickly, and continued his circling. "What do you want?" he yelled, knowing the answer, but there was no reply. They continued circling, and now the man was away from the window and fully in the shadows.

Suddenly, he lunged, and Henry brought his sword down, clanging against the metal and pressing it away, and just as quickly, the man was away, dancing lightly on his toes, looking for his next opportunity. A glimmer of light caught Henry's attention, and he saw that the man carried both the sword and a dagger. That was good to know, and he wished that he could avail himself of the same. Still, neither wore any kind of armor, so in that way, they were evenly matched.

He continued to circle, testing occasionally with his sword, but always the man had a quick response. Suddenly, the man slashed at his head and rushed in. Henry parried the sword strike, but felt the dagger bite into his left wrist, opening a deep wound. He pushed the man away, and stumbled back, taking an instant to look down at the red stain seeping out onto his shirt. "First blood," he murmured, and for the first time, felt a twinge of fear. He backed deeper into the room, taking advantage of the furnishings to block his path, hoping to gain his escape through the servant's doors. "Guards!" he shouted once again, this time hearing the frantic tinge to his own voice.

Once past the furniture, the room opened up into a large space, and he circled back toward the fireplace, where he grabbed at a poker with his free left hand, hoping to ward off the dagger, but the muscles in his arm wouldn't cooperate, slashed too deeply to respond. The poker fell to the floor, and he jumped back against the fireplace as the man lunged again, just missing him, the edge of his blade throwing sparks as it raked against the stones.

Now, however, the man had left a small opening, and Henry stuck, satisfied to feel his own sword part flesh. His opponent squealed and leapt back, reaching down to nurse the wound on his hip. And then he was up again, circling once more, but limping this time, favoring his left leg. Henry watched cautiously as his mind churned the possibilities. The odds had just turned. He may only have one useable arm, but he'd be able to move easily whereas his opponent was slowed.

Deeper in the room, he still tried to recognize his foe, but it was nearly dark here and both men were shadows. He circled, and then seeing the man wince as he bumped a chair, took his chance. He lunged forward, and when the man moved to parry, pulled up to the left and slashed down, feeling the sword slice fabric, and then flesh. And then he was away, jumping back before his opponent could do more than grunt. It was a shallow wound, but it would hurt, and bleed…